"It's hard for me to imagine this life without you," Finn said.

This life or his life? For her, it was both. He couldn't make the same leap. "I am ready to move on from this." But not ready to move on from him. She couldn't think of a way to keep him in her life and walk away from being a spy.

Finn's arms tightened around her. "I wish I could change your mind. The times I've spent with you were some of the best of my life. Even in this mission, having you with me has been great."

Sentimentality pulled at her heartstrings. Some of her most fun adventures had been with him at her side. He was the bright spot in her days. She had deliberately shut him out of her life during a time of enormous need, and that had been a mistake.

Hyde lifted her face. Finn brushed his nose lightly against hers and then lowered his mouth and kissed her softly.

* * *

If you're on Twitter, tell us what you think of Harlequin Romantic Suspense! #harlequinromsuspense

Dear Reader,

I've been fortunate enough to spend vacation time in beautiful tropical locations. The soft sand, the light breeze, the gentle (or sometimes not so gentle) waves, a cold bottle of water and a great book are a relaxing way to pass an afternoon. When I started writing Finn and Hyde's romance, I knew those locations and experiences would play a role in the story.

I've been receiving emails about Finn and Hyde since *Traitorous Attraction* was published in May 2014. Finn was part of a rescue team that pulled Hyde from one of the most dangerous prisons in South America. After meeting, both returned to their work as special operatives for the West Company and remained involved with each other in a steamy affair.

Keep your emails coming! Readers have a lot of influence over what I write, and I appreciate each and every one of you who take the time to let me know what you'd enjoy reading. If you're interested in reading more about the West Company, check out *Delta Force Desire* (June 2016). There's another West Company book coming in June 2017, so stay tuned.

Best,

C.J. Miller

cj-miller.com

SPECIAL FORCES SEDUCTION

C.J. Miller

HARLEQUIN® ROMANTIC SUSPENSE

Recycling programs
for this product may
not exist in your area.

ISBN-13: 978-0-373-40195-6

Special Forces Seduction

Copyright © 2017 by C.J. Miller

Printed in U.S.A.

www.Harlequin.com

C.J. Miller loves to hear from her readers and can be contacted through her website, cj-miller.com. She lives in Maryland with her husband and three children. C.J. believes in first loves, second chances and happily-ever-after.

Books by C.J. Miller

Harlequin Romantic Suspense

Hiding His Witness
Shielding the Suspect
Protecting His Princess
Traitorous Attraction
Under the Sheik's Protection
Taken by the Con
Capturing the Huntsman
Delta Force Desire
Special Forces Seduction

The Coltons of Texas

Colton's Texas Stakeout

Conspiracy Against the Crown

The Secret King
Guarding His Royal Bride

The Coltons: Return to Wyoming

Colton Holiday Lockdown

Visit the Author Profile page at Harlequin.com, or cj-miller.com, for more titles.

To Charlie (Char-Char), who shows me every day the meaning of family, hard work and dedication.

Chapter 1

Alexandra "Hyde" Flores caught a glimpse of undercover operative Finn Carter in her peripheral vision. But as she turned her head, she saw that he'd vanished. The orange candles and strings of white lights inside the wedding tent created shadows and apparitions. Hyde's life was haunted by ghosts of her past.

Her oldest sister Victoria was glowing and stunning in a thirty-thousand dollar, diamond-white couture wedding dress. Hyde knew part of her glow was that she was three months pregnant, and Hyde's niece Thea would soon have a cousin. For the first time in Hyde's life, seeing someone with the classic American dream made her envious.

She had been involved in complicated and dangerous missions for the last ten years and up until the end, she had loved it. Her psyche was changing and craving normal. Normal was good and safe.

Hyde claimed a spot for herself at a high-topped table in the corner of the white tent with a great view of the dance floor. It gave her pleasure to watch her parents, her sisters, her new brother-in-law and her niece dancing with the extended family. She had been on the fringes of the family for so long that her absence wasn't noticed.

A twinge of sadness nipped at her, but not enough to force her to mingle. Relearning social protocol in Bearcreek, Montana, was a throwback to her youth. Her job had trained her to read between the lines and to look for hidden agendas. She anticipated backstabbing and lies from the people she worked with. Her family, on the other hand, spoke plain and their only agenda tonight was to celebrate Victoria and Thomas.

Sensing someone watching her, Hyde turned and reached to where her gun was usually holstered. Her fingers came up empty and a mild panic threaded through her. The hair on the back of her neck stood on end. It was a slim chance, but possible that she'd been found by an enemy looking for revenge.

Instead of an enemy, Hyde's gaze connected with Finn's. She closed her eyes, waited until her thoughts cleared and her heart slowed to a normal rate. Thinking of him got her going, a shot of adrenaline to her heart. She blamed the weekends they had spent together. Quick, steamy rendezvous and abbreviated goodbyes were their trademarks. She and Finn had carried on their affair for three years without any commitment, without anniversary celebrations or promises of a future.

It had been great while it had lasted. It was no longer what she wanted.

When Hyde opened her eyes, he was gone. Or rather, her imagination had stopped playing tricks on her. Finn wasn't in Bearcreek, Montana. He was on his latest mission somewhere in the world. Hyde would never see him again. She was out of the spy game, and a life of secrets and lies was behind her. The pang of sadness that struck her had everything to do with her desire to have a normal, stable life and nothing to do with missing her former life—or Finn.

A masculine, strong arm slipped around her waist and though her instincts were to react defensively, she froze when Finn's familiar scent wafted over her, the smell of soap and sandalwood. Memories of him naked, in the shower, in her bed, flickered through her mind. Her heartbeat faltered, skipped, and her breath backed up in her lungs.

His voice cemented his identity. That deep, slow drawl that replayed in her dreams for months after she saw him. He appealed to her as no one had before or had since.

"You have never looked more beautiful than you do tonight."

Hyde whirled and came face-to-face with the man she had fallen for hard. A man she couldn't have a serious relationship with, a man who was almost as daring and wild as she had been. He embodied everything she had wanted in a man. Strength, cunning and excitement had been at the top of her list and now she wanted to add stable, honest and calm.

Despite not having been invited, Finn was dressed for the occasion. Black suit and gray button-down with a silver and black tie. Understated elegance. His tie clip and cuff links matched, small green gems adorning them. His dark hair was slicked back, every hair in place. He looked positively dashing.

Her heart overreacted, like it always did. "The most beautiful? You have a thing for canary-yellow and carrot-stick-orange dresses?" Her bridesmaid dress was bright and fun and in colors Hyde rarely wore.

"If you're the one wearing it," Finn said.

"What are you doing here?" She hoped she had pulled off sounding casual.

Finn could be working an operation. An op in rural Montana would be unusual, but spies worked in every corner of the globe. Hard to imagine terrorist plots afoot in this part of the United States, but Hyde was justifiably paranoid. She had been lied to and double-crossed far too many times.

"I'm looking for you." His hands slipped down to her hips and pulled her against his body. A mewling sound she recognized as hers escaped her lips. Their attraction was the one steady part of their relationship. Not a strong aspect to hinge a future on.

Hyde hadn't met a man who held a candle to Finn. Tall and muscled, his dark hair had a touch of gray at his temples. He looked good clean-shaven and with facial hair. He had about a day's worth of a beard.

"This is my sister's wedding." Even with the table between her and the throng of guests, someone would notice him. Finn was impossible to overlook. He hadn't been invited to the wedding and if Victoria spotted him, she would know it and ask questions. Hyde didn't want to answer questions about Finn. She had too many of her own. When it came to Finn, her emotions were a tangled mess.

Finn was an accomplished liar, but he wouldn't

know the details of the cover story she had told her family about her career. Her family believed she was a sales rep for a luxury car company and having become road weary, had made a career change. Believable, except when evidence to the contrary, like her former lover and world renowned spy, showed up out of the blue at a family function.

"This is a big day for your family, and I don't want to intrude. I've missed you," he said. He took her hand and led her away from the table and out of the wedding tent and into the open fields of her family's farm.

The farm spread over fifty acres, and her sister's wedding was being held in one of the most scenic areas. Hyde used to lay a blanket out under the stars in this exact spot and stare at the sky. The longer she gazed, the more stars she could see, and as a child, she had believed she could see outside the galaxy if she watched long enough.

"I can't leave my sister's wedding. It's not over," she said.

"I can't wait another minute to be with you. If you miss the bouquet toss, does that matter? Did you want to be the next to be married?" he asked.

For the first time in her life, Hyde did want to be married. She hungered for family gatherings and going to the gym and appointments at the salon. "I could catch it." She was the oldest unmarried woman in her family. Well, the oldest unmarried woman who had never been married.

"I had to see you. Kate West was right," Finn said, referring to the wife of the man who ran a black ops company they contracted with periodically. The West Company was a first-rate special operations firm that hired experts as the situation called for them. The West Company made it their business to handle problems quickly, efficiently and quietly. Hyde and Finn liked working for the West Company. They had professional and personal connections with the firm.

Hyde focused on what Finn was saying. "Kate was right about what?"

"You're not part of this life anymore," Finn said. "I see it on your face. I see it in the way you look at me."

Finn must know her better than she had believed. "I am retired from my former career." Hyde had a good relationship with the West Company and because she and Kate had formed a friendship, Hyde had wanted to do more than disappear and ignore phone calls. An explanation had been in order.

"Your sister is married. Is that what this is about?" Finn looked at her intensely and she had to catch her breath. She and Finn had always created fireworks when they were together: in the bedroom and when they fought.

Hyde linked her hands behind her. She didn't want to touch Finn or reach for him. They wanted different things and her new life would bore him. "I have decided I don't want to be in that line of work anymore." Her sister's wedding reinforced her decision had been the right one, but it hadn't been the initiating factor.

Finn folded his arms, and the bunched muscles in his biceps reminded her of how it felt to be held by him. A shimmer of desire piped through her. In Finn's arms, she had never felt safer and she could let down her guard for a few hours with him watching her back. He was a fighter. He was strong. He was passionate about everything he did, including his affair with her.

"I need to talk you out of this," Finn said.

"I'm not changing my mind," Hyde said. If he intended to rope her into taking another job as a spy, he would be disappointed.

Finn inclined his head. "What are you planning to do? Get a job in an office?"

Office work was on the list of possible jobs to investigate. She could work forty hours per week, clock out and spend the weekend binge-watching television and running errands and doing chores. "I have marketable job skills."

"I know you have job skills. I'm questioning if they apply to any jobs in this small town."

She hadn't had enough time to explore her options. She didn't want to think about her decision again or justify it. If anyone could talk her out of this course of action, it was Finn. "I'll be fine. Thanks for checking on me. Burn my address. I don't want anyone following me here." She had made enemies and some held grudges.

Finn drew her against him. "No one followed me here. Whatever happened, tell me and I'll fix it."

The pleading in his voice nearly felled her. He couldn't fix what had happened. She could not name the emotion that passed through her, but her heart clenched. "I don't want to be a spy anymore." Speaking the words was a relief. She realized she had worried about what Finn would think and she waited for the disappointment or an argument.

Finn's face remained frustratingly neutral. He blinked at her. "I'm going after Reed Barnett and I need you."

Reed Barnett, international drug kingpin, murderer

and all-around bad man. Hyde agreed he needed to be taken down, but she had no intention of getting involved. A Reed Barnett operation was far too dangerous and complex. After what had happened during her last mission, Hyde was staying on the safe side of the street.

"I can't be involved," Hyde said. She wouldn't consider it and she didn't want the details. Tracking and hunting Reed Barnett was a suicide mission. The man had money and a private army and arms en masse. It was rumored he owned a private island.

"I need someone I can trust at my back," Finn said.

Temporary loyalty on a mission could be bought. "I'm the wrong woman for the job." Questions about the mission swirled in her head. She wouldn't voice them. If she spoke them, she would get pulled into Finn's plans.

His jaw was tight. "Barnett killed Simon."

A spear of hurt struck her in the gut at the reminder. "I know he killed Simon." Simon had been a dear friend. He had once saved her life on an operation. He deserved better than what had happened to him.

"We can avenge his death. For Thea," Finn said.

Thea. With her name came a searing hot flash of regret and pain. Finn was one of the few people who knew that Simon was Hyde's niece, Thea's, father.

"It's the right thing to do," Finn said.

Hyde wrestled with her guilt. She didn't want to step back into this life. The adrenaline rush, the excitement and the danger were highs she would chase for the rest of her life. But to avenge Simon… "I don't know if seeking revenge against Barnett is right. I have thought about killing the man on many occasions, but the logistics and the reality is that I'd end up dead, not Barnett."

Finn took her hand in his. "This isn't an impulsive plan. We have the West Company backing the mission. We can take Barnett down. We can stop his drug ring. Protect more families from going through what Lydia and Thea are going through," Finn said.

He'd known the right angle to play with her. Hyde loved her sister and would do anything for her and Thea. To finally tell Lydia about Simon and what had happened to him, to give her a sense of peace and closure, would mean so much. Hyde was afraid to tell Lydia the whole truth about Simon. Her sister would dig around and land in Barnett's crosshairs. Or Hyde would reveal a piece of her life that was classified and open a can of worms. Could Hyde safely give Lydia the truth about Simon if Reed Barnett was dead?

Her mind was churning through her contacts, looking for an in with Barnett's crew and coming up short. Barnett was notorious for keeping his inner circle limited and forcing business associates to prove their loyalty in incriminating ways. "You make it sound easy. How will you get close enough to Barnett to strike?"

"I've laid the groundwork. I have a meeting with Barnett in a couple of days. Come with me. We'll destroy him and his enterprise."

A mission with Finn? Being together on vacation was different from being together on a complex mission in the field. She could scarcely draw a full breath thinking of being alone with Finn, of imagining days or weeks together. Emotionally complicated and fraught with problems.

Compounded with a face-to-face meeting with Barnett, it was unimaginable. What would stop her or Finn from killing him on the spot? Her heart thundered and warnings screamed in her head.

Finn was a passionate man and she was a fiery woman. Could they work together and get the job done?

Her hands itched to hold a gun. That quickly, she was ready to jump back in the game.

"If you were one of my operatives telling me you wanted revenge on Barnett, I wouldn't assign you to this op," Hyde said. Too many emotion-fueled decisions would lead to a mistake.

Finn ran his hand down her arm, letting their fingers linger together. "Does that mean you want me to take someone else?" He brought her fingers to his lips and kissed her knuckles. The fire in his eyes seared her to the core.

Finn didn't work well with others. He followed orders, but he preferred to be in command. This mission had a personal element and that would require extra vigilance. "I'm going. But you know we'll make more mistakes because this is deeply personal. Revenge is heavy baggage and I prefer to be light and nimble on operations."

Finn pulled her against him and she braced her hands on his chest. "I knew I wasn't wasting my time coming out here," he said.

"How'd you find me?" she asked.

He lifted a brow. "Former Army Special Forces."

"Right." His training as a Green Beret was exhaustive and had left him with an impressive list of skills. She had been careful to cover her tracks when she'd returned to Bearcreek. If Finn had found her, then her enemies could, as well. Hyde wanted to protect her family. "I need more than that."

"Small details I pieced together over the time I've known you. And begging Kate West for intel on you," Finn said.

Surprise struck her. "Kate gave me up?"

Finn winked. "Only because I told her I was in love with you and needed to tell you in person."

Hyde gasped. In love with her? They hadn't spoken of love, not once during their relationship. Standing in the warm circle of his arms, her heart overreacted.

Finn traced the strap of her yellow dress with his finger. "I told her what she needed to hear to give me your location."

It was like a hammer slamming down on a delicate flower, smashing it to pieces. Hyde shook off the disappointment that pressed on her. Finn, love and she didn't belong grouped together in the same sentence. It wasn't love she felt for him. It was desire, plain and simple. She would be smart to keep her eyes on the prize, which in this case, was the mission. "You think we have a chance of taking Reed Barnett down?"

"I do. Now stop talking about Reed Barnett and let's talk about something else. Like how we'll spend this beautiful evening."

She couldn't leave her sister's wedding. She wouldn't hear the end of it. "I'm staying at the wedding. My date will take me home."

Finn appeared a mix of hurt and surprised. "You have a date to this wedding?"

Her sister had fixed her up with George, a coworker of Thomas's. After suffering through fifteen minutes of awkward conversation, George had ignored her for the rest of the night. Stepping outside with Finn would have gone unnoticed by George. "I have a date." It was nice for Finn to believe she had moved on and wasn't still carrying a torch for him. A torch she was trying to extinguish. Finn was part of her spy life and after this mission, she was finished with that.

"Are you dating? Is your date the reason you're retiring?" Finn sounded indifferent, but he had dropped her hands and had taken a step away from her.

"George has nothing to do with my career plans." She had met him two days before the wedding at the rehearsal dinner.

"Is he taking you home?" Finn asked, folding his arms over his chest.

He wasn't. Hyde had driven herself to the wedding. That wasn't Finn's business. Hyde held up her hand. "Don't pretend to care what I do when we're not together, and don't act jealous. Territorial doesn't suit you."

Finn was perpetually confident and rarely questioned himself. He leaned back away from her. "That's an unfair statement. I care about you. I want to know what's going on in your life."

Hyde scratched at her head where a bobby pin was pressing into her scalp. "I can't get into it with you here and now."

"But I want to get into it." Finn lifted her hand to his mouth and kissed the inside of her wrist.

The caress of his lips nearly broke her defenses. "If we're working an operation together, we need to keep our relationship chill." They needed the reminder.

"Chill? What does that mean?" Finn asked.

It meant the opposite of what their relationship had been. No hot sex, no making out, no sleeping together. "It means we're working together professionally. Nothing else except the mission."

Lines formed around Finn's eyes. "I will respect your wishes." He released her hand.

Hyde was startled by Finn's acceptance of her statement. Disappointment pinged in her chest. He had let her go easily and it spoke volumes. "I should get back to my family. Are you planning to stick around or do you want to meet at the airport?" She wanted him to say *airport*. Being around Finn left her feeling like she needed to catch her breath and clear her head.

"I have nowhere else to be and we need to talk more about Barnett."

"We'll talk on the journey there," Hyde said. Finn's eyes didn't leave her. His gaze heated her from her head to her toes.

"We should talk now," Finn said.

"I can't now." The urge to cry struck her, which was ridiculous. Spies didn't cry when they were with their colleagues. Finn had churned up emotions she had worked hard to lock away. She needed time. "Goodbye, Finn."

As she walked away, she felt him watching her.

Finn remained at the table on the far side of the tent. He had unbuttoned his suit jacket and looked relaxed, as if he hadn't requested she go with him on a dangerous and complicated mission.

Hyde pretended the wedding held her full attention. She was thinking of Finn and Simon and taking down Reed Barnett. Guests talked and laughed and danced. Hyde worked to put a pleasant expression on her face. She strolled into the crowd and made small talk with her family. When she glanced at the corner table, Finn had disappeared. Regret speared her. She hadn't invited him to stay at the wedding. Perhaps she should have.

Finn was as much of an outsider as she was. She and her family were pretending that she was part of it, but her absence had taken a toll on her personal relationships.

Hyde caught a glimpse of Finn across the room. He was speaking to a distant cousin, who was laughing and touching his jacket sleeve. Jealousy nipped at her and Hyde suppressed the urge to stake a claim. Hyde turned away and searched for George. The DJ was playing a popular song that had filled the dance floor.

George was speaking to people she didn't recognize. Hyde looked around for Lydia or Thea. She needed a distraction. Possessiveness and jealousy didn't work in her relationship with Finn. She and Finn hadn't discussed their relationship in terms of commitment and exclusivity. This wasn't the time to make those demands. If they were working together, their personal relationship needed to cool off.

The song changed from a snappy pop tune to a slow love ballad.

"Dance with me," Finn said, coming up behind her. He slipped his arms around her waist and spun her to face him.

She leaned into him, chest to chest, and his cheek brushed hers. Lust hit her low and hard and she gripped his hands more tightly. Letting go seemed impossible. She had wanted to make a clean break from her spy life and that had included Finn. Now, in his arms, she couldn't imagine not seeing him again, not having him in her life.

She had been trying to build a new life in Bearcreek, feeling like an outsider. Five minutes with Finn, and she felt at home.

Chapter 2

Finn had imagined a number of scenarios on his way to Montana to see Hyde. The entire trip he'd questioned if he'd made the right decision. But worrying about Hyde had taken over his thoughts to an obsessive point, and if he didn't see her and talk to her, it wouldn't stop. Coming to Bearcreek was about more than her being the right spy to help with Reed Barnett. He needed to see with his own eyes that she was doing well.

Hyde was in his arms and that made the trip worth it. At least physically, she was fine. No overt injuries, obvious scars, limping or GSWs. He sensed something was bothering her and he would find out what it was.

"Alexandra, will you introduce me to your friend?" A woman's voice from behind him.

Hyde flinched in his arms and Finn tensed. Hyde

broke away from him and he missed the sensation of her soft body against his. He turned. Standing in front of them was a woman with Hyde's same dark hair, though the other woman's was cut short. Similar facial features, but hers were softer. The other woman's expression was also friendlier, her mouth drawn up in an unreserved smile. Hyde carried around the stress of her job and didn't smile often.

"Lydia, this is my friend Finn," Hyde said. She folded her hands in front of her and said nothing more.

Lydia looked between him and Hyde. "It's nice to meet you. Did you and Alexandra work together?"

Finn caught Hyde's subtle nod. "Yes, we did." He'd follow her lead about her cover story relating to where she had been the last decade. From what he knew of Hyde, unlike him, she maintained a cozy relationship with her family.

"What brings you to town? I hope you don't want Hyde to come back to work with you." Lydia slid her arm around her sister's waist and hugged her. "We're grateful to have Alexandra back with us. For the longest time, I felt like I only had one sister."

The guilty look on Hyde's face could have been about her frequent travel or it could have been because she had introduced Simon to Lydia.

Finn slid his hands into his pockets. "I'm passing through on business. I have a big job I'd like Alexandra to help me with. A short job. It will only take a few weeks."

Lydia looked at her sister. "I don't like the sound of that. Alexandra gets pulled into things. A short job turns into another and then another. She'll go missing for another ten years."

"It's the one job and nothing else," Hyde said. She pressed a hand over her stomach.

"That's right," Finn said, picking up on Hyde's anxiety and wanting to reassure her.

"I'm sure you have other associates who can assist you. Alexandra needs to be here," Lydia said. Anger colored the edges of her words.

Hyde tucked a stray strand of hair behind her ear. "Lydia, I'll talk with you about it later."

Lydia pinned her sister with a harsh stare. "Okay, Alex. Whatever you say." She looked over her shoulder. "Excuse me. My daughter is awake and fussing."

Lydia rushed off and Finn captured Hyde in the circle of his arms. He resumed dancing with her. She moved on the dance floor like she did in the field, sleek and smooth.

"She seems protective," Finn said.

Hyde swallowed hard. "They all are. They want me around. They were excited when I told them I planned to stay."

"Then your family is the reason you quit." He wouldn't stop pressing until he had the details. He needed to know what was going on in her life. She was logical and rational, and quitting abruptly didn't fit with what he knew of her. But then again, he might not know her as well as he thought he did. Spies lied. It had crossed his mind that he would arrive in Bearcreek and discover she had a husband and family of her own she had never told him about. Learning that wasn't the case, he was relieved.

"Part of the reason. I want to help Lydia. She deserves better than she's been handed. Thea is great, but being a single parent has been hard on Lydia. She's asked me about Simon on more than one occasion and I wrestle with what to tell her."

"What did you tell her happened?" Finn asked.

Hyde's shoulders tensed. "I told her that he quit and he stopped coming to work."

Finn saw the flaw in that explanation. "Not much closure for her."

"I should have thought it through. When she asked me about him, I was still reeling from the news of Simon's death and I wasn't sure what I was allowed to tell her. I couldn't believe he had been taken out. He was one of the best. He was careful. How did Barnett get him?"

Finn had been told parts of the story. He hadn't been directly involved with Simon's mission, and the details were classified. "I've asked questions and I didn't receive any answers."

Hyde looked over at her sister. "That's the main reason I'll do this. For her. For Thea. To give them answers and a way to move forward without being haunted."

Boots hit Hyde's second-story balcony. Finn was outside her sliding glass doors. No surprise, really. She had expected him, and Finn intended for her to hear his approach. Sneaking up on a spy was a quick way to catch a bullet in the head and the chest. Hyde still slept with a gun in her bedside table. And in her kitchen. And her living room. A woman couldn't be too careful about protecting herself.

She'd rented this place because of the many exit points. One day she would select a house because it made her feel at home. She would hang pictures on the walls and decorate it. It would take longer than a few months for her to stop thinking like a spy and return to being a civilian.

Hyde counted to five. The lock clicked open. Finn was fast with a lock pick. She was faster. She hadn't laid the jimmy bar in the door, anticipating his visit. He entered her room, closing the door behind him. Her heart raced and her fingers itched to reach for him. She counted his footsteps as he approached the bed. He dropped his suit jacket on the floor and loosened his tie from around his neck. Desire fluttered in her belly. Finn sat on the mattress, removed his shoes and lifted the sheet, sliding into the bed beside her. Heat spiraled through her. He gathered her against him. He smelled of laundry detergent and soap. "I couldn't sleep knowing you were here alone. I've missed you. I've missed holding you in my arms."

Tears sprang to her eyes and she curled her body against his. The tenderness he showed her was gentler than she had experienced with any another man. It struck her as odd because he was also one of the most brutal men she had met. "How did you know I was alone?"

His arm was slung over her waist. "I know you and I knew your date to the wedding meant nothing to you. You wouldn't take him home no matter how lonely you were. But you seemed sad. I couldn't leave you that way. I want you to tell me what's wrong so I can fix it."

She was sad. Hurting. Lost. Confused. Now that she knew about Reed Barnett, she felt pulled back into the world she swore was dead to her, but she also felt good having a purpose and a meaningful task. Given her skill set, fulfilling work had been hard to come by in Bearcreek. "I have a lot on my mind."

She couldn't tell Finn that she wanted a husband and a family and a life that involved footed pajamas, car pools and little league. A year ago Hyde believed a life of children and domestic duties was a prison sentence. She felt sorry for friends who organized playdates and spent their days playing cars and dolls. Now she wished she had considered her options sooner.

Telling Finn she wanted those things would be ice water on his libido and his feelings for her. And while it would have been a quick way to end the relationship, she wanted him to think fondly of her and remember her in a certain way.

Finn nuzzled the back of her neck. "I didn't believe Connor when he told me you weren't available for hire."

Connor, the leader of the West Company, had contacted her about a job while she was in Munich. She had impulsively told him she was retired, and after speaking the words, she knew they were what she needed. Thinking over the experiences she had lived through as a spy, she counted herself lucky she was alive and relatively unscathed. Running, hiding and lying were exhausting, but losing her baby had broken her. "I spoke to his wife about it." She could trust Connor and Kate not to spread it around. It was better for her enemies to believe she was in the game and not sitting around with her feet up, like a target with a big red bull's-eye on her chest.

Finn touched her hip, rolling her to face him. "You should have called me when things changed. You should have called me when you decided you didn't want to work as an agent anymore."

Her skin prickled where his hand rested. She couldn't get enough of him, but her desire was at war with her heart. "You would have pressed me for reasons why."

He shifted close, sliding his hips against her. "You're one of the best in the business. Why quit?"

She'd give the simple answer and leave out the stuff about love and marriage and a baby. "This isn't the life I want."

He tapped his finger against her leg. "Are you planning to stay in Montana and raise cattle with your family?"

He sounded sincere and she appreciated that he was trying to understand. He wouldn't understand this. What she wanted now was so over the invisible line of where their relationship ended, she couldn't voice it without feeling silly.

"I haven't decided what I will do." She had saved enough money to grant her the luxury of time to decide.

"What about your operatives and contacts?" Finn asked.

Hyde had turned away jobs over the last several months. She didn't have employees who relied on her, not in the traditional sense. She had referred operatives with special skills to jobs that warranted them and vetted agents in the field. When she'd quit, she'd washed her hands of it and had been comfortable with that decision.

Finn was the one open item on the past. She couldn't have Finn and a family. "Operatives I've worked with will work for someone else." It was how the game was played. The network she had painstakingly built from influential contacts now felt unfulfilling. She had made herself a warrior for the cause, any cause she believed in, and most important, causes where a woman was in danger. Those were the ones closest to her heart. She was walking away from those women who had needed her, often in crisis, but she would find other ways to give back.

He brushed at the hair at her temple. "When we last met, you loved your job."

When she had last seen Finn, they had spent three days in the Maldives Islands. She'd been fresh off an assignment, relaxed and excited. Stress relief, great conversation and mind-blowing sex wrapped up in one person were how she'd rejuvenated herself between missions. What he'd offered was everything she had needed, and for that, she was grateful. "I'm tired of this job. I want a simpler life."

Finn ran his index finger down her cheek. He was pure temptation. "You'll be bored."

Not if she found the right career or hobby. Plenty of people lived in the same town, drove to the same job each day and collected a paycheck every two weeks. She could do the same and she would be happy doing it. A husband and family could be in the cards for her. "I'll be busy."

"Busy isn't happy. I don't understand why anyone would want a house that breaks and a job that goes nowhere."

Hyde's brain spun. It wasn't as if she was thinking about marrying Finn, but to hear him describe the life she wanted in disparaging terms, Hyde was hurt.

She needed more than Finn could give her. Though she had known Finn wouldn't settle down with her, or anyone, hearing him speak the words felt like the death toll on their relationship.

Finn closed his eyes, oblivious to how she felt. That was one downside of subconsciously masking her emotions out of habit. No one could read her. "I don't see it that way. My new job will be exciting because it will be different. I'll have time off. I'll have friends I see more than once every few months or years."

"You are the most complicated woman I have ever known."

A compliment? Why the groan? "I don't think I'm complicated."

He shifted in the bed, moving the pillows. "The secrets you keep would make the average person insane. You hide them like you hide everything. But I have no room to criticize."

If he knew her biggest, most painful secret, how would he feel? He may blame her. He might be angry. If he was relieved, she wasn't sure she could handle that. She would interpret his relief as happiness not to be tied to a baby who would have been an inconvenience to him and his work. It wasn't fair to leap to that conclusion, but right now the only acceptable emotions surrounding her baby were grief, loss and sadness. Thinking of her baby, sorrow crashed around her. She put distance between her and Finn. "I can't be up late. I have a wedding brunch tomorrow morning."

"Isn't that what the reception was for?" Finn asked.

"Victoria and Thomas want to spend time with family, especially those who traveled a long distance, while they have the opportunity," Hyde said. She and Finn hadn't spoken much about their families. Did he get along with his?

In the last three months, she had been to a bridal shower, a bachelorette party, a rehearsal dinner, three dress fittings and a craft show. She had looped orange ribbons on bells and tied bows on bottles of bubbles while drinking wine with her sisters and mother. A different experience for her and she had enjoyed each. "Don't you want to spend time with your family?"

"Family is overrated," Finn said. Indifference emanated from his voice.

Red flags went up. Much about this conversation was telling. She hadn't realized how focused he was on his job. "I didn't realize you felt that way."

"Too much drama."

Hyde didn't press him. If family was unimportant to him, she couldn't change that with a conversation.

Finn shifted and adjusted the blankets. Though Finn rarely emoted, she sensed he was upset.

"Tell me what's on your mind." She set her hand on his arm and Finn covered it with his own.

"I was thinking about Simon. About his plans for the future. He wanted a wedding and a family. He met your sister and he fell hard. She and their life together were taken from him. Thea has Simon's eyes. Haunting."

She and Finn harbored guilt about Simon and Lydia's relationship. Hyde, for not warning Lydia to keep her distance from Simon, and Finn, because Finn believed he could have saved Simon from his untimely death.

Hyde didn't think any action on Finn's part would

have altered the outcome. She had voiced that sentiment before and he'd blown her off.

Death was a reality they faced daily. Spies accepted dangerous assignments in unstable places. Hyde had been close to death a few times. She had been shot. She had broken her leg and been left for dead. She had been imprisoned. She had defied the odds and felt blessed to be alive.

"Lydia will like to know that Simon cared deeply for her. I'll be happy when I can tell her the truth," Hyde said.

From what Lydia had shared, she and Simon had talked about a future. They'd discussed marriage. Lydia also believed that Simon had manipulated her, promising a life together as a line to get her into bed. Hyde had wanted to spill the truth. Simon's intentions had been genuine.

"She deserves at least that," Finn said. "When she tells Thea about her father, it shouldn't be to explain he was a loser who abandoned them."

They lapsed into silence, lost in their thoughts.

"Are you planning to be a spy forever?" Hyde asked.

Finn propped his head on his hand. "I'm good at it. I don't know if there's anything else that would make me as happy as this work."

She'd had similar thoughts in the past. "You might see it differently one day."

"You sound like my mother," he said, and he sounded exhausted.

Interesting that he'd mentioned his family again. "Does your mom know you're a spy?"

"She thinks I work as a contractor for a defense

firm. She doesn't know specifics," Finn said. "That's something I like about you. You know what I do. I don't have to hide much from you."

"We have secrets," Hyde said.

"When I'm with you, I can relax. You know the ground rules. You don't pry."

Prying was exactly what she wanted to do except she had no interest in pressing him for details about his missions, past or future. She wanted to know more about him, his life, his childhood. They had spent time together, and she felt like she had barely scratched the surface learning what made him tick. It may not change anything. Finn was against having a family, and having a family was her new dream. If she had an explanation, would that make parting easier?

Finn rolled and slung his thigh on top of hers, his leg between hers. "You smell good."

Whether his desire was taking over or he was avoiding delving into a deeper conversation with her, she couldn't tell. Sex was often on Finn's mind. "What you smell is soap and shampoo. I showered when I got home. My hair was sprayed into place and it was too stiff to sleep in and it was giving me a headache."

"I would have liked to help you," Finn said.

"Shower?" she asked.

He ran his nose along her jawline. "That and take the clips from your hair. Alexandra?"

He almost never used her real full name and it shook her and stirred her desire. Her stomach fluttered. "Yes?" She met his gaze. The fire in his eyes matched the heat in his voice.

"I want to kiss you."

Could she let him kiss her? Would one kiss change anything? A kiss wouldn't make her permanently decide to return to her life as a spy. A kiss couldn't change her feelings about the future. But a kiss could feel good and comforting. Comfort was something she was missing. No one knew how much she was hurting. No one had sensed her sadness and reached out to comfort her.

Finn was offering physical comfort and Hyde reached for him, drawing him close. His arousal pressed at the apex of her thighs. She ignored that and focused on his lips. His perfectly kissable, sexy lips. When their mouths touched, a hundred sparks lit in the air around them. His lips were soft and pliant. Unhurried and seductive, his tongue danced with hers. Heat smoldered inside her and she wished she knew how to cool it.

They had fantastic chemistry, and getting naked with him held a great deal of appeal. But that appeal was lost when she thought of the last several months. How lonely she had been in Bearcreek and how the time alone had affected her. Time to think was good, except when it brought to light unsettling questions. Her extensive traveling over the last decade had prevented her from being close with anyone, from forging close relationships or letting anyone inside. She wanted those things, and Finn wasn't the man who could give them to her.

A tear slipped from her eye. Finn pulled away, questions in his eyes, and then wiped at the tear with his thumb.

"I won't hound you to tell me what this is about. I know spies keep secrets close to the vest. But I'm here if you want to talk. I don't need to say anything. I can listen."

Hyde wanted to confess everything and bare her soul to him. But making herself vulnerable scared her. She kept her mouth shut.

Chapter 3

Hyde clasped Victoria's hands before she climbed into the limo with Thomas. "Promise me you'll be careful," Hyde said.

Victoria laughed and looked over her shoulder. "I will be fine. This will be the first vacation I've had in years. Don't worry so much."

Hyde shouldn't worry, but Victoria had never traveled outside Montana and now she was flying halfway around the world with her new husband. Hyde's paranoia pinged. She had learned to be suspicious of everyone. That suspicion was misplaced with Thomas. He was a good man and could be trusted.

Lydia was standing close by with Thea. Thea was sleeping in her arms, likely tired from the night before. Lydia had dark circles under her eyes, her clothes were wrinkled and her hair knotted in a messy bun.

As Hyde waved goodbye to her sister and Thomas, Finn strolled toward her. He had skipped the family brunch, choosing instead to sleep for two more hours. No details had been mentioned about his last mission, and Hyde hadn't reviewed the details for their upcoming one.

"Ready to leave?" Finn asked.

Hyde had assembled a bag that morning. She hadn't forgotten how to slip undercover and pack the essentials quickly. "Yes." Speaking the word held weight and evoked sadness. Leaving her family was harder than she'd anticipated. Staying away had been easier, jumping from one assignment to the next. Reconnecting had touched her more deeply than she'd expected.

She had felt a shift between her and Finn, as well. They were embarking on a mission together. Their career and relationship were colliding.

Hyde's father approached and Hyde braced for impact. She didn't want to lie to her family, but she didn't have a good, clear way to explain Finn's sudden presence in Bearcreek or why she was leaving.

"Alexandra, are you coming by for dinner tonight? The caterer dropped off the leftover food from the wedding. There's plenty for everyone. Even for your friend." Her father gestured at Finn.

No chance of avoiding an introduction. Hyde pointed to Finn. "Dad, this is Finn. We used to work together." Not a lie and didn't give away anything about the past.

Her father extended his hand. "Nice to meet you. Are you in town on business?"

Finn opened his mouth to answer.

Hyde jumped in. "Finn needs me to go with him on another job."

Her father stiffened and annoyance crossed his face. "Why? I thought you quit that job and were planning to stick around for a while. We've liked having you."

Finn looked from her to her father, his gaze assessing. Her stomach was coiled with tension. She didn't want her father to get the wrong idea about them. Having had a happy, forty-year-long marriage, her father wanted his three daughters to have the same. Hyde suspected he worried more about Lydia's happiness since she was under so much stress, but Hyde concerned him.

"I did quit. This is one last job. It requires my expertise. Big client and it's important."

Her father appeared resolved. He indicated behind him. "Make sure you say goodbye to your mother. This time, call from the road so we know you're safe. I don't like this. I think you'll get pulled back in by him." Her father looked at Finn. "I thought my daughter might have been involved in a relationship and that kept her away. She came home, quiet and lost and I figured she had her heart broken. You show up and it pretty much confirms it."

"Dad, Finn didn't—"

"Come on, Alexandra. I wasn't born yesterday. I have eyes and I have father instincts." Her dad looked at Finn up and down. "You're the type she'd go after."

Guilt ballooned inside her. How could she reassure her father that wasn't the case? She wasn't leaving Bearcreek to chase after a relationship with Finn. This was about taking Reed Barnett down and helping Lydia. "It's just work."

"It's never just work," her dad said.

Hyde looked away from her father, sure she would

spill the entire truth if she met his gaze. "I'll be fine, Dad. I'll be home soon."

Her dad wrapped her in a hug. "Don't stay away too long."

Hyde left Bearcreek with a heavy heart, but hopeful about the mission. She was doing this for the right reasons and for her family. Making Lydia happy would make this worth it. Being a spy for the last ten years, Hyde had learned to bury her emotions and when it came to Finn, she would do just that.

If she weren't working an op, Hyde would have enjoyed Reed Barnett's remote, private island, one of the nicest islands she had visited in the last ten years. Accessible only by private transportation via air or sea, it was the perfect getaway for two people who were harried, stressed and in need of some rest and relaxation.

What waited for them on the island was none of those things. The West Company had briefed them on the operation, and Hyde was in the zone. The sooner she could nail Barnett and bring down his enterprise, the sooner she could return home. Her father's words had stuck with her. He had seen something between her and Finn. Her feelings for Finn had delved deeper than she had realized if they were apparent to others. Keeping those in check would be part of the mission.

She had promised her parents she would call. She'd have to remember to do that and make sure she had a safe way to communicate without dragging them into this operation. Barnett was crafty. He could trace phone calls to and from his island. He could have her and Finn under surveillance. Hyde was prepared for anything.

The sea surrounding the island was crystal blue, the sky was dotted with white clouds and the weather warm without being humid. The island was ringed by white sandy beaches, blending into a picturesque foliage of palm, casuarina and prince wood trees. Nestled among the greenery at the tallest point on the island was Barnett's compound, the light tan of the walls and red of the roof gleaming in the sun.

Barnett was the king of his own private island. Though the island was officially part of a nearby chain, Barnett maintained its independence by paying off the authorities. On this island, Barnett was the law.

Barnett was staying on the island and cooling his heels. The heat needed to die down after his last big score. The sale and transfer of thousands of pounds of cocaine into Miami, Florida, had netted Reed Barnett millions. If he chose to set foot in the United States, the government would arrest him and try to make charges stick. Barnett let others take the fall for his crimes and he was slippery, sliding into hidey-holes whenever he needed to disappear.

Hyde exited the private villa where she and Finn were staying while on Barnett's island. The villa was located on the beach about half a mile from the main compound. The little house was spacious and well furnished with high-end finishes and an open floor plan. Bamboo reeds covered the exterior of the hut and blended with the sand.

She strode to a wooden lounge chair facing the ocean and adjusted the angle of the chair. Assuming her role as Finn's jet-setting lover, she mentally prepared herself to meet Reed Barnett.

Under other circumstances, taking him out quickly
might have been her preferred course of action. They
wanted to get off the island alive, and it was better
to conclude the operation with evidence against Barnett and his cohorts to bring them to justice. When
the opportunity presented itself to nail Barnett for his
crimes, she would take it.

Closing her eyes, she stretched out on the lounge
chair and lowered her sunglasses onto her face.

Finn whistled from behind her, and his shadow fell
over her as he approached. "You can wear that bikini
the entire time we're here."

Hyde rolled her eyes. She was wearing next to nothing. The bikini was light-colored, strips of fabric and
string, and left no place to conceal her weapon. She
felt feminine and pretty for the first time in months.
Though it had taken an extra twenty minutes, she'd
dried and styled her hair, smoothing it into soft curls.

She needed this op as a final farewell to this life,
a successful mission to give Lydia closure and to say
goodbye to Finn. Giving her sister peace of mind
would ease Hyde's guilt. Losing Finn in her life would
be devastating. She hadn't known a man as smart and
brave as he was. Their relationship was intense and
exciting. Back home in Montana, she wouldn't find
a man to replace him. Finn was one of a kind. "If
you like this, I have some equally fabric-challenged
clothes packed." The West Company had provided
her a suitcase containing everything she needed to
behave like Alexandra Morgan, the dim-witted girl-

friend of a major drug cartel leader operating on the East Coast in the United States.

The West Company had provided Finn a solid background, identity and large bank account as Finn Moore, as well. His persona would hold water as long as Reed Barnett didn't press or dig too hard. The experts at the West Company were good, but nothing was perfect.

Hyde lolled her head in Finn's direction. He was wearing a pair of red swim trunks and a navy T-shirt and he looked delicious. Her libido kicked up a notch. Flirting with him, touching him and being close was playing the part, but it was close to reality and what she wanted to do with him. She looked away, wishing she could confess the truth. The most intimate and passionate moments in her life had been spent with Finn. Her attempts to keep boundaries were challenged by how devastatingly handsome she found him. He walked into a room and he turned heads.

Hyde wasn't in her twenties anymore. She wasn't supposed to chase the handsome bad boy and hold on to the mistaken belief that dating him would lead to love and marriage and a family. She knew better, and every conversation with Finn cemented it.

How many more years would Hyde make a suitable mother? If her biological clock stopped ticking, would someone be crazy enough to let her adopt a child when she had no partner, no stable job and no home?

If she wanted a family, she had to make changes. A change in her career and a change in her personal life were in order.

Finn folded his arms over his chest. "Feel like

going for a swim?" He tensed and glanced down the beach. They were no longer alone.

Hyde didn't break character. "A swim? Maybe later. Why don't you come here and help me put on sunscreen?" She leaned forward in her chair to get a better look at who was approaching. Finn didn't seem alarmed, but she was curious.

Reed Barnett appeared, walking with two bodyguards. He was wearing a khaki-colored suit and pale green linen shirt. It was the first time she had seen the drug lord in person. His hands were tucked in his pants pockets as he strolled, talking to his guards and pointing at something in the ocean. Regardless of his casual behavior, he would not disarm her.

"Mr. Moore," Barnett said, coming close and extending his hand to Finn. "I was alerted you and your beautiful lady had arrived on my island. Welcome to both of you."

If he was rattled at Barnett's appearance, Finn didn't let it show. "I had planned to take advantage of your hospitality and enjoy the beach before our meeting tonight."

Barnett looked out across the water. "It's an incredible place. I don't get out here as much as I'd like. Work keeps me busy. You know how that can be."

Finn had made contact with Barnett through an operative from the West Company who was deep undercover in Barnett's drug ring. Finn was masquerading as a drug lord with extensive ties along the East Coast. Their communication had been indirect through the West Company's channels and their contact had indicated Barnett had a new drug he wanted distributed through Finn's networks to gain greater reach.

"New business is worth it. I like taking time off between big projects," Finn said.

Barnett asked a few more leading questions, trying to pry information from Finn. His answers were vague. The less they gave away, the easier it was. Barnett was assessing Finn and her, looking for a crack in their armor.

"Thank you for inviting us to your island. A couple of days out of the country is great," Finn said.

Hyde rose to her feet and walked toward Barnett, hating that he looked at her chest first before meeting her eyes. Wasn't even her best asset.

"Finn's right." Hyde came close to him and slipped her arms around Finn's waist. His arm went over her shoulders and the movement was so natural and unplanned, pleasure swirled through her. "This place is great. Even better than when you took me to Fiji. It was quieter, but this is so private." They had never been to Fiji, but it was on her list of places to visit.

Barnett studied them. He wouldn't find any reason to doubt their story or their carefully crafted backgrounds. She and Finn were the best, and their attraction to each other played well into the characters they were pretending to be. The surge of desire was real and strong enough that it caught her off guard.

"Please alert my staff if you need anything. I'll see you at dinner. It's formal, but she can wear that," Barnett said, pointing to Hyde's bikini and smirking.

She smiled like an empty-headed twit who took his words as a compliment. Hyde was careful to do nothing to put Barnett on the defensive or to raise his suspicions.

The closer she got to Barnett, the easier it would be to take him down.

* * *

Barnett sauntered down the beach away from Finn and Hyde with his guards on either side of him.

"I could shoot him in the back and he'd never be the wiser," Hyde said.

Finn's arm was still draped across her shoulders. He was enjoying the sensation of her soft skin against his. She had been cagey since he'd arrived in Montana, and she hadn't explained what had changed between them. Every other time they'd met, they'd had red-hot sex. She hadn't seemed interested. He didn't suspect she was involved with anyone else. Hyde would have been up front about that.

Hyde was internationally well-known and had a good reputation in their field. The number of successful missions she was rumored to have completed and her skill set was unmatched for someone her age. It didn't make sense to retire without a good reason. No one seemed to know why the legendary Hyde was unreachable. He'd heard a few rumors she was dead and others that she was undercover for a government agency.

Since they'd met, Finn had kept tabs on Hyde. He liked knowing she was safe. Her well-being was important to him and he needed her in his life. Accepting that she was a spy, as she had been from the first day they'd met, had become harder over time. When he'd heard whispers about a female spy being injured and he couldn't reach Hyde, he'd worried. He hadn't confessed that information to her. It would offend her, like his worry implied she couldn't take care of herself.

The last time they had been together, she had said nothing about quitting the business. It was a huge decision and Hyde wasn't impulsive. Why hadn't she mentioned it to him? Closeness and sharing personal details weren't central to their arrangement, but Finn thought of them as more than lovers. They were friends, too.

Hyde shrugged out of his touch. He didn't care for that, but let her go. He'd learned to hold his desire for her in check.

"Feel like a swim?" he asked again. The dark throb of need pulsed in his blood. Exercise would take the edge off.

Hyde pulled an elastic band from her wrist and wrapped it in her hair. "Sure."

She moved toward the water, not looking at him, saying nothing more, and Finn caught her around the waist. He brought his mouth close to her ear. "Don't be in such a hurry to get away from me. Someone could be watching."

Hyde met his gaze. Holding her this close and looking into her eyes, anyone watching would think they were lovers. She was holding her back rigid and arching away from him, her hands braced on his chest.

"You can't use that as an excuse every time you want to touch me," Hyde said.

"Why are you against me touching you?" Finn asked. He released her, but she didn't move away. Her chest was inches from his.

"If I were against it, it wouldn't be happening at all," Hyde said. She ran her hand down the side of his face and cupped his chin.

He loved her strength and her confidence. She had never played the damsel in distress. "You're right about that."

"Did you see someone?" Hyde asked. "Surveillance inside our villa?"

"The jungle behind the villa provides places to hide and watch. I didn't see any cameras or microphones in the villa, but I need to check more thoroughly." He had been unpacking and when he'd seen Hyde out on the beach, he'd wanted to be with her. That had felt more important.

She slid her hand down his chest and let it rest on his abs. He was already turned on and the gesture excited him more. "I wish this swimsuit gave me a place to tuck a weapon. Can I assume you have a weapon somewhere on you?" she asked.

"I have a covered blade in my pocket," he said.

She reached to his hip and smiled. Though it was a warm smile, the heat didn't race into her eyes. She was playing the part now, not flirting with him. "I could be the only woman in the world who finds it hot that you're armed."

"Then you'll love the holster I brought for you. Fits your inner thigh, so it can't be seen under a dress."

She smirked. "I already have one of those."

He drew her closer. Her breasts were pressed to his chest and her flat stomach against his. Every tiny movement brought sensation to his core and amplified his lust. "This one has a quick release on the snap and room for an extra round."

She made a sound of delight. "How did you get one of those?"

They weren't available on the open market. "The West Company's R and D department."

She smiled, and this time, the smile reached her

eyes. "If I could get Connor or his wife to owe me a favor, I would request a tour of their weapons closet."

Finn had seen the R and D department at the West Company headquarters. He had participated in a field test for them and had been given a tour. "At this point, it's not a closet. It's an entire floor of one of their secret facilities."

Hyde's eyes grew wide. "You're toying with me."

He shook his head. "I am not. I've seen it." He loved her passion for her job. Walking away from it didn't fit. He was missing something key.

Hyde pressed her hands together in front of her. "I know you can't tell me what you saw, but wow."

"Connor West had you in mind for a few upcoming ops. You could have asked for something new to accompany you on those ops."

Hyde pushed against his chest and walked closer to the water line. The waves were gentle and low. "I know. He called me. But awesome toys aside, I had to say no."

That fast, she was distant again. He had pressed her too hard.

They waded into the water. It was warm and felt great on his feet. "You might change your mind," Finn said.

"I doubt that. When my clearance comes up for renewal in a couple of months, I'm letting it lapse."

Not renewing her security clearance was a quick way to scratch her name off the United States' black ops-for-hire list. Finn had never seen the list and he didn't know who had access to it except likely the president of the United States, the vice president, a couple of senators and Connor West. Some of the best and the brightest were rumored to be on the list. Experts in absolutely everything at the government's beck and call.

If Hyde's clearance expired, acquiring another at the same level would take months, if it was granted at all. She wouldn't be eligible for special projects.

"After working for years to get where you are, you're letting it go." He couldn't get his head around it and he believed she would regret this decision.

"There are more important things than work."

Suspicion crept over him. Though he would never accuse her of being a turncoat, getting off the list and quitting the spy game made her a free agent. "Are you planning to go mercenary?"

She made a face of disgust. He was off the mark.

"I would never do that. What I have in mind entails Saturdays and Sundays off work, nights and holidays to myself and a steady paycheck. Reading the news about attacks and bombings and knowing someone else is handling it. No more calls at midnight to go wheels up."

"A small paycheck for boring work," he said.

"The paycheck doesn't matter," she said. "I'll embrace the mundane."

When they were ribs deep in the water, Hyde dove under. She surfaced ten feet out. Finn chased her. He slid his hand around her hips and lifted her against him. She wrapped her legs around his waist. He tread water for them. "Do you remember when we rented a room at the resort in Palm Springs and pretended to be spring-breakers?" They had stayed in the penthouse of a popular hotel. He and Hyde had loved being in the middle of that chaos. They had been close enough to hear the music, the lingo and the craziness, and far enough away to escape when they'd wanted privacy.

"We are too old for that now. I can't chug a beer from a funnel without getting reflux."

"It was two years ago."

"A lifetime," she said. She pushed off his chest and swam backward away from him.

If he could remind her of the closeness they'd shared, she may confide in him. They were friends first. He had told her things he hadn't told another human being. "What did you do with the bracelet I gave you?"

"I have it. In my pack. It fits my cover."

Was that all it was? Or did it still mean something to her? He had surprised her with the bracelet in Bora Bora, a diamond tennis bracelet in a platinum setting. "It was my grandmother's." He had been given it after his grandmother had passed away. She was the one person in his family who had understood what he did for a living and approved. The rest of his family wanted him to quit and go into politics, like his father and brother. The bracelet had a high sentimental value to him.

Hyde pushed her wet hair off her face. "The bracelet is a family heirloom?"

He nodded.

Hyde's brows were furrowed in confusion. "I thought it was a piece you picked up at the local market."

He had let her believe that. She wouldn't have accepted it otherwise. "I wanted you to have it. You're strong and brave like my grandmother was. If she had met you, she would have liked you and wanted you to have it."

"Finn, I can't keep a precious item like that."

It was important to him that Hyde have it. He didn't look too deeply into that thought. "You already accepted it. I would like if you wore it tonight."

Hyde touched her bare wrist as if considering it. "I could do that. But I want you to think about it. If you change your mind and want it back, please ask."

He wouldn't want it back. It looked great on Hyde and it belonged with her.

Hyde and Finn drove a sand buggy to Reed's house. It was huge and opulent, the four-story building boasting numerous balconies and dozens of gleaming windows. Storm shutters carved with elaborate scrollwork were pinned to the sides of the windows, and the front of the house was adorned with Roman-style columns and graceful archways. It must have taken an army of engineers to safely place such a large building this close to the water.

Inviting them to his home and this island, Barnett had an agenda. He had numerous politicians, police chiefs and judges on his payroll. He blackmailed people he couldn't pay off. Everyone had something to hide. Dig deep enough, and anyone looking would hit pay dirt. He'd want to know Finn's weakness.

Barnett was the master of getting dirty, getting the people around him dirty and then slaughtering anyone who threatened to expose him. His list of friends was long, but his list of enemies was longer. Many people would like to see him dead.

But many people would also line up to step into

his shoes. Finn wanted Barnett and his organization torn to the ground and the roots ripped up. He wanted Barnett to pay dearly for killing Simon.

They were escorted to the dining room. The walls and ceiling were painted with images of Victorian angels in the clouds, and the white floor tile was blinding. The room wasn't what Finn had expected.

Hyde squeezed Finn's hand. She was wearing a light blue dress, which looked painted on. Cut low in the front, it clung to her hips and thighs. The bottom of the dress was uneven, drawing attention to her strong calves. She was playing her part, and it was distracting to have her so close and know she wasn't available. The one thing he and Hyde had always done well was sex.

Why was it off the table? Hyde was different, but Finn couldn't figure out why. They were frequently apart and Finn missed much from her life. She had seemed to enjoy being close to her family. Had they convinced her to quit her life on the road?

"Don't frown, you look pissed off," Hyde said. She set her free hand on the crook of his elbow. Every muscle in his body flexed in awareness, and his lust elevated to nearly unmanageable proportions.

He leaned to kiss her cheek and they stared into each other's eyes. Heat snapped between them and Finn wouldn't buy this was an act. She played hell with his libido and it wasn't a one-way street.

Barnett was seated at the head of the table, no one at the other end. The brunette to his right had her body on display in a barely there orange gown. She was staring adoringly at Barnett. She looked like she was ready for a pageant, her hair curled and styled and makeup coating her face. Barnett was ignoring her, but she seemed unperturbed by it.

She had to be his latest fling. Finn didn't understand why women flocked to Barnett. His face was slim and his nose curved at the tip. He was wealthy and dressed well, but beneath his sophisticated demeanor hummed a quiet rage. Didn't women sense that and want to avoid him? Barnett had an explosive temper. He could turn on a dime. Anyone who had spent time with him would see it and rightfully fear it.

Barnett wasn't a man to be trifled with. Acquaintances and companions who displeased him disappeared.

Barnett stood in greeting. He gestured to the seats next to him. "Mr. Moore and the lovely Alexandra. Thank you for joining me tonight. This is my girlfriend, Ruby."

Finn held out Hyde's chair for her and she took her seat. Finn then sat next to her and between her and Barnett. Drinks were brought and after an exchange of pleasantries, Barnett took over the conversation.

"I am embarking on an exciting new opportunity. There are fortunes to be made. Before I share my grand plan, I need something from you."

Finn didn't like where this was leading.

Waiters in white gloves and black ties served appetizers. The longer Finn sat with Barnett, the dirtier he felt. And not dirty in a good way. Dirty as in, "my soul is being corrupted by the second." If he was the average of the five people he spent the most time with, with the exception of Hyde, Finn was being dragged into the depths of immorality.

"How about a show of your skill?" Barnett said.

"What did you have in mind?" Finn asked.

"Your reputation speaks to your skills as a marksman and as an explosives expert."

He was both, though he would rather Hyde handle explosives. Hyde was remarkable with them, having a sixth sense about timing and control.

Barnett stood and picked up a plate. "Shoot this."

Barnett pulled his arm back and let the plate spin like a disc. Finn withdrew his gun and shot the plate before it hit the wall. It shattered, pieces striking the floor.

Barnett's brows were lifted and the corners of his mouth turned up in amusement. Ruby's hand was over her mouth, staring at Finn.

"Good reflexes and it answers my question that you traveled armed," Barnett said.

"Safer to assume every person I meet is armed," Finn said.

"Even your beautiful lady?" Barnett said.

Finn touched Hyde's shoulder, as if she'd need his protection and reassurance. "Alexandra knows how to protect herself." Finn wouldn't let on how skilled a spy Hyde was.

Barnett snapped his fingers and pointed to the mess on the floor. Two waiters rushed to clean it up.

At the sound of breaking glass, Finn scanned for the source. Another test?

Ruby was on her feet apologizing.

Barnett pointed at her. "You clumsy cow! That's a five-thousand-dollar wineglass. How will you pay for it?"

Barnett was a moron if he paid five thousand dollars for a piece of glass. Finn hid his disgust at Barnett's reaction to what was probably a slip of her hand. Barnett had thrown a plate and had Finn destroy it for no reason. He had lodged a bullet in the ceiling, an expensive repair. Barnett wasn't a man who cared about wasting money. But he obviously enjoyed humiliating his girlfriend.

Ruby brought her hands to her mouth, and her body trembled. Hyde moved as if she planned to go to the woman's side, but Finn clamped a hand on her forearm. If Hyde interfered, she could get Ruby killed. It had to be killing Hyde to see this. Since he had known her, Hyde had harbored a passion for protecting women who could not protect themselves. Rumors had swirled about Hyde's actions to protect others, and Finn had witnessed it himself over the last several years.

Humiliation was survivable. As long as Barnett didn't throw a punch, Finn would let it play out.

"I suggest you go to our room. You can make this up to me tonight." His grin was lascivious and Ruby looked at Finn and Hyde, her face red, and then fled the room in tears.

Barnett appeared composed. This was the hair-trigger temper Finn had read about. One moment Barnett was relaxed and jovial, and the next he was tearing someone to shreds.

Hyde was seething, twisting her linen napkin in her lap and tapping the gun at her thigh, but she was keeping her facial expression in check. The rest of the meal passed without incident. Ruby did not return to the table and Finn didn't blame her. He hoped she had found a boat and was hightailing it away from Barnett.

When dinner was over, Barnett invited Finn to his private office for drinks and cigars.

"Are you okay on your own?" Finn asked, turning to Hyde at the table. It would be like Hyde to use the time to look around the house under the guise of admiring the decor and artwork. He ran his hand down the side of her face and she leaned into the touch. Their eyes connected and heat and anticipation arced between them.

She gripped her clutch in her hands. "If our generous host agrees, I'll enjoy some wine on the portico."

Barnett nodded. "I like a woman who can entertain herself."

Hyde must want to stab Barnett. Everything the man said to her sounded like a slight or an innuendo to sex. Finn credited her with staying calm. He put his hands on her shoulders and kissed her lightly. She allowed the kiss, but she didn't return it. He sensed she wanted to and was overthinking this. Finn would break through her walls and find out what was bothering her. It was a matter of time.

"Mr. Moore? Are you coming?" Barnett asked.

Though he hated splitting up from her, Finn followed Barnett into his office.

Hyde had worked as a spy long enough to have seen every type of relationship and had learned to categorize them quickly. Some were good, some were awful and most were somewhere in between. She placed Reed Barnett and every woman he dated in the awful category. He had humiliated and verbally abused Ruby. The idea made Hyde's blood run red-hot with rage. If there was anything that elicited a reaction from her, it was a woman in trouble.

However Ruby had come to be involved with Barnett, she had to regret it. She could feel trapped or know she couldn't leave with her life. Perhaps she was waiting for the right opportunity to escape to safety. Or she had been someone's victim for so long, she didn't know how to be anything but one. Though it wasn't the mission's primary objective, Hyde wanted to get Ruby safely out of her entanglement with Barnett when she was ready to take that step.

In her field, Hyde was often underestimated and men tried to push her around. She had pushed back and struggled for every scrap of respect she had. She'd had examples of strong women in her life. Her father treated her mother with respect, and Hyde expected nothing less from the men in her life. After a decade of missions, her reputation preceded her. Now, when a man learned her name, they reacted with the right amount of awe.

Barnett's butler led Hyde out of the main house to a large patio overlooking the ocean. Citronella candles surrounded her.

Ruby appeared, having changed from the orange evening gown into pink yoga pants and a matching zip-up sweatshirt. Her hair was long and loose around her shoulders. She folded her hands in front of her and lifted her head. Hyde read her discomfort in the tightness of her shoulders, but Hyde also saw strength in her eyes.

Hyde would break the ice first and let Ruby know that she was a friend. "I'm glad you came out tonight.

Who knows how long the men will be talking? It's nice to make a friend on the island."

Ruby touched the ends of her hair. "I'm embarrassed by what happened at dinner."

It must be her first event of this nature, or she was playing a carefully scripted part to gain empathy. Hyde didn't let her guard down until she was sure of someone and it was rare for her to be sure of anyone.

Hyde's plan was to be as kind as possible to get close to Ruby without giving away anything about herself or Finn. "He overreacted. I'm sure he'll be over it by tomorrow."

Ruby touched her bare left ring finger. "He was pretty mad."

"He seemed fine at the end of dinner," Hyde said.

"Whenever he gets mad like that..." She let her voice trail off.

If she finished that statement with "he hits me" or any variation of those words, Hyde would kill Barnett. She and Finn would have to come up with a Plan B to destroy the rest of his network. Her retribution for Barnett was ready to be taken off its leash with the slimmest notice.

"He what?" Hyde prompted.

Ruby pressed her hands to her sides. "It's the best sex I've ever had."

Not what she'd expected, but Hyde rolled with it. She could be a friend to Ruby and leverage her for information. Allies came in handy. When the time came, she would help her escape Barnett's network.

Hyde giggled. "They get worked up, don't they?"

Ruby relaxed and Barnett's staff brought a bottle of wine and glasses out to them.

Hyde accepted a glass of wine, but didn't drink it. She brought it to her lips, but she was listening, gathering every detail Ruby was willing to share.

She needed to figure out if Ruby could help them or hurt them and if she could be trusted.

After several hours of speaking with Ruby about everything from music to travel to books they enjoyed, Hyde pretended to be drunk. She had dumped a fair amount of wine into the bushes around the patio. It was almost one in the morning, and Finn was still talking with Barnett. When Ruby begged off to get some sleep, Hyde couldn't think of a reason to linger without raising suspicions.

One of Barnett's guards drove her wordlessly to the villa on the beach. Hyde thanked Barnett's guard and stumbled into the house, closing and locking the door behind her. Her feet crunched over the gritty sand that seemed to coat the brown tile floor.

Hyde swept for bugs. Thinking of Ruby, she hoped Barnett's anger would disappear before bed. If their villa was closer to the main house, she could have kept a better eye on Ruby.

Hyde hit the shower. Ten minutes in, the sound of the front door opening and closing interrupted her thoughts. Finn was home. Hyde shut off the water. She wrapped a plush white lavender-scented towel around her.

Her time with Finn was the closest thing she'd had to a vacation in the last ten years. Finn had once needed to cancel plans with her when his mission went sideways, and Hyde had been utterly disappointed. That lingering displeasure had been an eye-opening experience. She needed Finn after a mission. It was how she bounced back from the soul-wrecking events that were her job.

When this was over, Hyde wouldn't have Finn. Instead, she would take a vacation. A weeklong getaway to somewhere warm where she could relax without fearing for her life.

Keeping her towel around her, Hyde met Finn in the main room of the house. Achy, needy and unexpected desire swelled inside her.

He was removing his tie and it was one of the sexiest things she had seen in months. Finn in dress pants, his shirt rumpled and the sleeves rolled to his elbows, his hair askew and now the tie loose around his neck.

His brown eyes blinked at her. "I won't be presumptuous, so I'll ask. Were you waiting for me?"

Her clothes were hanging in the closet. "Just getting pajamas."

"Can I watch you change?"

Seeing her naked wasn't a novelty for him. "That's unfair since I have no intention of letting you touch me." The words were a boundary she needed. If she followed her impulses, she would be in his arms in minutes.

A playful expression crossed his face. He removed his tie and shirt. Buff and muscled only began to describe him. A tiger was tattooed across his side. The tattoo covered a scar he'd gotten on one of his first missions when a poacher had shot at him.

Though his appearance wasn't the sole reason she liked Finn, it was impossible to ignore. Finn's dark and brooding, bad-boy-meets-secret-agent, tough-guy image appealed to her.

Broad across the shoulders, tanned skin from hours spent in the sun and lean muscles that she liked to touch, beckoned to her. To feel his body tighten beneath her hands and to lie against him, his arms around her, was the safest she had felt in her life.

When she had been in the worst emotional pain in her life, she had thought about being with Finn, his arms offering comfort and security she desperately needed to fill the gaping hole in her heart and emptiness in her soul.

Her excitement slowed when she thought of Munich. Her stomach clenched and she touched her midsection, feeling like she was less than she had been before, like something important was missing. Finn was the same man she'd been attracted to six months ago. She had changed. What she wanted from him and for her life was different.

Falling into bed with Finn would be easy. If she crossed that line with him, at the end of the mission she was still alone and without a family of her own. That dream was far out of reach, but not lost to her.

Hyde was beyond the point where she could have sex with Finn for recreation and pretend it meant nothing. She couldn't put her finger on the precise moment it had happened, but sleeping with him had become about more than sex. She cared for him and he couldn't—wouldn't—give her what she wanted.

She took her pajamas to the bathroom and dressed. He joined her after several minutes, changing and brushing his teeth at the sink across the bathroom. She was momentarily thrown by the simplicity. They weren't a couple in their home getting ready for bed. They were operatives on a mission where people would die to achieve their goal and even more people would die if she and Finn failed. Hyde wouldn't let herself get caught in a fantasy. They were working. This was not real life.

Hyde left the bathroom and tossed a bed pillow onto the settee.

"That's where you're sleeping?" Finn asked, turning off the light in the bathroom.

It was late, the end of a long day, and she didn't want to have a lengthy conversation about it. "Yes."

He sighed. "Get in the bed."

"I'd rather have some space."

"We slept in the same room in Montana," he said.

"I know." She had liked it. Too much. It had been too tempting to cross the limits she had set.

He put one hand on his hip and rubbed his forehead with the other. "When are you planning to tell me what's going on with you? Why are you acting like this?"

"I've told you. I want a life with words that scare you. Words like husband and wedding and babies and mortgage." No point in dancing around it and pretending she was okay with sex with no strings, at least not when it came to Finn.

Finn straightened. "Those words don't scare me. They just aren't in the cards for me."

He sounded certain. Case closed. Not even a hint that in the future, the distant future, he may want those things. She lay on the settee and closed her eyes. She couldn't have this conversation with him. The intense longing swallowing her to hear him say those words clarified that she needed more from him. She wanted him to say he would give her a life and home together, if not now, in time. That he was capable of being the man she needed.

"Did you see Ruby?" Finn asked. The worry in his voice prevented her from ignoring him.

A change in the subject and she let go of her foolish hope about Finn changing his mind. "I did. We shared a few glasses of wine. She was shaken, but okay. This wasn't the first time Barnett lost his temper with her, and she seemed fine."

Finn made a sound of disgust. "Until Barnett takes it to the next level and he gets violent with her."

She'd had similar thoughts. "He is a wretched human being. I can't imagine anything he does making up for how he humiliated Ruby or why she would forgive him and stay."

Finn flopped on the bed. "If you change your mind, I'm here. I know you want to sleep next to me. I can feel it."

Hyde shifted on the settee and stared at the ceiling. "If I get in bed with you, will you stop questioning me?"

"For now. But Hyde, I know there's something going on and I want to understand. I want you to let me in."

She looked over at him. He lifted the blanket and patted the bed.

She crossed the room, the floor cold under her feet. She slid under the covers with him. He didn't reach for her and she didn't move closer. Sharing the same bed was close enough. They had an invisible wall as a barrier and neither was ready to tear it down.

Chapter 4

Despite his many bad qualities, Barnett had the best amenities on his island. Swimming pools, golf courses, fully equipped gym, day spa, restaurants and coffee bars. It had to cost a small fortune to keep and maintain this small island for Barnett's personal pleasure. He and Finn were meeting on one of the island's golf courses to play a round while Hyde and Ruby had treatments at the day spa.

Finn was amused thinking of Hyde receiving spa treatments. She would be antsy and bored. Then again, golf bored him, so they were in the same boat. By pretending to enjoy an activity they disliked, but that Barnett and Ruby found enjoyable, they'd get closer to their targets. Now, if only Finn could get closer to Hyde.

He had tried. Every time he asked her what was wrong, she shut him out. It wasn't the mission she was upset about. There was more to it and he was going crazy with her putting so much distance between them.

More to his disappointment, when he and Barnett finished their round, Finn had learned nothing except that Barnett hated to lose. Finn let him win by a few strokes, sensing he would be a bad sport, possibly to the degree of ending their partnership over it. Finn might not be learning about the business, but he was learning a great deal about Barnett. Except for his ruthlessness and utter disregard for others, Finn saw nothing that should have propelled Barnett to the top of his game.

"Feel like checking on the ladies?" Finn suggested, unwilling to pretend to suck at golf for another round.

Barnett removed his golf glove and handed it to his caddy. "Ruby needs rest after last night. She didn't get much sleep."

Finn made a sound of acknowledgement. Barnett's need to make innuendo about how he and Ruby spent their time together revealed an insecurity, but Finn hadn't figured out the specifics. His impotence, some deep-seated woman issue, his inability to satisfy a lover in bed or a combination of all three.

"What about you? Did your accommodations put Alexandra in a good mood? The villa you are staying in has one of the best views on the island."

The villa and the setting did nothing to warm Hyde. She was still freezing him out. Finn didn't think she was angry. She wanted space. For spies, that wasn't unusual. Being aloof was a way to stay safe. He and Hyde hadn't been distant with each other in the past and that was what made it hard for him. "She was asleep when I returned to the villa." The lie was easier.

Barnett was looking for a masculinity-measuring contest and Finn preferred details of his personal life remain private. Even fictionalizing details about him and Hyde in the bedroom made him uncomfortable. Given his penchant for winning, better for Barnett to believe he was the superior man in bed. It didn't matter to Finn. He wanted to work things out with Hyde, but not because he was in competition with someone.

They drove one of the golf carts to the spa. Finn spotted Hyde and Ruby lying poolside, each reading a magazine, frozen cocktails on a table between them, and sunglasses covering their eyes. Finn's heart leaped to his throat. From this distance, Hyde took his breath away. They parked the golf cart and strode onto the pool deck.

Hyde waved as he approached, and he itched to touch her. Ruby greeted Barnett with a kiss and he reached to her rear end, squeezing and pulling her close.

"How was golf?" Hyde asked. She looked stunning in a bright yellow string bikini accenting her curves and the cut angles of her stomach and leg muscles. She appeared relaxed. She looked that way after great sex, too.

"Great views of the ocean," Finn said.

Hyde set aside the magazine she was reading. It was a bridal magazine. Was it her pick or the only selection offered by Ruby? Hyde had mentioned wanting a husband and a family. How long had that been on her mind? She hadn't mentioned it at their prior meetings. Was she putting distance between them because she knew that Finn would make the worst spouse and parent? For that reason, he had no intention of being either. He traveled too much and his plans changed week to week. He missed birthdays, anniversaries and holidays. He couldn't put a wife or children through that.

His father was a politician. Finn had hated how often his dad had been pulled away on business. To subject his wife and children to that lifestyle struck Finn as unfair.

"I was planning to take a swim. Interested?" Hyde asked.

The water would feel great and distract him from obsessing about Hyde. "Let me get changed."

Hyde stood and tossed her sunglasses on the lounge chair where she'd been sitting. "I don't feel like waiting." She grabbed his shirt and pulled him into the pool with her.

They came up laughing. Hyde delivered a wet kiss to his lips. "You have to be more spontaneous."

Ruby and Barnett were watching them. Ruby looked like she was considering tossing Barnett in the pool and then thought better of it.

"I'm plenty spontaneous," Finn said. He should be enjoying this, but it bothered him that this might be for show and nothing about her casual touch meaningful.

Hyde swam away from him. "Now do you want to change?"

"What did I do to deserve a dunk?" Finn asked. He wanted to discuss the golf game, but he couldn't in front of Ruby.

Hyde shrugged. "You needed to cool down." She brought her mouth close to his ear. "You looked like you wanted to stab Barnett."

Had he? He thought he had been hiding his feelings well. "I was thinking about you."

She leaned away from him, surprise registering on her face. "It's me who you want to stab?"

Never. Hurting her wasn't his objective. "I want to figure you out."

Hyde pushed off him, diving under the water. She appeared in the deep end of the pool. Her long hair was slicked back and she looked positively gorgeous. He wanted to give chase, snag her and kiss her. He put a lid on his desire for her. If he gave her space, would she confide in him, and let their relationship resume on the path it had been before?

Barnett's phone rang and he stepped a few yards away to take the call. When he returned, a frown pulled down the corners of his mouth.

"We have new suits in the pool house," Barnett said. "I apologize, but something has come up that I need to attend to. Enjoy your day." He put his phone to his ear and hurried away.

Ruby climbed into the pool and sat on the stairs. Her arms were wrapped around her midsection and her eyes cast downward at the water. Should he say anything? Finn didn't know how Barnett would feel about him talking to Ruby. Best to leave that to Hyde.

Finn dragged himself out of the water and changed in the pool house. When he exited, Hyde was by the stairs, talking to Ruby. Hyde could be extracting valuable information from her. Finn sat on the lounge chair next to Hyde's. He looked at the bridal magazine, a picture of a brunette bride glancing over her shoulder, a bouquet of pink puffed flowers at her side and the yellow pastel of the background glaring.

This was what Hyde wanted? A day in a white dress and a big party followed by years of commitment and obligations was no adventure. The life they had, the travel and the excitement, was far more fascinating.

Hyde strode to him and he set the magazine down, his cheeks flushing. He felt like he had been caught red-handed.

"Find something you like?" she asked.

Finn shook his head. "I don't understand the whole idea of it."

Ruby joined them, wrapping a towel around her waist. "You sound like Reed. He thinks marriage is a waste of time."

Hyde made a sound of empathy. "Finn, too."

Their cover dovetailed with reality. Finn kept his cool. Was Hyde angry about that? He hadn't promised her anything he couldn't deliver. He didn't want to put down roots. He liked to travel and see new places. He couldn't be tied to one person or one place forever. He had chosen his career because he loved adventure and challenges.

His father had been committed to his job and neglectful of his family. He'd had unrealistic expectations about the way his family should behave when they were together and no intention of putting in the time to make them a cohesive unit. Finn's commitment to his job would mean ignoring his family. He couldn't—wouldn't—do that to anyone. Until he had met Hyde, he kept his affairs light and brief. Now that she was in his life, he wouldn't become his father and try to maintain a commitment to her and his career. One would inevitably suffer and he'd lose the work he loved, or Hyde would grow to hate him. He couldn't live with either outcome.

* * *

Ruby set her towel on the lounge chair and sat. "It would be nice to have my family and friends see that Reed is a good man. They know little about him, yet they have plenty of bad things to say."

Hyde could understand why. Ruby seemed blind to how dangerous Barnett was. "How did you meet?" Hyde asked. An innocent question, but might tell her more about where Barnett traveled.

"In the south of France," Ruby said and sighed. "I was working in a hotel as his chambermaid. I brought him towels and he asked me to stay the night with him. I could have been fired. I turned him down three times before I agreed to stay. I never left. Reed took me away from that job and has given me everything I could wish for."

Not everything. Ruby wasn't seeing the big picture or the opportunities that awaited her out from under Barnett's thumb. "Sounds like a fairy tale," Hyde said, trying to inject warmth into her words. She had developed a genuine affection for Ruby, and pretending to like Barnett and how he treated Ruby was becoming harder.

Ruby stared out across the pool. "He swept me off my feet and I fell for him fast. We've been together about three months. He's been busy and it's hard for him to find time for me. Whenever I ask to travel with him, he says it's too dangerous."

"Reed and Finn want to protect us. When they get involved in things, we get pulled into them, too, and then they worry. That additional distraction could cost them," Hyde said. Ruby might know something about Barnett's work, and Hyde wanted to nudge it out of her.

Ruby sighed. "I get bored on the island. I know it seems picture-perfect and like I have an ideal life, but there's no one to talk to."

A beautiful bird in a gilded cage. Hyde didn't envy her position. "I understand."

"I hope when Finn and Reed are finished with their new project, he'll have more time to spend with me."

"I miss Finn when he works too much, too. It comes with the territory," Hyde said. She tried to appear empathetic.

"How long have you and Finn been together?" Ruby asked.

"Almost three years," Hyde said. That information had been documented in their operation notes. It was close to the real amount of time they had known each other. Over the three years, when they had been together, Hyde had felt like she was transported to another time and place.

"Wow. I've never had a relationship last that long. Maybe with Reed it will?" Ruby said. Ruby's phone beeped and she jumped to her feet. She dried her hand on a towel before looking at her phone. "That's Reed. I've got to go."

Had Barnett been listening to their conversation? Was he worried about something that Ruby might say? Hyde waved goodbye and Ruby dashed off in the direction of the main house.

Finn climbed out of the pool, droplets of water running down his muscular form. He strode toward her, snagging a towel off the rack of clean, dry ones.

"What was that about?" He sat on the end of a lounge chair.

Hyde joined him. "She was meeting Barnett. He snapped. She came running." A situation she had seen far too often. She had been assigned an operation years before that reminded her of this one. Different dynamics, and in the other case, the boyfriend had been an assassin. He had used his girlfriend Rayna to provide his alibi. Perjuring herself, Rayna had sunk deeper into her boyfriend's crimes. Hyde had warned Rayna that it wouldn't end well. Hyde had tried to provide resources and offer her protection if she told the truth about her boyfriend's murders. Rayna hadn't listened. The boyfriend had killed her and dumped her body in a lake. They'd found it months later. It had broken Hyde's heart. Until the body had been found, she had been hoping that Rayna had escaped.

Finn set a hand on her calf. "Take it easy. I know you don't like the dynamics between them, but it will be okay." He kept his voice low.

This was Hyde's last mission. She wanted for once, just for once, for her experience to save someone before something bad happened. Too often, she had to pull someone out of the fire. Few heeded the warning when she smelled smoke.

Barnett could have video cameras anywhere. She and Finn kept their conversation to banal topics while they gathered their belongings. Once they were away from the pool and possible surveillance, they could speak frankly. They exited the pool area and decided to return to their villa on foot. The walk would give them time to talk. About the mission. Finn had hinted that he wanted to discuss their relationship, but Hyde was still collecting her thoughts on that. Focusing on what she wanted in the future was more important than delving into the past.

"Did you get anything from Barnett?" Hyde asked.

Finn slipped his arm over her shoulder. Hyde instinctively leaned toward him. While on this island, they had to appear and behave as lovers. Hyde hadn't calculated how long it had been since they'd actually been lovers, but it was recent enough that those emotions, the intensity and the intimacy, still bowed between them.

"Barnett received two phone calls while we were golfing from someone he called Sydney," Finn said. "They discussed meeting tonight. No mention as to why or where from what I heard."

"Hard to pick a place. By the main house?" Hyde asked.

"We may hear the approach if it's close to the main house," Finn said. "I'll call the West Company and see if they can reroute a satellite to do a flyover. We can look at the images and pinpoint possible places for a boat or chopper to land."

"Maybe it's a supplies delivery," Hyde said, though she hoped Finn caught a lead into Barnett's new endeavor.

"Perhaps. But Barnett wouldn't need to be involved in routine supplies deliveries. He has about fifty employees who could handle that for him," Finn said. He moved his arm from around her shoulder and took her hand in his.

At the steps leading to the villa's porch, Finn brought her hand to his lips and kissed the back of it. Their eyes met and held. A swell of emotion billowed inside her. Hyde swallowed, thinking of all she should say to him and hadn't.

The memory of being with him the last time simmered in her blood. When she opened her mouth to speak, the words wouldn't form. She pulled her hand away and whirled around, fleeing into the villa.

"Want to talk about it?" Finn asked, following her inside.

She didn't. Not yet. "We need to see if anything looks amiss." Plus, exploring the island would prevent them from being alone in the villa. "I'll be ready in a minute." She changed into a sundress and donned a wide-brimmed hat, sunglasses and a gun strapped to her thigh. Finn changed into board shorts and a T-shirt.

They walked along the beach, close enough to hold hands, but not touching. The sand was hot and soft beneath her feet. The sound of the waves was the background to their conversation.

"When I retire, this is how I want to spend my days. Minus the interacting with a criminal part," Finn said.

"I thought you didn't want to retire," Hyde said, surprised to hear Finn suggest slowing down. Most of the time, he spoke of the next mission, the latest gadget he had acquired for said mission or the exciting new place he was working.

"I can't do this work forever. Enough injuries and I'll be out of the game or I'll get slow. A newer, sharper guy will come along and show me up and take my jobs," he said.

"New guys don't have experience," Hyde said. Experience had gotten her through difficult situations.

Agents who had been in the field longer than she had saved her life on more than one occasion.

"Experience slows me down. I know what can happen. If I stop and think about the consequences for too long, opportunities pass me by. Pretty soon, no operation seems worth it when looking at the risks."

Hyde brushed away a strand of hair that had blown across her face. "That's what I'm afraid of, too." Except she wasn't afraid of losing jobs or operations. She was terrified of waking up one day, her career over, and her life hollow and empty.

She felt his gaze on her. Did he finally understand why she'd retired? When Finn looked at her, a thrill skittered over her. With their backgrounds, they had understood each other and the life they led. Only recently had she felt disconnected from him when she'd realized she wanted something else for her life.

"Until I can't do this work anymore, either physically or mentally, I'll stop as many bad guys as I can," Finn said.

Hyde wouldn't get him to see the advantages of changing his plans. It depressed her to know that after this mission, they wouldn't have a reason to see each other. She would find stability, he would chase the next mission and they would drift apart.

Though the sun was relentless and hot, as they walked back to their villa, Hyde felt ice-cold.

Chapter 5

Hyde had to cover some distance to watch the shore-line. Her phone was connected to a satellite feed that was monitoring the area. Moving back and forth along the beach, it would be easier to spot approaching boat lights in the dark. Without a dock, any ship of large mass would need to stay offshore and send a smaller boat to reach land.

Finn would message her if Barnett excused himself or indicated he had a problem. If Barnett was meeting with Sydney himself, Hyde would have warning and hopefully be close enough to capture the interaction on her camera.

Every terrain presented challenges, but Hyde hated the bugs and nocturnal predators that came with tropical island life. Too many hazardous surprises lurked.

She was wearing head-to-toe black and had coated

her skin with bug spray. The temperature would drop over the course of the night and she would be more comfortable when it was cooler. She could be watching for hours.

Moving through the trees, she estimated about thirty yards of sand between her and the water. Despite the dark and unknown, it was serene sitting alone. Underscoring that sense of peace was the knowledge that Barnett had a plot afoot.

Hyde had a soft spot for protecting women in danger and when she thought of Ruby, she wished she could speak plainly about her loser lover and convince Ruby to leave him. It wasn't the first time Hyde had met a beautiful woman who had clung to the first money that came by. The luxuries it afforded seemed great until the real cost was revealed.

Giving a man complete control was dangerous and in Ruby and Barnett's relationship, Barnett dominated. He had control of the house, the money and the business. Did Ruby have any assets? She should set aside expensive gifts in case they needed to be pawned for cash.

If Ruby's relationship with Barnett ended, if he didn't kill her, would she feel like she could go home? Hyde couldn't imagine feeling unwanted by her family. Her parents' house in Montana had remained a soft place to land. It was part of the reason Hyde hadn't worried about the future. If a situation got too hot, she could bail and go home. How did Finn cope? He didn't have a place to call home and his family issues seemed to extend to more than annoyances.

Hyde caught sight of lights across the water. Her heart rate escalated and her adrenaline fired. Controlling her muscles, she took slow, deep breaths. She waited and watched. It took twenty minutes before a dinghy came into view, moving toward the shore. A lantern was hanging from a post on the back of it, providing her a shadowy view. The moon was bright, but at the wrong angle to illuminate the faces of the arrivals.

Hyde snapped pictures so she wouldn't miss anything. She and Finn could review them later and the West Company could look in detail at the photos.

Four men climbed out of the small boat. Three were built tall and broad across the shoulders, like bodyguards, and from the bulges around their sides, they were heavily armed. One couldn't stand still, looking around and shifting on his feet. They surrounded the fourth person. Sydney? Whoever he was, he didn't trust Barnett. Without the bodyguards, the man was easy pickings for a sniper attack.

Hyde watched, wishing she could get closer to hear what they were saying. The beach provided no cover.

Another man came into view on the beach, driving a dune racer. Hyde snapped his picture. Was it Barnett? Her photo software could sharpen the picture to confirm his identity. From the height and build, it wasn't Reed Barnett, but figures in the dark could be misleading. A detailed analysis would confirm.

Hyde's phone vibrated and she glanced at it.

A message from Finn. "Get back to the villa. Barnett's sending guards."

Hyde wouldn't panic. She was on foot. The fastest way to the villa was on the beach, but if she ran along the water, she'd been seen. She made the only choice she could.

She ran through the trees and foliage. Her night-vision goggles helped, but she couldn't stop to be careful. Branches and vines cut at her skin, swiping her chin and cheeks. She stumbled and caught herself, urging her legs to move faster. Her heart was racing and sweat dripped down her back. Long sleeves and pants protected her from bug bites, but made cardio a killer. She dumped her canteen of water over her head as she ran.

She faltered again, twisting her ankle. Precious seconds were lost. She stood, hobbled a few steps, giving her ankle time to stop throbbing and then sprinted, struggling for balance. Her ankle burned and she ignored it. A sprain wouldn't kill her, but Reed Barnett catching her in a lie would.

When she reached the villa she was sharing with Finn, she approached with caution. She was too late. Two guards were at the door. They were knocking. They had keys, so they'd enter if she didn't answer.

Her clothes and equipment would give away she hadn't been on a moonlit stroll.

Circling to the rear of the villa, she looked for another way inside. The bathroom window was open. She jumped for it, catching the ledge with her fingertips and scrambling for a better grip. She fought her way in through the window, squeezing into the narrow space. She braced her arms on the vanity and lowered her body into the bathroom. She stripped out of her clothes, shoving them in the shower stall, and wrapped a towel around her.

For effect, she took a second towel and dabbed at her hair as she entered the main room. They had turned on a light by the door, but the room was shadowed.

She screamed as if startled by the presence of the two guards. They drew their guns and she shrieked louder. "Get out of my room! Who are you? My boyfriend will kill you for this!" She retreated into the bathroom, figuring that was what a scared woman would do.

The men were apologizing in French to her, but she pretended not to understand. Shouting for dramatic effect, she made more threats about her boyfriend and tried not to laugh at her drama. Grabbing her phone, she dialed Finn. "Finn, someone is in the villa. Please help me. I'm locked in the bathroom." She added an edge of hysteria to her voice, though she tried not to overdo it. The girlfriend of a drug lord would have some confidence in her safety.

Hyde dabbed some makeup over her scratches and then sat on the ledge of the tub and waited.

When Finn arrived, it was with a stream of curses. Hyde also heard Barnett's voice as he ordered his men to wait outside.

"Finn, is that you?" Trembling voice: nailed it.

"Yeah, baby. I'm here," Finn said.

Though they were playing a role, the endearment rattled her. Finn sometimes called her *baby*. And it wasn't just the word, it was the way he said it, like a caress. The softness in his tone was like a stroke down her body. But desire and attraction hadn't been and still wasn't her and Finn's problem.

Hyde exited the bathroom and threw herself into Finn's arms. She was playing the distraught girlfriend to the max and it was fun. Most of the time, she was her own protector. "Finn, men were in our room.

Thieves. Perverts. Or murderers. I came out of the bathroom and they terrorized me!"

Finn arched a brow at her. He hugged her. "Calm down. It was a misunderstanding. When I told Barnett you were sick, he sent someone to check on you."

"You could have called and checked on me. I was doing better until this," she said.

"You didn't answer the phone in the villa," Finn said. "He was worried about you."

Hyde huffed. "I was in the shower and meditating. I didn't hear it. I'm fine, but look at my hair. I didn't even brush it. Now I'll need another bath. I'm tense and stressed out and I look a mess. They better not have taken any pictures." She patted at her hair as if that was her biggest concern.

"You'll be okay and you look great," Finn said, hiding a smile.

"My apologies," Barnett said, stepping forward. He didn't feel bad enough to not look her up and down, but at least he'd spoken the words and was pretending to care he had upset her. "I will direct my security staff to be more reserved in the future. I feel responsible for my guests. If anything had happened to you, it would be a tragedy."

He ended his statement with a drip of sarcasm and Hyde wondered if a threat didn't hide in his words. Hyde pretended to be soothed by his statement. "I was shaken up by two strangers in my villa. We've had incidents before…" A girlfriend of a drug lord would have experiences with potentially deadly situations. That didn't mean she had to be calm about it.

"Why don't you get dressed and I'll stay here with you for the rest of the night?" Finn asked.

She didn't want Finn to miss anything important that transpired with Barnett. "No, no, please go back to your guys' night. I'm fine here," Hyde said. "I'll be presentable when you return."

"I planned to call it a night soon anyway," Finn said.

He was begging off from more time with Barnett. They were on the island to learn as much as they could about him and cement their business relationship. Wanting to spend time together wasn't the plan. Her heart banged harder against her ribs.

"I'm sorry for the intrusion. Finn, we'll speak about those matters in more detail tomorrow. Good night to you both," Barnett said.

After he left and Finn locked the door behind him, Hyde shivered. She maintained a healthy fear of Barnett. He was phony, nothing he said could be trusted and he wouldn't hesitate to kill either of them if they crossed him.

She returned to the bathroom, feeling like she needed a shower for real this time. She sat on the edge of the oversize tub.

"That was well played," Finn said, following her. He closed and locked the open window.

"If the window hadn't been open, I would have been forced to manufacture another lie. I doubt it would have been as believable."

"Quick thinking," Finn said.

She would need to plan better in the future. Barnett was keeping his eyes and ears on them. "I saw something at the beach. Before you messaged me, I snapped a couple of pictures of a conversation." She reached into the shower stall and handed him her camera that was waded in the pile of clothing.

"Did you see anything change hands? Money? Guns?"

"It was dark and I had to leave in the middle." She checked her weapon and night-vision equipment for damage. She removed her clothes from the stall. Turning the shower on, she let the water heat and she stepped into the stream, slid closed the glass door and removed her towel.

The casualness in which she had gotten almost naked in front of Finn struck her. Granted, a shower door was between them and she had been distracted, thinking about the mission.

Being naked with him felt natural. Hyde wasn't prudish, but she was usually more reserved around men she had no intention of sleeping with.

"Did you send the pictures to the West Company?" he asked.

"I did while I was waiting in the bathroom for you. I want to take a look at the pictures myself, though, and see if my photo software can do anything to sharpen the images."

Finn chuckled. "I have to say, I never realized how good of an actress you were."

She was a chameleon. "I lived as a man for almost six months in a prison, remember?" Her jailbreak was how she had met Finn. Lowest point in her life. She hadn't showered in months, she had been starving and thirsty and had a broken rib from a prison fight in which someone had thrown a table at another inmate, but it had struck her. Living in the prison, she had felt close to death several times, and it was only through alliances and luck that she had survived.

"That you lived in that prison is unbelievable. How could someone think you were a man?" He'd expressed similar thoughts before, though he rarely brought up her prison time. It was a source of anxiety for her.

It was a time she didn't like talking about. She was grateful she had pulled it off. "I can do anything to survive. It's a unique talent." She had blocked out a number of events from her time in prison. Being imprisoned had made her rely on her animal instincts. All that had mattered was protecting herself and surviving. She wouldn't live like that again.

"Is there room for someone else in the shower?" Finn asked.

Hyde froze. She'd showered with Finn before, as a time saver and for pleasure. She wasn't ready to confront her feelings for him tonight. She chose the safe option. "Give me a minute. Then the shower is yours."

He left the bathroom and closed the door. It snicked shut firmly. He was mad. Finn hadn't been mad at her before. She needed to say something to defuse the tension. When she'd had relationships in the past and they went bad, she'd ended them. She and Finn needed to get along for this mission. She couldn't tell him goodbye and beat feet and allow Simon's killer to be free and clear.

Hyde hated conflict in her professional relationships. It made her uncomfortable and unsure. Though she and Finn were dedicated to the mission, their private life was interfering.

Finn wanted reasons why she had erected a wall

between them. She wasn't ready to talk about Munich and the baby she had lost. A pregnancy she hadn't known about until she was eleven weeks and had started bleeding. The miscarriage had landed her in the hospital during a mission. The doctor had said that "these things happen." He had been matter-of-fact about it. Hyde had tried to hide her emotions and had pretended she was fine with it.

She hadn't been taking prenatal vitamins or sleeping eight hours a night or being especially careful with her body. She had been running and lifting weights, as was her routine. What if she had caused the loss? She was devastated to have lost something she hadn't known she'd wanted.

She'd considered calling Finn and telling him about the baby, but black ops agents weren't easy to reach. More than that, it wasn't a conversation she'd wanted to have over the phone.

Spies kept emotions locked away. Spies learned to handle them in private in their own way. Finn couldn't reasonably expect her to bare her soul to him. Hyde struggled to be honest with herself about what had happened and her feelings about it.

Hyde shut off the water and grabbed a fresh towel. She wished she had thought to bring clothes into the bathroom with her. Facing Finn fully dressed would have made her feel more in control.

Shoring up her confidence, she entered the main room. Finn was gone. Disappointment struck her. She wasn't interested in fighting with him, but she wanted to resolve their issues before they spun out of control. Though she was grappling with her emotions, she was sure she could find a way to explain how she was feeling, if not why.

Hyde dressed in a white sweat suit the West Company had provided. It was impractical, but surprisingly comfortable. She stepped out onto the front porch. The wind was blowing gently and the smell of salty air made her feel alert. Finn wouldn't have gone far. In the dark, she scanned for him. He was sitting on the small porch in a wood chair, watching the water. His elbows were resting on the chair's arms and his hands were steepled together in front of his mouth.

Hyde debated going back inside, but instead, pulled the other chair closer to him and sat beside him. "Want to talk about it?"

He didn't look at her. He stared at the water. It was a knife hit to the heart. She had been freezing him out to protect herself. Having that treatment turned on her rattled her. "Come on, Finn. You need to talk to me."

"I've been asking you to talk about it since Montana," Finn said.

She had explained as much as she could. She tried another way. "Have you ever been on a mission that changed you? Deep down, changed you? Made you a different man?"

He tapped his heel in an even beat against the wood porch. "Every mission changes me." His hands dropped from his mouth.

Hyde touched his elbow. Though she had his attention, she wanted him to look at her. His eyes met hers and emotion slammed into her. She couldn't name the emotion that accompanied the intensity and heat, but she felt it burn through her. "Then you understand. I was on a mission and it changed me." The unbearable loss and the heartache haunted her.

"What mission and what happened? Because I'm thinking the worst. Almost anything you say would be better than what I'm imagining happened. For you, one of the world's best spies, to suddenly decide she wants out, I know whatever it was, it was bad," Finn said.

He was probably thinking about altercations with enemies, near loss of life. "I'm okay. I am handling it," she said. She struggled to find the right words.

"Being here with you makes me worry," Finn said. "I know you can protect yourself, but since I don't know what's going on with you, I feel like I need to do something. Step up and be overprotective to make sure you're okay."

"This could go sideways at any point. I won't give you the disturbing details of the stories Barnett told tonight, but he is a psychopath." Finn sounded distressed and Hyde was sorry that she couldn't tell him more. She wished he would accept that she was fine and would talk about it when she was ready.

"Promise me you'll consider talking to me," Finn said. "You've confided in me before. I can be a friend."

Hyde didn't want his friendship. She was looking for more. Hyde caught her breath. That truth had hit her like a ton of bricks. Nowhere near ready to be finished with Finn, she wanted more from him than they'd had in the past. It was a long shot, but she was clinging to the dream of a future with him and she'd need to let that go to move on with her life.

Finn adjusted the phone on his ear as he poured his coffee. He'd slept terribly the night before. Too many worries and not enough solutions weighed heavily on him.

"We've been running the facial recognition software. No matches, but we're cleaning up the images and removing shadows to see if that helps," Abby said. Abby was their contact at the West Company. She had been assigned to provide remote support in whatever manner she could while Hyde and Finn were in the field.

It was probable that the people Hyde had seen on the beach were in the United States' facial recognition system as special agents, special ops or wanted criminals. In addition to international criminal tracking systems, the West Company had access to the United States' Department of Motor Vehicles systems from each of the fifty states, and their analysts had run the picture against those images.

Finn couldn't imagine a more trustworthy person than Connor West wielding so much power. As the leader of the West Company, Connor was the definition of a patriot and he wouldn't abuse the power bestowed upon him. He had been tossed around by the government when he had worked as a spy years before. Those experiences laid the groundwork for his commitment to running honest and fair operations.

After Finn hung up with Abby, he found Hyde in the bathroom doing something with her hair, twisting it and clipping it with flowers. He had never seen her take such care with her appearance. She was a naturally beautiful woman and adding a dress, high heels and the hair and makeup, she was breathtaking. She leaned forward over the sink to adjust her hair, and her profile was feminine and alluring. Her hair was gathered at the side and the ends were curly. With the print of her dress and the way it moved around her legs, she reminded him of a dancer.

It was driving him to distraction that she had shut him out of her life. She was here with him, but she was slipping away. He couldn't bridge the distance with her. When he felt close to her opening up, she shut down.

Hyde patted her hair and slid another clip into it. "Ruby messaged me this morning. She wants us to meet her and Barnett for brunch. I think he's planning to tell you about his loyalty test."

Given what Finn knew of Barnett, the test would be twisted.

As she turned from the sink, she winced.

He caught her expression in the mirror. "What's the matter?"

She lifted the hem of her green dress and showed her swollen and bruised ankle.

"Did that happen last night?" he asked.

She nodded. "I cut through the trees and I fell a couple of times. It ached last night, but it hurts pretty bad now. I had some light scratches on my face and neck, but makeup covered those."

"Do you want to cancel the meeting with Barnett and Ruby?"

Hyde looked repulsed by the idea. "I don't want them to be suspicious about what happened last night."

"Won't they see your ankle?" Finn asked.

Hyde shifted the fabric of her dress. "I hope not. If they do, I'll cop it to a sprained ankle and blame my clumsiness. I'll say I woke up in the middle of the night for a drink and fell. Unfamiliar surroundings."

Finn didn't like the look of the injury and he didn't

like that she was planning to walk on it. "Let me get you some ice."

She nodded. It must hurt badly if she was willing to accept help. Finn wrapped ice in a towel and brought it to Hyde. He knelt on the floor at her feet and set it against her ankle. She reached to hold the towel, and their hands brushed. The connection lit a fire through him. Why was she fighting this so hard? Their attraction was strong and persistent. Ignoring it was only making him burn hotter for her.

"When will you talk to me about this?" he asked.

She blinked at him. She didn't ask what he was referring to. They knew. "When I can."

It was the best answer he had received from her and he didn't push. She'd tell him the truth eventually and he was prepared to deal with whatever she said. Whatever had happened, he would be supportive and helpful and perhaps kill the person who'd hurt her.

Hyde and Finn drove a dune buggy to Barnett's compound. Hyde was in heels, intensifying the ache in her ankle. Though the ice had helped, it was swollen. Hyde reached to it, rubbing. She would be careful not to draw attention to her injury at Barnett's house. The more questions, the more likely she would be caught in a lie.

Finn parked outside Barnett's compound. He stepped out of the buggy and circled around to help her. Hyde leaned on him, grateful he had taken her arm on her injured side.

"These steps," Hyde said. The last time they had taken the stairs, they hadn't bothered her. Now, putting her full weight on her ankle—in narrow heels—

was killer. The heels had gone perfectly with her floral-printed wrap dress. She should have forgotten about fashion and worn comfortable sandals.

"You can do it," Finn said.

Hyde hid the pain. She had been in worse agony. Her time in prison came to mind. This shouldn't be a big deal.

They reached the front door and it opened before they knocked. They were escorted to the dining room. The doors that lined the walls had been opened, letting in a soft breeze that smelled of sun and sand. Sheer white curtains had been pushed to the sides and they billowed, waving in a random pattern, keeping time with the wind.

Finn poured her a cup of coffee from the carafe on the table and she accepted it gratefully. They kept their conversation about the artwork in the room and general pleasantries. Every word they spoke was likely being listened to. At least with the conversation staying on neutral ground, avoiding difficult topics was easy.

Barnett and Ruby arrived ten minutes later holding hands. Ruby was wearing a green dress, low cut in the front with a short, full skirt falling to her knees. It was the most conservative clothing Hyde had seen Ruby wear.

The woman sat across from Finn and Hyde, but Barnett stood. He took a sip of his water and stood to the right of his chair, forcing Finn and Hyde to turn to face him. "Finn, I've enjoyed having you and Alexandra here. Our discussions lead me to believe we could have a very lucrative business together." Clasping his hands behind his back, he paused, watching Hyde and Finn.

If he was trying to make them uncomfortable, he was succeeding.

"Cheers," Finn said, lifting his cup to Barnett and breaking the awkward silence.

"I have requirements for the people I work with," Barnett said.

Ruby was staring at Barnett, her hands folded on the table. Hyde watched her eyes. She looked bored.

Barnett sat, angling his chair toward Finn and Hyde. "I will not waste your time further. You need to prove your loyalty to me in order for us to continue with our plans."

Hyde had been holding her breath and let it out slowly. She dreaded the words that would leave Barnett's mouth next. Proving their loyalty could mean anything.

"I need five million dollars from you. We'll call that your buy-in to my venture, some start-up capital."

Five million was a relatively small amount for someone like Barnett. What was the purpose of requiring the money?

Barnett waited, as if wanting a reaction. Hyde blinked at him and hoped her expression was appropriately vacant.

"I don't want the money from your personal accounts. You'll need to prove that the money is stolen," Barnett said. The corners of his mouth lifted. He was enjoying this.

Hyde had expected a catch. Giving him the money was too easy.

Barnett tapped his finger on the table. "I want the five million to be accompanied by a dead body."

Hyde and Finn exchanged looks and Finn patted her hand as if reassuring her. Money was one problem they could solve using the technology skills available to them through the West Company. Killing someone was another matter.

How was Finn planning to play this? Reasoning with Barnett seemed unlikely. Finn could explain that he didn't get his hands dirty and killing was out of the question.

If Barnett refused to compromise and Finn refused the loyalty test, this was finished.

"View this as an opportunity to take out the competition or other obstacles in our way. I'll fly you from the island to Florida. You'll have seventy-two hours. If you choose not to return, I'll send an assassin to ensure your silence on this matter."

Finn and Hyde killed as a last resort: to stop heinous activity, to stop a terrorist or to stop a mass murderer. They did jobs that others wouldn't do for the greater good. They had a personal code of honor and that code said nothing about killing for sport.

"I'm not an assassin for hire, Barnett," Finn said.

"You've killed before," Barnett said.

"Not on someone's command."

"If a situation arises over the course of our business that requires you to do something unpleasant, I need to know that I can count on you to handle it," Barnett said.

Finn leaned forward, setting his elbows on the table. "I can handle it. I wouldn't be at this table if I couldn't. What about you, Barnett? What sign of loyalty will I have from you?"

Barnett appeared amused. "What do you want? You know what cards I hold."

"I have influence on the East Coast. It's why you brought me on. If you have enemies you want handled, you need to handle them on your time," Finn said. "I can get your product where no one else can. Why do we need bodies to pile up? I don't like involving the authorities in my business, and a murder investigation will do that."

Finn was playing a good angle, appealing to the logic and business side of the arrangement.

"I consider this nonnegotiable. But I will make you the same offer. I'll give you a body if you want it and I'll steal five million, too."

Not what Hyde was hoping Barnett would say.

Finn remained quiet. He rubbed his jaw. Was he considering this? If he said no, Barnett may kill them. Limited their options. But they couldn't murder someone on Barnett's say-so.

"I'll give you the five million and a body," Finn said.

Barnett broke into a grin. "Excellent. I'm thrilled to hear this." He handed Finn a piece of paper. "These are the identities of the men you may choose to kill. Pick one."

Hyde's stomach turned. Ruby appeared unfazed. She must know that Barnett was a murderer. She would have a much different reaction if this were the first time she had heard this request.

Finn lifted a brow and looked at the list. "You have

a number of men on this list who will be challenging to reach, much less to kill."

"You have resources. Use them," Barnett said.

Finn pointed to the list. "Julio Ramirez? What's your quarrel with him?"

Hyde was familiar with the name and his work. He was a lifelong criminal with a vast history of drug trafficking, murder and theft.

"He's tried to move in on my territory. He's too greedy and unreasonable. I can't have it. Every person on that list is in my way. Think long-term. If we want our venture to be rewarding, we need to get obstacles out of the way. Those men are obstacles," Barnett said.

Barnett was using Finn to take out a rival. How did that play into their business arrangement? Barnett could have taken out a hit on Ramirez without involving Finn. He must derive some satisfaction from forcing Finn into a difficult situation. More than that, Barnett would have leverage over Finn, evidence of a murder he committed to release to either the authorities or the dead man's gang.

"I'll handle it," Finn said. Finn stood and extended his hand to Hyde. He drew her to her feet. "We need to get moving. If I have three days, I'll make use of them."

Finn and Barnett exchanged curt goodbyes.

As they left the house, Hyde couldn't read Finn. He was walking quickly, a snap in his step, his brows drawn together and his shoulders tense. Processing what Barnett had said would take time, and speaking of the situation was too dangerous. They would need to be off the property before they discussed their options.

"Alexandra!"

Hyde turned at the sound of Ruby's voice. "Hey, Ruby. Sorry to depart so abruptly."

Ruby flipped her hair over her shoulder. "Are you sure you don't want to stay for brunch? We have a new coffee I'd love for you to try."

Hyde wasn't sure how to answer that. It was almost like Ruby was pretending the last five minutes hadn't happened and her boyfriend hadn't just asked them to kill someone. Was denial how she stayed with Barnett? Guilt and sympathy mushroomed through her. "Sorry, Ruby, next time."

Ruby glanced at Finn. "Are you going with him? You could stay on the island with me while Finn deals with this."

Ruby's eyes were pleading with Hyde, and compassion twisted in her gut. Staying to protect Ruby had merit, but Finn needed her. Either he would choose to end the mission and flee for a safe place where Barnett could not find them or accept the mission and go after one of Barnett's targets.

Hyde set her hand on Ruby's arm. "I'm going with Finn. We travel together."

"I told Reed that he could trust you. I don't know why he wants to involve you like this," Ruby said.

Finn put his arm around Hyde's waist. "We'll be back. You heard Barnett. Three days."

Ruby opened her mouth as if to say something and then snapped it shut. She leaned toward Hyde. "I told him the money was enough."

A multimillion-dollar theft would be enough for most. The dead body was a gruesome twist. How did that make Ruby feel? She knew about Barnett's demands on the people he did business with. What else did she know about his enterprise?

Hyde debated saying anything more. She couldn't trust Ruby to maintain her confidence, but she wanted to give the other woman a way out. "When the flight leaves the island, you should come with us. We could go to a spa while the men work and get some rest and relaxation."

Finn's eyes twitched. She was going off script and he didn't approve. Involving Ruby would complicate matters, especially if Barnett blamed Hyde and Finn for Ruby's disappearance.

Ruby shook her head. "I already asked Reed if I could visit my family." She bit her lip, and tears sprang to her eyes. "He says we have things to do here." Ruby blinked and wiped at her eyes, smearing a small amount of eyeliner to her temples.

Hyde squeezed Ruby's hands. "We'll be gone three days. Maybe less." Though Hyde had no idea how they would accomplish Barnett's ridiculous request. She had doubts that Finn would want to. If they went that deep with Barnett, the line was blurring and they were venturing into a morally questionable area.

Finn looked at Hyde. "We need to go."

Hyde said her goodbyes to Ruby and they walked away from the compound to their dune buggy. When they were a good distance away, Finn stopped and looked at Hyde. "Ruby has to stay on the island. Do not invite her to come with us again. I was afraid she would take you up on your offer."

Hyde glared at him. "She doesn't have to stay here. I could help her hide. Once she's on US territory, I have contacts and assets to help her."

Finn ran his fingers through his hair. He didn't get rattled easily, but Barnett's demands were over-the-top. "You can't. Barnett would blame us."

"Are you still planning to do this?" Hyde asked. She was expecting him to call it off.

"What choice do we have?" Finn asked.

Plenty of choices. "We could not do it."

"You mean, we could quit."

Barnett had presented the tasks as an ultimatum. "Yes."

Finn let out a low growl of frustration. "If that's what you want to do, I won't force you to be part of this."

Finn was bent on continuing down this path. Could she leave him alone when he might need her help now more than ever?

Alone in their villa, and after checking for listening devices, Finn grabbed his bag and tossed in the items he'd need for an operation. "Tell me what you're thinking."

Hyde had been quiet on the drive. She was packing slowly, folding and rolling each article of clothing before placing it in her suitcase. Finn didn't know if she was working up the nerve to abandon him or if she planned to stay on the island to protect Ruby. Both options riled Finn. He needed to know she was safe.

"I don't know how well we can fake someone's death and I don't know if I'm prepared to kill. Even if it is someone like Ramirez." Hyde looked pale when she spoke the words.

Involving her in another mission tangential to this one was how mercenaries and spies were caught in this life. No mission existed without ties to a dozen others. Like their relationship, it quickly became complicated. Hyde and Finn's relationship had started as a no-strings-attached series of flings and had escalated into what they had now. Finn didn't have a word for their current situation. He cared for her, his affection for her was strong and yet they were standing on opposite sides of an impenetrable wall.

"I don't know what's feasible in three days." She sighed and punched her suitcase. "This is why I want out of this game. I don't want to work ops. They go askew and we have no way out. If we quit, Barnett will send a hit squad to take us out. If we move forward, we're the hit squad."

The heaviness of her words landed on his shoulders. He looked at the list Barnett had given him. "We have five names here. The only one I recognize is Ramirez. I don't know enough to decide how to proceed."

"Get the list to Abby. See what she knows," Hyde said.

Their contact at the West Company might offer some ideas.

Within ten minutes, they were on the phone with Abby, discussing their options. Of the four other names on the list, three worked in law enforcement. Those agents and agencies were being alerted to the threat. The remaining two names were criminals, one whose location was unknown.

"We could get one of the agencies to cooperate with us and fake a death," Hyde said.

"Those agents are unlikely to have five million dollars to steal," Finn said.

"Then this is a trap," Hyde said. Barnett had given them a list of five names, but only one was possible. They had no options. They were hunting a criminal.

Chapter 6

Hyde checked that her head scarf covered her hair, and she stayed close to Finn. He was wearing the light-colored, loose-fitting linen clothes common in the region. They had to get from the airport to the mountains and make the journey to find Julio Ramirez.

They had already burned twenty-four of their seventy-two hours planning and preparing and traveling to Selvan. They had good intel that Ramirez was in the area, hiding in a remote mountain lodge.

Ramirez ran the drug trade in the area. His business was international. The West Company had received the necessary authorization from the American government to shut Ramirez down and had provided information on the target. He would be stopped and his business torn to shreds. They couldn't kill him unless he posed a direct threat to them. The West Company was working to find a body that could double as Ramirez. The one benefit in their favor was that Ramirez was relatively unknown by law enforcement and for anyone, including Barnett, to confirm his identity was a difficult task.

Hyde mentally sealed herself against the heaviness in her chest. Ramirez was scum of the earth. He killed addicts who couldn't pay their debts to him and he ruthlessly cut down competition. In a town near where he lived, he kept the poorest under his thumb and lived high on the hog from the profits of his business.

"You look like you're going to kill the next person who glances in your direction," Finn said.

Hyde lowered her head. She had forgotten where she was. "I was thinking about our subject." His picture was burned into her brain. He had a long face and small eyes, clean-shaven except for a small patch of hair below his thin mouth. Short, stocky, with prominent neck and arm tattoos. He kept his dark hair long and tied at his nape with an orange strap.

"Sick piece of crap, isn't he?" Finn had read the same file.

It was rare for her to have someone to discuss operations with. Usually, she took the lead on missions and when she hired operatives, she doled out small bits of information as needed. In this mission, she and Finn were equals. "I've dealt with people like him for ten years. For every one I stop, ten more begin their enterprise. I'm tired of dealing with people like him. I'm tired of dealing with liars and killers and cheaters. I can't promise that I won't go berserk on him," Hyde said.

"I feel the same," Finn said. "Except my version of berserk will mean taking down him and every person who works for him."

Selvan was recovering from a recent civil war. During that time, crimes had gone unchecked while factions battled each other for land and resources, and no single, stable government had control. The economy had collapsed and the country was relying heavily on foreign aid to meet their needs for food, clothing and rebuilding their infrastructure. That chaos had opened the door to illegal activities and crime bosses rising up and exploiting the people around them.

Finn and Hyde had their rock-climbing equipment, camping gear and survival provisions in their packs. Ramirez was heavily guarded and traveled with security and decoys, but they'd find a vulnerability.

They set up camp at the base of the mountain near a small village. It was too dark to climb, but they would start moving at first light.

Hyde peeled the orange she had bought at the local market and handed a slice to Finn. "When this is over…" She almost said she would come back and see what remained for her to clean up of Ramirez's enterprise. If anyone had the bright idea to step into Ramirez's shoes, she would tear that person down. And repeat until everyone knew that a vigilante would relentlessly and brutally stop anyone who tried it.

"When this is over, what?" Finn asked.

When it was over, she was finished. She wouldn't come back. That was what retiring meant: walking away from a job that would never be finished and turning her back on the people whom she had worked with over the last ten years.

Hyde couldn't imagine saying goodbye to Finn. Their other goodbyes had been spoken with the knowledge they would try to see each other again. After this mission, it was over. *They* were over.

"The West Company can send a team here to keep an eye on things." Passing the buck to someone else didn't feel right.

"You don't have to feel guilty about it," Finn said.

But she did, about the thought she had expressed and her internal dialogue about Finn. "This isn't the life I want, but it's the only job I've ever known. Not everyone can do what we do." The burnout rate for spies and mercenaries was high. Few made it past five years. It was tough on a body, hard on a soul and made a normal life with a family and friends impossible.

"You've been fighting the good fight. You can pass the torch," Finn said. He removed their tent from his pack and started assembling it.

Was it selfish to want a life that didn't involve constant travel to unknown places, weapons, killing and lying? She knelt to hold the stake for Finn so he could hammer it into the ground with a rock.

"I'm not passing the torch as much as throwing it down and hoping someone picks it up," Hyde said.

"The West Company's training facility will produce its first class of graduates in a few weeks. Thirty men and women looking for a torch," Finn said.

That made her feel better. At least the West Company had a handle on things.

When the tent was erected, Hyde slipped inside.

It was large enough to accommodate them without touching as long as neither of them moved.

Finn joined her in the tent. He lay next to her, hands at his sides. After several minutes she listened to his slow, deep breaths. As her ears adjusted to the sounds around her, she could pick out various noises and she categorized them: animals, foliage, wind, water and Finn.

"Finn?" she asked, rolling to her side. She set her fingers on his stomach. Her hand rose and fell with each breath he took. He was strong and warm and she wanted to move closer to him and rest her body against his.

"Hmm?" he asked.

Too many questions weighed on her. "Will I have a way to get in touch with you after I retire?" He had found her in Bearcreek, but how would she know where he was? They had used their mutual associates to locate each other and had exchanged contact information through an ever-changing series of email addresses and phone numbers. She wouldn't be part of that world, a world that was silent from the outside.

"I can leave you messages where I am. Or the West Company can get me a message from you."

Throughout her time as a spy, Hyde had kept a phone number and associated voice mail for her family to contact her. It had been part of her cover. "You can't leave detailed information on my voice mail." It wasn't secure. It was hackable. Finn knew that. If anyone connected them, they could use her weaker position to find Finn.

"I can check in so you know I'm alive. I know not to leave any information," Finn said.

"Will you visit?" She was pushing. Spies couldn't safely return to the same location over and over. Too easy to track and find them. She had known spies who had not seen their families in years because they needed to protect them.

"Do you want me to visit?" he asked, sounding indifferent.

"I don't know."

"Are you thinking that telling your future husband about me would be awkward?" Finn asked.

Hearing him mention the words *future husband* was awkward. "I wasn't thinking about a husband, but the people in my new, normal life. They won't understand what you do or what I did."

"We can rendezvous from time to time."

Same as they had until now. Thinking of him and of seeing him had kept her company in the loneliness of the night when she had been on missions.

If she was meeting with Finn occasionally, she wouldn't be able to move on in her personal life. Though she and Finn hadn't made commitments to each other, she was a one man type of woman. "It would be harder to let you go if you were still in my life."

Finn sighed. "Do you want me around or not?" He sounded irritable.

What she wanted wasn't black-and-white. She wanted him in her life, but not as a spy, and resolving that was complicated. She craved a normal relationship, where they went on dates and talked and saw each other on a regular basis. She couldn't have that. "Aside from my family, you've been the one constant in my life. Unlike my family, you know what

I've done and who I am. You accept that part of me." Her job had required keeping secrets and they had to be kept forever.

Finn set his hand on her side. "You don't need me in your new life. I don't fit."

Where his hand rested, heat flowed through her. "Do you think I would make a good mother?" The words shot from her mouth. Some subconscious part of her had wondered how he would perceive her as a future parent. It was a delicate question traipsing over a fragile part of her psyche. Before she could verbally void the question, he answered.

"Of course you'd be a good mother."

"Really?" she asked. She had her doubts.

"You're smart and strong and brave. Your kid will be the most protected kid on the playground and you'll figure out all his secrets before he tells you. I have no doubts when you meet the right man, it will fall into place."

Hyde blinked back tears. "Thanks, Finn." They were words she had needed to hear.

He kissed her forehead. "You're welcome. Now, get some sleep."

She moved closer to him so her forehead was resting against his chest, and her hands were tucked between them.

The sun rose, casting rays of light across the tent. Exhaustion leaked from Finn's every pore, but they needed to keep moving. Three days wasn't enough time. Barnett was short on forgiveness.

The river was the only place to clean up. Kneeling at the river's edge on tan pebbles and beige sand,

Hyde splashed the cold, moving water on her face and arms, washing away sweat and dirt.

Finn removed his shirt and rinsed it. Same with his boots, socks and pants. Everything was quick-dry fabric. A few minutes in the hot sun and he could redress.

Hyde wasn't moving. She'd brought her hands to her face, but then she'd frozen. Finn stalked toward her, wet clothes in hand. He set them next to her on the rocky shoreline. "Hyde?"

She dropped her hands, and her body sagged. Her brown hair hung around her shoulders and she looked forlorn, sitting on the shore, facing the water, her legs tucked close to her.

Finn sat next to her. She glanced at him, letting her eyes travel up and down his body. "Not feeling modest?"

"Not really."

"I know you didn't want this," Finn said. Guilt plucked at him. He had talked her into avenging Simon's death. He had convinced her that Reed Barnett had to be taken down. Had he made a mistake by involving Hyde?

She ran quaking fingers through her hair. "I do what I believe is right and I don't feel bad about it. Some people think our work is immoral or that we're broken inside to carry out these missions and keep moving on with our lives. I wonder…"

Her eyes welled with tears and she stopped speaking. She rubbed her hand across her chest.

"You wonder what?" Finn asked.

"I wonder if I've been punished for the lives I've taken and the things I've done." She wiped at her eyes and then reached into the cold water of the river, splashing her arms again. The water wouldn't unburden her soul. Her sadness was pervasive, clinging to every inch of her.

A dark sense of foreboding shadowed him. "In what way do you think you're being punished?"

She looked out across the river. "This is not something I planned to tell you. This isn't something I've told anyone."

She was about to pull the pin on a grenade and launch it. This was the reason she was planning to retire. This was why she was cagey around him. He swore to himself no matter what she said, he would stay calm. If someone had hurt her, he wouldn't fly into a rage and kill them. She needed him and his support. His anger could add to her pain. Even those reminders to himself weren't any guarantees.

She looked at the water and then lifted her eyes to meet his. "When I was in Germany, something happened."

Finn waited. Hyde wasn't a melodramatic person, but each word was being dragged from her mouth as if hard to speak.

"I was pregnant," Hyde said.

Finn felt like the air was being sucked from his lungs and at the same time, he was dizzy with confusion. Every syllable bounced around in his brain. "Was?" Past tense? What had happened?

Her mouth quivered. "I had a miscarriage. I hadn't even known I was pregnant. I was taken to a hospital when I started bleeding. The pregnancy was confirmed."

Finn had questions, most of them selfish, but one stood out in his mind. "My baby? Was it my baby?"

He had to ask the question, but he knew the answer. His chest felt tight and his heart was racing.

Hyde looked at him in surprise. "*Your* baby?"

He had been faithful to Hyde and though they hadn't talked about it, he had assumed she had, too. The parentage of the baby wasn't the most important, but he had to know.

"Was it our baby?" he asked. He felt sure about Hyde and their connection, and he realized that he had come to think of her as his and vice versa.

Hyde closed her eyes and took a deep breath. She clenched her fists at her sides. "Yes. I should have told you when it happened. I felt guilty. I thought you would be happy that I lost the baby, which I couldn't have handled."

Shock, grief and loss mixed in a volatile cocktail. Shouldn't he feel relief? He waited, but no sensation of reprieve or happiness struck him. "I am definitely not happy."

He sat next to her, not touching her, resting his arms on his knees. He watched the water, and the sunlight glinted off it. Thoughts drifted in and out. He imagined Hyde pregnant with his baby. He imagined her holding a child in her arms. She would be a natural, loving mother. Hyde cared deeply about people. She was loyal and fierce. People in the mercenary community admired her.

But he was a mess. He didn't get along with his family and he didn't have a place he called home. His plans for the future included chasing another mission. His devotion to his job was something he had been proud of and now it bothered him to admit it. "Why did you feel guilty?" Shredded emotionally, sure. But guilt was misplaced.

She picked up a pebble and tossed it into the water. "I should have been more aware of my body and what was going on. We should have been more careful when we were together."

His insides clenched. Finn set his hand on her back, softly. "No guilt. This happens sometimes. You didn't do anything wrong."

She turned her head and met his gaze. "Should I have called you?"

The pain in her eyes nearly knocked him over.

"Yes." He would have come to her no matter where he was. They could have gone through it together.

She looked away from him, pulling her knees tighter into her chest. "Nothing could have been done."

"I could have been a friend to you when you needed it."

He slipped his arm around her shoulders. He didn't know what reaction she had expected, but he needed to comfort her. He didn't have a word to describe precisely what he was feeling, but she was hurting and it burned into him, like another of his failures.

"I'm sorry, Alex. I'm sorry you went through that and I'm sorry I wasn't there when I should have been," he said.

A tear slipped down her cheek. "If I hadn't passed out and been taken to the hospital, I may never have known. And after I knew what I had lost, I wanted the baby. With everything in my soul, I wanted a baby I didn't know I'd had. That sounds silly, but losing the baby left a hole in my chest," Hyde said.

He now understood her behavior of late and he was

riddled with guilt. He should have been there for her. Going through the ordeal alone seemed unfair.

"I would have kept the baby and raised him," Hyde said.

Her statement was needless. She would have. They had never discussed a family or their views on children, but her pain made it clear.

"I know," Finn said.

"It's screwed up. I thought I couldn't have children. I had a horseback riding accident when I was eight and the doctor told my mother than it had left scars. It changed how my parents raised me. They encouraged me to have a career and put everything I had into it. I guess they figured if I would never be a mother, I could have work I loved."

She had never shared that detail of her life with him. "The doctor was wrong. If you were pregnant, you could be again. You could have the family you want," Finn said.

Hyde wiped at her eyes. "Or this baby was a freakishly lucky chance and it will never happen again."

Finn left almost nothing to chance and he had learned to make his own good fortune. This sounded important to her. "You can't think like that. It happened once. It could happen again."

She met his gaze. He read gratitude and hope in her eyes.

"Are you mad?" she asked.

No anger for her in his heart. "Not mad. I'm not sure what I feel." His shoulders felt heavy with guilt and worry. She had gone through the experience alone and it had been hard enough on her that she had made a drastic life change.

They sat on the shore for a long time, listening to the water and the wind in the trees.

Hyde finally stood, brushing off her pants. "Thanks for listening. We should clean up and get moving."

Her body was tense and her gaze cast downward. She took a shuddering breath in. He sensed she needed something more, more time, more conversation, but they were on a tight timeline. He wouldn't close the book on this yet. When she was ready to talk again, he would listen. In the meantime he would try to process his emotions. "Let's clean up and cool off. We have a day of climbing ahead of us."

They walked into the river. Finn pulled her shirt over her head, cleaned it and tossed it over to his clothes. Next, her pants, socks and shoes. She dipped down in the water and let it run over her hair.

Letting go of her hand wasn't an option. He was also saddened by what she had told him about their baby. A baby deserved better than him for a father. Knowing what he did, he wanted Hyde close, wanted to hold her in his arms and reassure her that it would be okay.

Trying to convince himself this was fine, he couldn't shake the idea of what might have been.

Chapter 7

Scaling the Quinn Range Mountains was slow and tedious work. Though Ramirez's camp was only a few hundred yards from the base of the mountain, getting there and staying off the winding road leading to it meant climbing. Losing their way was possible, and the rock face didn't provide many cliffs where they could rest. At least the rocks on this side of the mountain were dry enough to grip onto. If it started to rain, they would have trouble maintaining a strong hold on the smooth rocks.

The blowing wind was chilly, but Hyde's muscles burned. They had changed into dark clothing, long sleeves and long pants. Not only would it protect their skin from scrapes, the cold came on fast as they rose. Every few yards, Hyde glanced over her shoulder, taking in the view. Beautiful fields of purple and yellow wildflowers, the river intersecting the trees and rocks jutting from the ground, beds of green surrounding them.

Hyde and Finn were using stakes to secure their ropes, making it an exhausting climb. The lack of sleep added to their fatigue. With Hyde's revelation settled on their shoulders and lingering between them, it was a quiet and solemn ascent.

Hyde questioned whether confiding in Finn had been the right idea. He hadn't said much about the baby, and reading him was difficult. He wasn't happy about the loss and he'd been concerned for her.

Not the easiest way up the mountain, this was the best way to approach Ramirez's headquarters unde-tected. Ramirez had the main roads covered and she and Finn didn't have enough firepower to blast their way to him.

The higher she and Finn rose, the thinner the air. Hyde stopped on a ledge and took several slow breaths. The cold was bracing. When Finn stopped beside her, he groaned.

"See that?" He pointed above them.

Hyde shielded her eyes and looked up slowly, careful not to disorient herself. A ledge along the path extended straight out from the mountain. They would have to navigate around it, costing them time and energy.

"We're burning through our hours." Progress wasn't happening as fast as she would have liked.

"We have another option." He patted his pocket where he had a stash of C4.

Hyde liked explosives. When done right, they could break down a barrier. "If I make a mistake, it will blow us off the mountain. The explosion could set off an avalanche and we could be crushed. And the sound will alert Ramirez that we're coming." Assessing their options on the fly didn't leave time for dancing around the risks.

"How often do you make a mistake?" he asked.

When it came to explosives, especially C4, Hyde was careful and precise. She didn't make mistakes. She considered her options. "I can do it. What about the noise?"

"The immediate blast may alarm him. He'll send scouts to see what happened. He won't see us and by the time we're close enough, he'll have written it off as a minor avalanche."

"Avalanches are never minor," Hyde said. Especially when they could be underneath one.

"You'll do this right. I know it."

Hyde trusted her skills, but with Finn close, they'd need to be extremely cautious. Hyde pointed away from them. "Climb that way, secure yourself with stakes. Give me a few minutes."

Finn handed her the C4. Hyde had blasting caps and twine. Moving up the mountain, she posted a slab of C4 to the base of the boulder. She'd have to estimate how much to use. Too little would be useless and too much would kill them.

After setting the explosive, she clutched the twine and climbed to where Finn was waiting.

Hyde found a good position to secure her footing and her hand grips. Finn had chosen an excellent location. The shape of the mountain would protect them from flying debris. Finn had staked them deep four times and tied ropes to each post. He had two around himself and two around her.

"Ready?" she asked.

At his nod, she lit the end of the twine. When it was burning strong, she released it. Finn tucked her against him.

She waited for what felt like minutes. Her fatigued muscles were tense. The boom shook the air around them. Hyde's foot slipped and she grabbed for something to secure herself. A tumble of rocks struck her, knocking her farther off balance and sending her off the ledge.

One of her stakes had shaken loose. Hyde stayed calm as she dangled from one rope and struggled for her footing.

Finn dropped beside her. He had made a harness and pulley out of his ropes. Quick thinker. Hyde reached for him. Taking his hand, he pulled her against him. They worked together to move up the mountain, their path clear toward the top.

When they found a place to rest, Hyde squeezed Finn's hand. Her nerves were rattled and her hands were still shaking. "Thank you for what you did back there."

"We're partners. I wouldn't have let you fall."

Hyde rested her head on his shoulder. Her muscles quivered from the rush of adrenaline, fear and exhaustion.

Was he thinking about what she had confided in him at the river? She kept waiting for a visceral reaction from him. He was putting a lid on his emotions, but they were simmering, waiting to be addressed. She knew Finn too well to think he was indifferent.

As they resumed climbing, Hyde focused on not slipping.

* * *

Once they reached the large plateau where Ramirez was supposed to have his camp, they checked in with Abby at the West Company. They ate their MREs while they talked to her.

The clock ticked louder the closer they were to their deadline.

"We cleaned up the pictures from the beach Hyde sent," Abby said. "Looks like Barnett is involved with an import and export tycoon named James Sydney. Sydney works in Miami and while his company has been investigated many times, no charges have been filed because he's politically connected. We suspect he helped Barnett on his last score and will be helping him on the next one."

The name matched the one Finn had overheard when he was playing golf with Barnett.

"What political connections?" Finn asked.

"His father is Senator Eli Sydney," Abby said.

Irritation plucked at him. Finn knew Eli Sydney. He and Finn's father ran in the same political circles and played golf together. Finn wondered if his father knew what James Sydney was involved with and how his illegal dealings—convicted or not—were kept out of the spotlight.

The sound of rumbling, like a fleet of motorcycles revving to ride, cut through the air. They were close to Ramirez's camp. Disconnecting their call, they moved toward the direction of the sound, keeping to the trees for cover.

Hyde smoothed her hair away from her face. She had twisted her hair into a braid and it hung down her back.

Finn had put pressure on Hyde to partner with him on this mission. He regretted that now. He couldn't have done this without her, but he hadn't known about the baby. That detail was wedged in his thoughts. "I'm sorry about the baby," Finn whispered. It had been hours since she had mentioned the baby, but he had thought about it nonstop.

Hyde touched his forearm. "I know you are."

Wearing dusty black pants and a purple tank top, black long-sleeved shirt tied around her waist, she was beautiful. She drove the breath from his lungs. The urge to pull her to him and kiss her pulsed through him. He beat it back. With his attraction to her came the strongest sense of wanting to protect her. It was a bad emotion to harbor in the field. He would do his best to keep her safe, but he needed to trust that she could hold her own. Watching her too closely was a distraction.

They were taking extra care to be silent. They heard the noise first and then the camp came into view between the trees. Olive canvas tents sat in a cluster among tall grasses, about five off-road vehicles were in sight and narrow path beat through the tents. Around the camp were poles mounted with unlit lanterns.

According to the West Company's intelligence, Ramirez sent instructions from this location and he didn't involve himself in the drug trade face-to-face.

Hyde moved toward the camp, and Finn extended his arm to stop her. He shook his head and pointed to his eyes. He wanted to observe first and assess what they were facing. Being rash would blow the operation. They should count the number of men in the camp and if they could locate Ramirez, assess how to get to him.

Hyde obeyed him, which surprised him. The field

wasn't a place for arguments, but Hyde hadn't been the type to cow to him.

Crouching low in the bushes, they circled the camp, searching for Ramirez and staying together. The first glimpse of Ramirez was less than impressive. His propaganda painted him like a modern-day warlord, tall and muscular with a menacing stare. In reality, he was about thirty pounds overweight with a doughy face. He was armed, but he carried himself lazily, arms swinging, gait slow. Finn and Hyde exchanged looks. She had seen him, too.

A group of eight men left the camp on foot, heading down the mountain path. Finn and Hyde needed to act fast before the men could be called to return to protect their leader. Though they hadn't seen inside every tent, by Finn's count, eleven men including Ramirez remained.

Hyde leaned to the left and her shoulder brushed his. She didn't jerk away or acknowledge the casual touch. When she moved, he missed the softness of her skin and the heat of her body. Finn slid his arm around her waist. Hyde glanced at him in confusion, looking from his hand to his face. Many words sprang to mind. Those words would need to wait. Releasing her, he pointed to the camp.

They had discussed their plan and they needed to act on it. They hurried around the perimeter to the large canvas tent where they had seen Ramirez exit. Finn gestured for her to stay behind the tent, next to a small, humming generator. He crept up the side and peered in through the flaps over the entrance.

The tent was empty. Finn waved to Hyde to join him. She moved on silent feet to his side. Most of

Ramirez's soldiers were likely on patrol or selling drugs in nearby towns.

Inside the canvas enclosure was a small desk and a computer. They slipped inside. Hyde plugged her phone into the computer port. The software the West Company had provided would download the data from the computer and uploaded it via satellite connection to headquarters. For extra measure, the phone installed a virus to scan the computer disk and continually send data to HQ. Finn snapped pictures of documents laying on the desk.

Ramirez was their target, but he was also the head of a drug cartel, and information about his drug ring would help the West Company destroy it.

Hearing voices outside, Hyde grabbed her phone, pulling the small cord from the computer. They dove to exit the tent through the back, sliding beneath the canvas. Hyde moved like a snake. Finn had to struggle more with his size.

"Do you think we got anything?" Hyde asked. She slipped her phone into a pocket on her pants and had her hand on her gun.

"The virus will do the rest," Finn said. "Now we bring him in."

When they had the right opportunity, they would grab Ramirez, steal one of the off-road vehicles that was parked outside his tent and hurry to the chopper waiting for them at the rendezvous point. Nightfall was two hours away. If they could manage this before sundown, they wouldn't need to navigate an unfamiliar area with night-vision goggles.

They had seven hours to return to Barnett's island. They could make it. It would be tight, but they could do it.

Finn waited for silence inside the tent. He slipped a small mirror under the canvas to view the space.

Ramirez was sleeping in a chair, a bottle of whiskey empty on his table and his food half-eaten. Finn withdrew the syringe he had brought to sedate the man. Carrying his dead weight would prove challenging.

Hyde squeezed Finn's arm before he moved inside the tent. She was wishing him luck. Finn ran a finger down her cheek. This would be over soon. What would become of their relationship was undecided, but the more time he spent with Hyde, he didn't want it to end.

Finn entered the tent by slipping under the back. He moved toward Ramirez. But before he could get close enough to inject the sedative, two guards rushed into the tent, waving their guns and shouting in French. Sunlight poured in, blinding part of his vision. The guards were wearing green fatigues and speaking so quickly, Finn was catching every other word. They were threatening him and demanding to know who he worked for, the same questions repeatedly.

More on instinct than anything, Finn lifted Ramirez, holding the man in front of him like a shield. Ramirez awoke, struggling. He kicked his desk, sending Finn backward and the desk tumbling. The syringe was knocked from Finn's hand.

Hyde entered behind the guards. One of them whirled to face her. The other aimed for Finn and discharged his weapon.

Ramirez jerked and Finn felt searing heat on his

upper arm. Finn fired back, aiming for the guard's knee. The guard crumpled to the ground, shouting for assistance.

More guards would come. He and Hyde needed to get gone.

Hyde had dispatched with the other guard and rushed to Ramirez, kneeling next to him and looking from him to Finn. "He's still alive. But he's going to bleed out if we don't get him help."

Finn swore. This operation was lacking the finesse it would have had if he and Hyde had been given more than seventy-two hours to accomplish it. "Get his legs." Finn lifted him under the arms. Ramirez's shirt was wet with blood and sweat and he was heavy and awkward to carry. Together, they carted him to the vehicle they had selected for their escape. Finn and Hyde placed Ramirez in the back of the vehicle. Hyde stood in place, staring at the body.

"Hyde!" Finn said.

She didn't respond. He rushed to her, giving her shoulders a shake.

As if coming back to the present, Hyde blinked and ran to the driver's side seat. She opened the door and bent low, hotwiring the jeep. Finn jumped into the back. Blood was pouring from Ramirez's shoulder. After removing his shirt, Finn pressed the fabric hard over the wound, trying to stop the bleeding.

With a roar from the engine, Hyde scrambled into the driver's seat and they were taking off down the steep trail.

"Maybe no one has figured out what happened," Hyde said.

"What happened back there?" Finn asked.

Hyde glanced behind her at him. "I froze."

"I saw that. Why did you freeze?"

She didn't respond.

The sound of gunfire filled the air. It sounded like bullets were pelting the car. Finn slid lower in the seat, sitting on the floor of the vehicle and trying to help Ramirez. "They know we have him."

Hyde navigated the twisting road. Darkness was falling, but using their headlights would call attention to their position.

They came to a fork in the road. "Which way?" Hyde asked.

Finn glanced at the GPS on his phone. The roads were unmarked and the trees prevented them from getting a good picture from the overhead satellites. "Left." He was guessing, following his instincts.

"How is he?" Hyde asked, turning the vehicle down the left path.

"Breathing," Finn said. "We might have gotten lucky."

"A medic was already on board the chopper in case we were injured. We might get him help in time," Hyde said.

They bumped along the narrow, rocky road. Finn let out his breath when he heard the sound of helicopter rotors. They were close to help.

As they reached the rendezvous point, a bed dropped down. Finn and Hyde stopped the off-road vehicle and, as carefully as they could, carried Ramirez's body out of the back.

Gunfire peppered the air and they ducked. "Where's it coming from?" Hyde shouted.

It could be echoes, or Ramirez's guards closing in on them.

Finn's phone beeped and vibrated. He pulled it from his pocket. "Missile launcher spotted." Dread swamped him.

The message was from the West Company, possibly the pilot of the helicopter. A missile launcher would shoot the chopper out of the sky. Hyde and Finn hurried to strap Ramirez onto the stretcher. He and Hyde climbed on top, perched at the edges of it.

As the helicopter dragged them toward it, Finn and Hyde's eyes connected.

This flight was similar to how she had escaped prison. This was how he and Hyde had met. Under fire, being lifted into the air, not knowing how far away safety may be.

Hyde shivered and Finn read the fear in her eyes. She didn't talk about her time in prison often and when she mentioned it, she glossed over the details. This had to bring back terrible memories. Is that what had caused her to freeze when they were leaving the camp?

"I won't let anything happen to you," Finn said.

"If we're caught…"

They would be sent to prison, he finished to himself. "We won't be."

Reaching the helicopter, Hyde clambered in and they maneuvered Ramirez inside. Finn was last. As the medic worked on Ramirez, Finn sat next to Hyde.

"Want to tell me what's going on?" Finn asked.

Hyde shook her head.

Finn let it go for now. It was too loud to have a conversation and Finn was counting on her confiding in him when she was ready.

* * *

Ramirez was recuperating in a hospital in the United States under an alias while the body of a recently deceased man matching his description lay in a casket between them. Barnett wouldn't have access to dental records or DNA for comparison and with the stories of Ramirez being shot and taken from the camp, his crew believed he was dead.

The experts at the West Company had also recreated the tattoos on their dead body similar to ones that Ramirez had on his biceps, shoulders and neck.

Finn's shoulder had been bandaged. The bullet that had struck Ramirez had grazed him. Finn was lucky it hadn't been worse, but it had to hurt.

Finn and Hyde sped in their borrowed boat toward Barnett's island. Having the boat provided them a luxury they hadn't had before: an escape route. The boat was small, fast and could be brought to land.

The West Company's technology department had used the documents Hyde and Finn had found inside Ramirez's tent to locate one of Ramirez's bank accounts and withdraw the five million dollars Reed Barnett had required as a buy-in to his venture.

The West Company hackers had left the appropriate traces so Barnett would know Finn had stolen the money, but also covered their tracks such that Ramirez's cartel couldn't connect the theft to the West Company. Creating an international incident wasn't on the West Company's to-do list.

"Are you ready to face them?" Finn asked.

Hyde slipped her arms around his waist and rested her head on his good shoulder. The boat skimmed along the water, bouncing on waves. "I don't think

we have a choice." She was slipping back into character, but part of her need to touch Finn was her fear.
He had been bleeding heavily in Selvan and it had
scared her. He could have bled out. She could lose
him in her life. Sorting through those thoughts, even
in the few hours she'd had, she'd realized that losing
Finn in her life in a real and permanent way wasn't
something she could face. Not now. She wasn't ready.

But she couldn't be a spy anymore. How could
those two deep desires coexist? The impact of her
emotions rattled her. The slight tremble in her hands
gave away she was standing on the edge of something
much too deep.

Finn and Hyde slid into shore and Hyde helped Finn
pull the boat onto the sand. She hauled hard, knowing his injury had cost him. They anchored the boat
with stakes provided for this purpose.

"We've got fourteen minutes until the deadline,"
Finn said, sweat dripping down his temples.

Hyde took a cloth from her handbag and dabbed
at his face. "Told you we could do this," Hyde said.
Fourteen minutes was cutting it close, but as far as
they'd come, they'd make it.

They wheeled the casket onto the dune buggy and
secured it with bungee cords and ropes.

On the drive to the mansion, Hyde inspected her
nails and tried to keep her eyes off the man next to
her. Sharing with Finn the story of their baby had
unleashed a dam of emotions and she was trying to
hide it. Hide it from him, from Barnett and to protect herself.

She must look a disgrace. Her hair was knotted in
a messy bun, her clothes were rumpled and she was

in need of a shower. In keeping with her character, she made a mental note to complain about the physical labor involved in moving the casket and demand time at the spa.

Taking a deep breath, she cleared any panicked thoughts. Showing weakness was unacceptable. She held on to her story that the body in the casket belonged to Ramirez. If Barnett smelled a lie, he would kill them.

Finn didn't knock as he strode into the house. Barnett's staff met them in the entryway.

"We need to see Barnett," Finn said.

Barnett's butler nodded and escorted them to Barnett. He was lying next to Ruby on lounge chairs poolside, drinking yellow cocktails, a tray of fresh-cut fruit set on the table next to him.

Watching them, Hyde felt a stir of irritation. She and Finn had been through physical and mental challenges over the last three days whereas the criminal was relaxing comfortably, sipping drinks. Hyde wouldn't miss this part of the spy life. Karma was supposed to slap bad down, but Hyde didn't think it worked fast enough.

Ruby smiled and sat up, waving. Barnett looked at his phone. He smirked. "Almost didn't make it."

Finn touched his bandaged shoulder. "You didn't give us much time."

"I assume since you are here, you've done as I've required," Barnett said.

Finn handed Barnett a device with the money-routing information. "Casket is out front. Bank information on the device."

The West Company deposited the money into an

untraceable account offshore. Barnett would have no trouble accessing it. If he moved the money into his accounts, the action would have the added bonus of allowing the West Company to track Barnett's accounts, too.

Barnett took the device from Finn. He called someone on his phone. Two men came from the main house and Finn reached for his weapon, his body tensed.

Despite their willingness to play Barnett's game, she and Finn didn't trust him. Barnett had created a difficult task to prove loyalty. They were experienced spies, but without their resources, they may have had to kill Ramirez and they wouldn't have been able to move the money in time.

Barnett held up his hand to Finn. "They will not shoot you." Addressing his guards and tossing them the bank account device, he said, "Confirm the identity of the body and the amount in the account." The guards left and Barnett returned his attention to Finn and Hyde. "Have any troubles?"

His tone put Hyde on alert. He couldn't have uncovered their identities. They were careful. The West Company were master spies. Barnett could have had his lackeys kill them.

Finn stared at Barnett. "I had three days. It wasn't easy. I took a bullet in the shoulder."

"Did you accomplish the task alone?" Barnett asked.

Hyde's instincts screamed warnings. Her gun was at her thigh. She moved her fingers toward it.

Barnett knew something. He was testing them. He couldn't know about their connection to the West Company.

"I didn't work alone," Finn said.

Barnett waited. Finn remained silent.

"Was she with you?" Barnett pointed at Hyde.

She and Finn hadn't discussed how they would address her involvement if questioned about how they had found and tracked Ramirez. To this point, they were pretending she hadn't been.

Finn nodded. "She was for the final leg of the journey."

Barnett rose to his feet. "I want full disclosure of what happened on the mission."

"Revealing my methods and resources weren't part of the arrangement," Finn said.

"If you work with me, I don't cut other people in. I like to know exactly who is involved with my business. No subcontractors who I can't control."

Hyde sensed a standoff. She needed to say something or Barnett would boot them out. They'd come so far.

She stepped forward, setting her hand on Finn's arm. "It's okay, Finn. You don't have to protect me or who I am."

Three pairs of eyes swerved in her direction. Ruby's eyes were wide. Barnett stared at Hyde, his gaze drilling into her.

Finn's hand was near his weapon. "You don't need to out yourself."

Barnett was looking for them to reveal something. "I don't like to discuss this and Finn knows that. But I sense I will have to tell you the truth if we want this business partnership to work." She took a deep breath for dramatic effect. "My father was a thief. He taught me to be adept with a gun in a fight. So while I have no interest in being a petty crook, I helped Finn. I knew he was against the wall with the timeline and what he needed to do, so I had his back."

Barnett assessed her. "You don't seem like someone who gets her hands dirty."

She lifted her chin and squared her shoulders, setting her hand on her hip. "It's not the life I want and I've made that clear to Finn. My dreams are different than carrying a gun. I do what's needed to help my man. He had three days and the task was difficult. I've known Finn long enough to know when he's under the gun and I wanted to help. Making this deal would be a life changer for us. But now that you mention it, I don't like being dirty and I want a shower and some spa time."

Barnett stared at her. Was he wondering if she was lying? Hyde wouldn't babble. She had said her piece. If Barnett didn't buy their story, they would shoot their way off the island. Her fingers tingled, thinking about the gun at her thigh.

"Barnett, they did what you asked," Ruby said. She set her hand on his arm.

Barnett's gaze swung to Ruby. "I didn't ask you."

Ruby snapped her mouth shut and lowered her head. In their absence, nothing had changed between Barnett and Ruby. He was dismissive and rude, but at least Ruby was alive.

Barnett looked at Hyde and scowled at her, perhaps trying to intimidate her. "Then you aren't the helpless damsel you pretend to be."

"I've never pretended to be helpless. I am capable of protecting myself and the people I love. But don't mistake my involvement here. I support Finn. If this is what he wants to do, I'll be here for him." The truth of the words flustered her.

She met Finn's gaze. Heat flowed through her and having him close, some of her edginess dissipated and was replaced with confidence and trust. Confidence that together they could do this and trust that he had her back.

"I couldn't ask for a better woman," Finn said.

She hadn't known true companionship until she had met him.

Barnett sniffed. "If the body and money check out, I'll send someone to escort you to dinner. If it doesn't, I'll send someone to your villa to kill you."

"You didn't unpack this time," Finn said.

While she'd showered, he'd finished sweeping the room for bugs and had turned on a device to block un-authorized signals from monitoring their room.

Even knowing they weren't being watched, Hyde couldn't bring up what was weighing on her mind. She kept to mission-related details. "It might not be worth it. Barnett could have wanted Ramirez dead and be happy to have us take care of it. Our partner-ship with him might end here."

Barnett screwing them over wasn't unexpected. Barnett claimed to want Finn's help with distribution of his drug, but Hyde wouldn't put lying past Barnett. They were lying, too.

Finn slipped his hands into the pockets of his cargo shorts. "He'll invite us. We bring value to his orga-nization."

"Do you think he believed me?" Hyde asked.

"I almost believed it."

Hyde rubbed her eyes. She wanted to be flat-out honest with Finn and then go home. To say those difficult words that were taking her over. A future could be on their terms, compromise, bargaining and discussing. They would have to come a great distance to find middle ground.

Like she had done for the last ten years, she stuffed those thoughts away into the darkest corners of her heart.

"Was it prison?" he asked.

Her heart beat fast and she felt ill, the way she did anytime someone mentioned La Sabaneta. "What about prison?"

"You froze. In the field. Was it because of prison?"

Her time in prison would haunt her for the rest of her life. Working hard to make her peace with it, she had come a long way. But she would never get over what had happened there. "I didn't freeze because of prison. Or maybe I did, at least in part. My time there affects every moment of my life. I wasn't thinking about La Sabaneta." It was Finn. She had been thinking and worried about Finn.

Finn crossed the room to her perhaps sensing she needed him. He slipped his arms around her waist. Heat spiraled between them and she didn't want to push him away. He knew her most painful secret and he was still here. Leaning into him, it felt right and good to be in his arms. She had worried she would feel misunderstood or judged. She felt neither.

"It's hard to imagine this life without you," Finn said.

This life or his life? For her, it was both. He couldn't make the same leap. "I am ready to move on from this." But not ready to move on from him. She couldn't think of a way to keep him in her life and walk away from being a spy.

Finn's arms tightened around her. "I wish I could change your mind. The times I've spent with you were some of the best of my life. Even this mission, having you with me has been great."

Sentimentality pulled at her heart strings. Some of her most fun adventures had been with him at her side. He was the bright spot in her days. She had deliberately shut him out of her life during a time of enormous need, and that had been a mistake.

Hyde lifted her face. Finn brushed his nose lightly against hers and then lowered his mouth and kissed her softly. He made a sound of contentment.

He leaned away. "Don't tease me, Alex," he said.

"I'm not teasing you," she said. What was she doing? It was hard to think with his arms around her. Lust overrode clearheaded thinking.

He kissed her again, deeper, more thoroughly, their tongues brushing each other, his hands moving to her lower back. He pulled her against him, holding her along his long, muscular body. The kiss consumed her, and Hyde arched to be closer to Finn.

He walked her toward the bed and with every step, another article of clothing hit the floor.

When she felt the mattress at the back of her thighs, she sat, pulling Finn with her. Shirtless, he was a sight. She drank him in, the hard planes of his body, his sculpted jaw and cheekbones, the strength in the rippling muscles of his body. She lightly touched the edges of the bandage around his upper arm. "Does this hurt?"

"It's manageable," he said. He had refused to take

heavy-duty painkillers in order to keep his thinking clear.

Finn moved fluidly, like a predator, and Hyde enjoyed that. Positioning himself over her, he let the weight of his body press her to the mattress. Her bra and panties were frustrating barriers between them.

He rocked against her, mimicking what he planned to do, reminding her of the steamy, long nights they had spent together. Heat streaked through her and she felt relaxed, as if being with him transported her to a different place. A place where only pleasure and happiness existed. Meeting him after missions was therapeutic. Even when they could only be together for a few hours, those few hours were as rejuvenating as a week at a five-star resort.

If these were their last days together, they should enjoy them and each other. That may make the heartbreak more profound when they parted ways, but based on how she was feeling, that pain would run deep. Finn's hand brushed her hip and Hyde stopped moving.

"Stop." She spoke the word on a whisper. All she could imagine was losing him and how taking this step would make it worse.

Finn moved off her immediately. He sat on his haunches, confusion plain on his face. His hair was mussed. Had she done that?

Before she could say anything, they heard a knock on the door.

"I thought we had a few hours," Finn said, sounding irritated.

Barnett could have decided that she was lying and

had sent a team of men to kill her. But murderers didn't knock. Finn grabbed his gun and Hyde rose from the bed, searching for her clothes and her weapon. When she had on her shirt, pants and gun, she answered the door.

A man Hyde had never seen stood at the door. Close-cropped dark hair, clean shaven, dark eyes and shorter, but stockier, than she was, he extended a tan envelope to her and said nothing. When she took the envelope, he turned to leave.

Finn came to her side as she opened the envelope. Their shoulders brushed and heat traveled up and down her spine.

"Barnett is inviting us to dinner." Relief washed over her.

"Does that mean we're in?" He seemed skeptical.

"I suppose. For now." Enough time hadn't passed for Barnett to confirm their story and the details of Ramirez's capture. Hyde didn't like having that hanging over their heads. How would Barnett react if he learned that she and Finn were playing him?

Hyde closed the door and slipped the letter into the envelope. "I need to get ready."

She wanted to put distance between her and Finn. If they hadn't been interrupted by the door, what would have happened between them? She had put the brakes on what they'd been doing, but she couldn't deny her attraction to Finn or the urge to connect with him in a meaningful way.

This space was too small, their history too deep. That sense of connection, that rightness, stretched between them. After this mission, she would say goodbye to Finn. Hyde kissed his left cheek. She kissed his right cheek. Then she pressed a kiss to his mouth.

A million emotions sprang up inside her when their lips met. Lust and desire escalated out of control and in the span of a few seconds, she relived some of the most amazing experiences of her life. Horseback riding in Barcelona, blueberry picking in Lima, water-skiing in Sydney, and whale watching in Hawaii, all with Finn. Finn's sense of adventure, his bravery and his compassion were some of his best qualities. Their connection was unmatched.

Finn knew how to touch her, what she liked and how to please her. A confident and strong lover, he met her exuberance, stamina and ferocity and was gentle when she needed it.

Finn ran his hand down her bare arm and interlaced their fingers. Bringing her fingers to his lips, he kissed each knuckle and then knelt on the floor in front of her.

He was almost down on one knee, and her heart fluttered, but Finn wasn't and wouldn't ever propose. Family and commitment weren't in his future. The life he had was all he wanted. She was the one who had changed and she couldn't fault him for that. From the start of their affair, he had been honest about loving his work. Settling in one place for any length of time didn't fit the job description.

"Round two? This time I can win you over," he said.

He unfastened her pants and slid them down her legs. With quaking knees, she stepped out of them. His hands parted her thighs and he moved between them.

"Tell me to stop and I will," he said. He had when she'd spoken the word earlier.

His whiskers brushed her inner thigh and he kissed higher to the apex of her thighs.

"Pink. Cotton. Practical and sexy," he said.

He didn't remove them. Her heart was pounding and she felt like she was watching him in slow motion. It would feel good to strip off every article of clothing and writhe naked in bed with him. Her emotions were a jumbled mess and she couldn't resolve her desires with her worry.

He stood. "I wondered." He ran his finger along the top of her underwear.

"About my underwear?" she asked.

"Whenever we've met in the past, you had the most incredible underwear. I wondered if that was an everyday ritual or something for me."

Both. When she bought new clothes and shoes and packed to meet him, she thought about Finn and what his reaction would be to seeing them. She enjoyed his happiness and fascination with her. "After pretending to be a man in prison, I promised myself that when I escaped, I would take every opportunity to embrace being a woman. I like beautiful things."

"You're an amazing woman. Gorgeous. Smart. Talented." His finger grazed languidly along her skin, teasing her.

"Thank you."

"You blush when you're given a compliment."

"I don't," she said. She was in careful control of her emotions and while Finn's praise has pleased her, she understood the limited value of flattery and compliments.

"That's what makes you even more beautiful. You're not vain about your looks."

Finn rose and pressed a kiss to her lips. He didn't deepen it. His mouth lingered against hers. Something inside her gave way and she looped her hand around the back of his neck and pulled him against her. She jumped and wrapped her legs around his waist.

His hardness pressed against her core and she moaned. She opened her mouth wider and her tongue sparred with Finn's. Forking her fingers into his hair, she felt the silky strands between her fingers. How did he feel so good and soft, while being so hard and strong?

He walked her toward the couch and dropped her onto the cushions. He lowered himself on top of her. When their bodies collided, she rolled, forcing him onto the floor and underneath her.

Kneeling across him, she stared at him. His hair was mussed and his clothes rumpled and she fell for him more.

She had always liked and wanted Finn. But after her pregnancy, Hyde had to face two emotional revelations, one about her desire for a family and the other about her feelings for Finn. He was more than sex to her.

She brought her leg over his hips and perched on the edge of the couch, embarrassed she had started and stopped this. Finn sat and set his hands on her knees.

"It's okay. We won't do anything you don't want. If you're not ready, I understand."

Hyde met his eyes. "It's gotten complicated."

"I know," he said.

Hyde stood and strode to the table where she had left her phone. She checked for new messages, anything to distract her from the confusion and desire ping-ponging around her mind.

Chapter 8

Hyde couldn't shake the feeling that something would go wrong tonight at Barnett's dinner. If he was planning to kill them, he would have done so already. But Hyde didn't trust Barnett or his plans.

Finn didn't trust Barnett, either, but he held steadfast to his goal. Fear wouldn't dissuade him.

"Why don't you stay here tonight? If Barnett tries anything, I'll send you a message. Use the boat and get as far away from the island as you can," Finn said. Concern edged his voice.

They were a team and the more time she spent with him, the more deeply that word resonated. She had Finn's back if this mission went sideways. "And leave you here to die? We'll attend together. We'll be ready." And armed.

After discussing their plan, as well as contingency

plans, they prepared for the occasion. Finn was wearing a tuxedo and Hyde a long, emerald-green dress, which hugged her body until it reached her knees and then flared.

She tucked a gun in her clutch and strapped another one to her leg. Accessing the second gun would be difficult, but Hyde was ready in a pinch.

Finn drove the dune buggy down the beach to Barnett's mansion. They were escorted into a long, glass-enclosed sunroom overlooking the beach. The window trims were painted yellow and orange, and the dark wood table in the center of the room sat twenty-two. Only four of the chairs had place settings. Fans whirled overhead, cooling the room. It was quiet and that worried Hyde. Her fingers itched to reach for her gun.

Barnett was waiting in a chair that reminded Hyde of a golden throne, with red velvet wrapped around the arms and intricate scrollwork across the high back and sides. It was how Barnett likely saw himself, a king of his island. "Welcome," he said. He was wearing a silk robe, and a cigar burned in an ashtray in front of him.

Just the one word? That was unusual. Was he hoping she or Finn would talk to fill the silence and give something away?

Ruby was absent. She may have been warned to stay away from this meeting.

A waiter brought Hyde and Finn each a glass of red wine, but Barnett was without a drink of his own. Hyde set hers down, wanting her hands free. This could be a bloodbath in the making.

Folding his hands in front of him, Barnett cleared his throat. "We believe you've brought me Ramirez. I've sent teams to authorize your stories. If I catch a whiff of a lie, I will kill you and I won't give second chances or ask questions."

Finn hadn't moved though he seemed tense, his shoulders hiked, his knuckles white. He was poised to strike. They both were. No matter what happened here tonight, she would keep Finn safe.

Hyde's hand drifted toward her gun. Pulling a weapon in this room would bring Barnett's guards, and Hyde was sure they were being watched. She considered killing Barnett and taking her chances. Ending his miserable life would mean she could return to hers. With their leader dead, Barnett's organization could be systematically destroyed.

"Enough talking in circles, Barnett. I've done what you've asked. You might have something I want, but that wind blows both ways. I want to know more about the master plan. Stop jerking me around," Finn said.

Barnett frowned. He didn't like a show of strength from Finn, but he must realize that Finn wouldn't wait indefinitely. Though Barnett was influential and ruled unreservedly on the island, Finn could lash back.

"My new drug is one of a kind, absolutely spectacular," Barnett said.

That wasn't news. The illegal drug market, much like the pharmaceutical drug market, was flooded with new drugs every day. Every street dealer with a Bunsen burner and a mortar and pestle thought he could manufacture the next big moneymaker. A drug's success was dependent on many factors. The drug had to be sold in the right clubs to the right people who would spread the word. It had to bring its customers back to the table, wanting another fix.

Finn leaned forward and folded his hands on the

table. "I gave you five million for a buy-in to a new drug? I'm not impressed. You'd better have more than that, Barnett." Finn gestured to his shoulder. "I took a bullet to get this job done."

For the first time, Barnett seemed nervous, his heel tapping against the ground. "Imagine a drug that makes you feel better than ecstasy, but with the addictive power of cocaine. It's cheaper than heroin to manufacture, about one dollar and thirty-three cents, but in my test markets, the pills sold for forty dollars apiece."

"I like those margins," Finn said. "Where are they manufactured?"

Barnett appeared smug. "I've set up manufacturing plants in many places. I deliver the ingredients, I keep control of those ingredients and my labs create the drug. I can relocate if pressure from the local authorities becomes too strong. The process is safer than meth, meaning less waste and fewer casualties."

"If this drug is as amazing as you claim, you should be able to distribute it without push from me," Finn said.

Barnett pressed his hands together. "I've been in this business a long time. I don't want my formula replicated and my profits cut into by knockoffs. I'll lose market share and customers. I need control. I need to dominate the market."

Hyde suspected more to the story than he'd let on. But Barnett wouldn't give away his full plan. A new drug, easy and safe to manufacture, with high profit margins and a high rate of addiction meant hundreds of millions of dollars in Barnett's pockets every month.

"I'm a person of interest to several American law

enforcement agencies. I can't step foot on American soil without risking arrest. I need you to be my liaison," Barnett said.

"Meaning you use my network to distribute the drug fast and it's my neck on the line if the Feds make the connection to the drug, or you, to me?" Finn asked.

"Arrest is a risk. You've stayed out of jail and avoided prosecution this long. Based on what I read about you and what my network has told me, you are the right man for the job. My last big score could have been bigger. But someone I trusted made a series of mistakes. We lost money. We wasted product. That won't happen this time," Barnett said.

Finn drummed his fingers on the table. "Tell me what you need me to do. Specifics. I'm not your errand boy."

Barnett looked like a lion about to spring. "I need you to fly to Miami and negotiate some business for me. I need you to set up the deliveries and the infrastructure. Do it fast. I have a shipment of highly volatile chemicals coming into the port soon. I need you ready to receive. In return, you'll have ten percent of the profits."

"Twenty-five," Finn said. "My contacts. My experience. My neck on the line."

Barnett nodded. "Twenty. No mistakes, though, Finn. During my last transaction in Miami, my partner wound up dead."

Hyde and Finn took their boat to a nearby island and waited to board a private plane to Miami. They were running on fumes.

Their plane took off at 3:00 a.m. When the plane

was in the air, Hyde took out her nail polish and worked on her nails. The mindless task gave her time to think and in Miami, frequenting nightclubs required a certain look. Tired and bedraggled wouldn't cut it.

Barnett could be leading them into a trap. Or more likely, planning to use them and have Finn take the fall for Barnett or have them outright killed. She and Finn were in the weeds with the snakes, and being bitten was highly probable.

Hyde had been in situations where she wasn't safe and where she couldn't trust anyone. She too vividly remembered those long days and nights in La Sabaneta prison. She'd had to be sharp every moment to conceal her identity. She had been lucky enough to form alliances that had helped her to survive. Through some of the tightest security, she had a friend on the outside pass her cigarettes and cell phones to use as currency. Those had kept her alive on several occasions. She had worked out relentlessly to hide her small frame, though with the terrible nutrition, every person in La Sabaneta looked famished.

In her retired life, she wouldn't miss that fear or the rush of adrenaline that had accompanied her on missions or the panic that overtook her when she thought about being imprisoned again. Her background had made her who she was today, but she wanted to leave those experiences behind.

Finn sat next to her on the plane. "You okay?"

She had told him she wasn't feeling well. An excuse to put distance between them. She needed to think. "Nothing a hot shower, a good meal and a night on a decent mattress can't fix."

Finn pushed his chair into a recline position. "We could sleep here."

Her body was tired, but her thoughts were running wild. "Go ahead. I'll wake you when we land."

"Relax, Hyde. There's nothing we can do now except dig up what we can in Miami. When we have enough, we'll nail him."

They didn't know the direct path to do that and the longer they were on the mission, the more out of control she felt. This assignment tested her relationship with Finn.

"Are you upset with me?" Finn asked. He blinked at her with those expressive eyes.

She was contemplating the mission and her future and her feelings for him. "Just thinking."

"I'm worried about you, Alex. I forced you into this mission. I know you have other dreams and goals. I have every intention of making your dreams come true. I'll return you alive and happy to Montana," Finn said.

Was she happy? After making her decision to leave the spy world, Hyde had been fumbling. She hadn't found her new world yet. "Thank you for acknowledging that this isn't the life I want." He had transitioned from questioning it to accepting it.

"It's hard for me to fully process it. But it's your life and your choices."

Hyde faced him. He was staring at the ceiling of the plane.

Hyde put the nail polish lid on and screwed it tight. "While we're on American soil, why don't you call your family and have them meet us in Miami?"

Finn shot her a look of disgust, the same look he

might have given her if she had suggested he lick the bottom of her shoes. "They can't see me. I won't bring them into this."

Was he concerned about their safety or was he maintaining distance? "We could find a way to meet them safely," Hyde said. "Unconnected to the mission."

"We?"

The word had popped from her mouth before she'd considered the implication. Meeting Finn's family wasn't a good idea. They might get the wrong impression about her and Finn. They'd navigated Finn meeting her family skillfully enough. "I will go along as your bodyguard."

"No visits with my family," Finn said. His tone left little room for negotiation.

Hyde wouldn't let it drop easily. "You don't know the next time you'll be in America. Why not extend the olive branch to them now?"

Finn rolled to his feet in one smooth motion. "You don't know what you're talking about, Hyde. Let it go."

It wasn't like Finn to sprint away from a challenge. Speaking to his family was a far different problem, than say, avoiding missiles in the field. "You're running from them and given how you live, you're probably hiding, too."

Finn was staring out one of the airplane's windows. "Not running. But involving my family in my life won't bring me anything except more headaches."

"You could let them know you're safe."

"They know," Finn said. "They would be alerted if I was dead."

Hyde had pushed a hot button. She wanted to understand what he was going through and perhaps get to the heart of the matter. Suddenly, this issue felt important to her, like talking about his family was letting her inside his life in a real way. "They'd like more than that. They might want to know how you are and what you've been doing."

"I can't tell them about anything I've been doing," Finn said.

"You could tell them about me," Hyde said.

Finn stabbed his fingers through his hair. "Except what would be the point? You won't be in my life long. You don't want to be an operative and you've made it clear there's a personal obstacle between us."

She had sorted her feelings while on this mission and had come to the conclusion she wanted him in her life. Not clear on the specifics, but losing him felt devastating. "I've been going through something difficult, Finn. I wasn't ready to talk about it."

"You talked to me about it, but you've been distant."

She didn't have a good explanation for that. They were holding back. She didn't want to do that anymore. An actual connection with Finn would mean so much to her.

Finn turned. "We'll be in Miami in a couple hours. We're meeting a few of Barnett's contacts in the nightclubs. Doesn't give us much time. You should sleep now." He closed his eyes, not giving her a chance to respond.

Getting into a conversation about his family wasn't happening, not today and maybe not ever.

Rather than argue with Finn, Hyde found a comfortable position in her chair and shut her eyes. She had her own demons. She didn't need to chase away Finn's.

Finn and Hyde arrived in Miami without issue and gathered their bags from the trolley on the runway. Overhead, a plane took off. They had been the only passengers on their flight.

Finn had arranged for a car to be waiting for them. A man was standing at the exit, holding a sign with their aliases written on it. Finn approached and the man handed Finn a set of keys, giving a small bow as he backed away, almost like he was afraid of Finn and couldn't flee fast enough.

Hyde slipped into her role as a drug lord's girl-friend. The car parked at the curb was worth well over a hundred thousand dollars and was ostentatious and mysterious, with dark tinted windows that concealed the interior. Hyde had driven in astoundingly fast and well-appointed cars before, but this one was the most luxurious.

Hyde took a seat in the passenger side, the softness of the leather seats like a caress. Even though she would have loved to drive, Finn's character wouldn't let his girlfriend take the wheel. When she closed the door, the car was nearly silent, blocking out the sounds of traffic and voices.

"I called ahead to the hotel, and Abby sent over some new outfits for you," Finn said. He set his hand on her knee and gave it a squeeze. Hyde looked from his hand to his face, but just as quickly, he removed it and took the wheel. Reading too much into a casual touch would drive her crazy.

Hyde could imagine the type of outfits a drug lord's girlfriend would wear clubbing in Miami. "Looking forward to it." She'd enjoy the wildly sexy clothes and stiletto heels. In Montana, she wouldn't have many opportunities to dress up.

"We have a meeting at 10:00 p.m. tonight with the owner of a club along the beach," Finn said. "Tables at Illumination start at twenty-five large per night."

This was the flashiest operation she had been on. Most of her work as a spy involved wading through dirty conditions. Hiding out in run-down buildings and digging through Dumpsters for information had been the norm.

The car moved smoothly along the road like it was made of polished glass. Finn was tapping the leather steering wheel with his right pointer finger.

"Want to tell me what you're worried about?" Hyde asked.

Finn's hands gripped the wheel, turning his knuckles white. "Are you planning to bring up my family again?"

She had tried and failed. "No."

"You think I should contact them."

She was worried for him. He was making a mistake. "It's your family. Handle them how you see fit."

Finn made a noncommittal noise. "We have enough problems. Let's not add my family to the mix."

"I'm your friend. I wasn't trying to add more concerns to our plates. I was trying to smooth things over with your family for your sake and peace of mind."

"It's complicated and you wouldn't understand. Your family is close. They care for each other. I was with them for less than a day and I could see it," Finn said.

"You don't care for your family?" Hyde asked.

"I care for them," Finn said. "But being away from them is better. Do you know who my father is?"

Hyde hadn't heard him speak of his father much. "Not really."

"He's a politician. He's worried about fund-raising and his contacts and getting elected, and everything else is a distant second. My mother, brother and I don't rate as high as golf games and fancy dinners if there's a connection to be made. I escaped that life. I have no interest in going back."

"I'm not suggesting you take up a post as a politician. I'm saying you could speak to your family."

Finn adjusted the air conditioner, dropping the temperature inside the car. "They'd try to suck me into that world. A veteran for a son makes a compelling line item on my father's résumé and he'd like to trot me out to certain factions to win their favor. I won't give him that satisfaction."

The venom in his voice spoke to a deep-seated hurt. "You think any part of his life, even having a family of your own, means sucking you back in?"

Finn said nothing. He stared straight ahead. "My father wasn't there for me or my mom. If I had a family, I wouldn't treat them that way."

Hyde heard something different in his words. He could have been speaking hypothetically or generally, but he had stated that he would be a different husband and father if in that position. Was it a sign he had relented on his earlier statements about not ever having a family? Her desperation to keep him in her life made her grasp at straws.

"There's a reason I don't like to talk about this. I don't want to overthink it. I don't want that life and I won't let anyone force it on me," Finn said.

The last comment was directed at her. Hyde fell silent. The air in the car was suddenly frosty. She had made a mental leap, dissecting every word Finn spoke. But he had said it before and he was saying it again. He was a spy for life.

The dresses the West Company had sent for Hyde to wear were long enough to be decent and cover her completely, but in them, she felt like a celebrity. For tonight's jaunt, she picked a deep purple strapless dress that fell midthigh. She was impressed by the designer label on the dress. Her heels took a bit to get used to, but after finding her stride, Hyde felt confident she could look natural, like she wore five-inch heels everywhere she went.

Finn was still grumpy about their conversation regarding his family. She had dug too deep. They should appear in public as a happy couple. Seeming at odds might make their contacts uncomfortable and, therefore, wary of working with them.

Hyde grabbed Finn's hand and spun toward him. He looked drop-dead sexy in a black suit, white shirt, open collar. Like hers, his clothing was designer label, modern and fit well. "Try to relax," she said.

Finn slipped his arm around her waist. "I am relaxed."

His tone was light, but his body was tense, the arm around her tight.

"It doesn't seem that way," Hyde said. "Is your shoulder bothering you?"

He shook his head but touched the injury. The slight narrowing of his eyes indicated he was in pain.

"Are you worried about meeting Barnett's partners? I read the file from the West Company. We can do this." Part of Barnett's business plan was to keep his new drug flowing through the most popular clubs in the region, using word of mouth to spread the drug's popularity and increase demand.

Finn shook his head. "I'm not worried about the meeting. I expect Barnett to stab me in the back and I'm prepared for it. It's you. You're worrying me."

Hyde dropped her hands. "Me? What am I doing?" Her defensiveness rose. Despite her monthslong hiatus, she had been solid on this mission.

Finn ran his hand through his hair. "You've changed. You're asking me questions. It was never like that between us. You just accepted who I was."

Hyde straightened. "I accept who you are."

"You're trying to change me. Just because you've changed doesn't mean I will."

Hyde stepped away from Finn. She had thought she'd hidden her conflicted feelings well, but her questions were enough to let Finn know that everything was not good. "I'll stop pressing you. I'm sorry."

"We need to leave soon. We're expected at Illumination."

After ten minutes of stilted conversation on the drive to Illumination, they valet-parked. Finn was high confidence, arrogant swagger, devil-may-care attitude in a hot package.

Entering the club through the front door, they skipped the line that wrapped around the block. The bouncer nodded at them, and a hostess escorted them to a small, two-person, glass-top table with a great view of the dance floor.

"This table costs twenty-five thousand for the night?" Hyde asked.

"That's the going rate."

Hyde had never been to a nightclub outside her operations. The women around her were standing as if posing for a picture, and Hyde mimicked their posture. Shoulders back, chin up, ankles crossed and a hand on her hip.

"That's a terrific dress," Finn said.

Hyde smoothed the fabric. "Are you making fun of me? This isn't my usual style." Kicking and running in the dress would be difficult.

"Not making fun. I've been thinking it since you put it on." He was initiating a truce, trying to put their relationship on solid ground. Arguing about his family and the future was getting them nowhere fast.

"You look handsome tonight, too," Hyde said.

She and Finn's gazes caught and held. Some of the awkwardness between them disappeared. Finn reached to the side of her face and ran his fingers along her jawline.

He opened his mouth to speak and with a glance over her shoulder, snapped it closed.

Hyde turned slowly. A man approached, all smiles, slicked-back dark hair and carrying a drink in his hand. His suit was tight and his shoes too shiny. The first three buttons of his dress shirt were open. This was Finn's contact Damien Winslow, appearing far more polished in his club than the police booking pictures from the file the West Company had provided. Winslow had served time in a federal penitentiary following drug charges. Based on his connection to Barnett, he had returned to the same line of work that had gotten him in trouble years before.

The men greeted each other with a handshake and sized each other up. Hyde looked around, pretending to be fascinated by the people in the club. This was Barnett's test market. The drug could be making the rounds tonight.

Winslow gestured for a waitress to bring them drinks. Finn and Winslow exchanged pleasantries until their cocktails appeared. Hyde lifted her glass to her mouth and pretended to sip.

Finn pushed his cup a few inches away from him. "Not while I'm working." Finn leaned close to her. "We have some business to discuss. Why don't you go have fun? I'll join you shortly."

Hyde smiled and nodded but wondered if she should have insisted on staying with Finn. She was his backup and depending where she went in the club, she might be out of eyeshot of him. Hiding her annoyance that he had asked her to leave, she sauntered away. She felt eyes on her and unease danced down her spine. She turned to see Finn and Winslow watching her.

Hyde circulated through the club, looking at the dancers, watching the young, happy faces as they gyrated and bounced to the rhythm of the music. Entirely too much alcohol was being consumed. Hyde had missed this in her twenties. She had been too serious and deeply involved with her work and her training to take nights off to party. The only time she was in a club like this was for a mission.

A man approached, crowding her space. He was bodybuilder-huge, his skin tanned and shiny and his hair cut short around his square-shaped head. Hyde didn't recognize him. Was he a friend of Winslow's?

"Dance with me," he said.

He could work for the West Company and be here to deliver a message. Hyde stayed in character and played it safe. "I'm here with someone," Hyde said, extending her hand to put distance between them.

The man looked around and gestured to the empty space next to her. "I don't see anyone."

Pushy didn't jibe with her. "He had some matters to attend to," Hyde said.

"I don't know what that means, other than he left a sexy woman alone for the taking."

Hyde didn't care for his wording and had the impression he was not from the West Company. "I am not someone who likes to be taken."

"That's because you haven't been with me." The man reached for her hand to lead her onto the dance floor.

She pulled away. "No. Thank you." Her thanks had an edge.

"Your loss," the man said and strode down the bar to the next woman.

Hyde shook off the conversation and watched, looking for the discreet exchange of drugs. Given that Barnett had sent them to this space and Winslow's criminal record, this place had a number of drugs on the premises.

Finn appeared at her side. "See anything worth talking about?"

Relief passed through her at the sight of him. "I think you'll have the better story."

Finn slipped his arm around her waist and drew

her against him and onto the dance floor. Locked in each other's embrace, they moved where fewer people would bump into them. His thigh brushed between her legs as they danced and she felt waves of pleasure pipe over her.

"Why did you send me away from the table?" Hyde asked.

"We were talking business. You may be my partner in many senses of the word, but here, I'm working the business angle for Barnett," Finn said. "Winslow wants a huge order from Barnett."

Hyde pressed against Finn, wanting to be close to him, her body tingling. "How big?"

Finn arched a brow. "As much as we can get him."

"What did you tell him?" Hyde asked, trying to focus on the problem at hand and not the heaviness in her breasts or the heat pooling at her core.

"That I'm in Miami working on it, but it would be at least a week."

"How did he take it?" Hyde asked.

"He was annoyed I didn't offer it to him now. I didn't admit that I don't know much about what he was talking about. He called it Whiteout. He was walking carefully with me. He doesn't want to piss me or Barnett off. He knows there's money to be made," Finn said.

Finn's strong arms held her and in the circle of his embrace, she felt safe. She was pretending to be his girlfriend, but this felt real. Her attraction to Finn was scorching hot. She couldn't separate her emotions from her physical attraction to Finn.

"Are you okay?" Finn asked. "You look upset." His eyes were fastened to her.

She slid her hand down his tie. "Do you have more business to conduct? Would it be rude if we left?"

"No to both questions, but why? We might meet some of Winslow's associates. We haven't been here long," Finn said.

Hyde's heart was racing and she wanted to be alone with Finn. She had been resisting him. The rightness of being in his arms convinced her that surrender was inevitable. "I want to be alone with you."

Finn's eyes blazed. She brushed her fingers across his forehead, moving a stray strand of hair to the side. Reaching to the back of her head, Finn forked his fingers into her hair at her nape. He pulled her close to him, holding her an inch from his mouth. Their eyes locked and Hyde realized she was holding her breath.

She let it out slowly.

"You are driving me out of my mind," Finn said.

"I'm not doing anything."

"You're doing everything. That dress. Your mouth. The back and forth. It makes me simultaneously unsure what you want while being absolutely sure what I do."

He closed the distance between them and his amazing mouth moved seductively over hers. Hyde closed her eyes, focusing entirely on what he was doing to her. His tongue traced the outline of her lips.

"I can't think. But we are being watched. We'll give Winslow enough to know why we're leaving," Finn said.

Then his mouth plundered hers and she gave herself to him. Finn kissed his way to her ear. His hands hadn't moved south of her waist, yet every nerve ending in her body tingled. She wanted to let her desires make the decisions. The longer Finn kissed her, the more she wanted him.

Finn nibbled on her earlobe. "We need to leave now or I'll take you on this dance floor and not care who sees."

Chapter 9

Hyde slipped her hand into Finn's and they hurried through the crowd toward the exit. Finn led her from the club to the valet. While they waited for their car, Finn whispered in her ear the many things he wanted to do to her. Some they had done. Others were new experiences.

No one could hear them but Hyde's cheeks heated at his ideas. He was a creative and adventurous lover. If she let this happen, the night could be long and amazing.

The valet held open Hyde's door and she climbed inside the passenger seat. Finn switched the car into drive.

"Ready?" he asked.

She nodded. He took off from the club.

Hyde ran her finger down his arm and slid her fingers between his. Stretching her seat belt, she moved closer and kissed his cheek and caressed his thigh, massaging the muscles in his leg.

"Hyde, I'll get in an accident."

"You won't," she said. "You're an excellent driver even with distractions. You've driven with guns being fired at you."

"In those situations, my concentration was absolute. Now I want to take my hands off the wheel and put them on you."

She kissed the underside of his jaw and his neck. "I know you like when I kiss you here." She pressed a kiss behind his ear.

He accelerated the car. "Alex, are you sure about this? Because I know you've been through some things and I'm trying to be sensitive and understanding. I'm about to cross the line and stopping will be hard."

She couldn't put her finger on the precise moment it changed, but she wanted Finn and she could compartmentalize the past, the present and the future. The past was behind her and it had opened a door in the future she hadn't believed she would have. She was with Finn now and that was enough in the present. "I wouldn't get you hot and bothered if I wasn't."

Finn pulled to the front of the hotel and tossed the keys to the valet. Hand in hand, she and Finn hurried to the elevator. After inserting her key in the control panel, the elevator brought them to their hotel suite directly.

The room was dark and quiet. Finn switched on the lights. They drew their weapons and swept the room. Alone for the first time that night. Rushing together, they met in the middle of the room near the coffee table.

Finn gathered her brown hair and lifted it, giving him access to her neck and backside. He skimmed his hand to the base of her spine.

His lips brushed her nape, and her hair fell down her back. Finn lowered the zipper of her dress and peeled the fabric down slowly. The tightness of the material held the dress around her hips. With a wiggle and some help, the dress pooled on the floor.

Hyde stepped out of it and her heels clicked on the hardwood.

Finn sucked in his breath as if seeing her naked for the first time. "I've been waiting all night to do that."

Hyde reached for Finn's shirt. She unbuttoned the shirt, parting the crisp cloth. When it was unfastened, she removed his suit jacket, careful over his upper arm and shoulder. She did the same with the shirt. His clothes joined her dress on the floor.

Finn reached for her, his eyes intense with longing. He cupped her breasts in his hands and brought his mouth to each, licking and sucking. Heat spiraled through her. She forked her hands into his hair, wanting to feel the strands between her fingers. They had been together many times before, but this time felt different. Finn wasn't wrapped in mystery; Hyde had begun to understand him. She wasn't looking for some fun between missions; she knew what she wanted out of life. This didn't have long-term potential and that made time with him more precious to her. Walking away from Finn untouched and unchanged was impossible and she embraced that.

Finn stood. "You're the most beautiful woman."

Hyde reached for his buckle. Never breaking eye contact, she undid it. Finn removed his pants.

He was a perfect specimen of a man. Tall and bronzed, ripped muscles and tight abdominals, she wanted him. Hyde guided him with her outstretched hands to the couch. Pushing on his chest, she sent him back onto the cushions.

She knelt over him, setting one leg on the couch and the other on the floor.

"What's the plan?" he asked.

"No plan. We have enough orders and plans. This is you and me," Hyde said. She didn't want their work and their colleagues and enemies between them tonight. "I can't stop wanting you."

She lowered herself and ran her hands down his chest, enjoying the hardness of his body.

"Alex, it's been a long time," he said. "I want this to be good for you."

She didn't respond. It had been a long time for her, too. Months had passed. She'd had no interest in sex. She had been dealing with a terrible blow to her heart and her soul, and reconnecting with another person hadn't interested her. She had wanted to grieve and keep her own company.

Being with Finn had wakened that slumbering part of her until it roared to be fed.

She positioned herself over him and slid down, taking him deep. She moved her hips, adjusting to the sensations and relaxing her muscles.

He grasped her hips and she arched her body. Her name escaped his lips. She rocked against him, sensuous feelings flooding her. Desire consumed her. She moved wildly on him, exhilaration escalating. There was something familiar about being with Finn, but also fresh and arousing.

She was on the brink in minutes and then tipping over the edge in his arms. Finn watched her and then moved their bodies, flipping her onto the couch. With slow, deep glides, he built her excitement again.

He rode her hard and she closed her eyes, enjoying the sensations he evoked. His body tensed and he kissed her. A shudder racked him and he collapsed on top of her.

Finn traced his hand down her side, stopping at her hip. "Tell me we don't have to get up."

She shifted. "At some point, we'll have to."

"I blame the dress," Finn said.

"I blame the dress, too," Hyde said.

Finn's face turned serious. "Are you all right?"

She pressed a kiss to his lips. "Yes. I promise. I'm okay."

Finn groaned and stood. "Arm cramp."

He reached onto the couch and gathered her in his arms. "The bed. The bed is more comfortable."

He carried her into the bedroom and laid her on the king-size mattress. He scooted close to her and wrapped his body around hers.

Hyde closed her eyes, her muscles relaxed, the lingering sensations of making love with Finn leaving her calm and in control.

She let sleep pull her into darkness.

Finn's phone rang at 6:00 a.m. with a call from a blocked number. He wanted another few hours of sleep, but that wasn't in the cards.

"Yeah. What?" Finn wasn't obligated to be polite to anyone calling before seven.

"Finn, it's me." It was Reed Barnett. "I need you to

head out to Coconut Beach. There's a shipping yard nearby and one of my associates needs to discuss our distribution plans."

"I'm on it. Text me the address and information," Finn said, shaking the sleep from his voice.

"How did it go with Winslow?" Barnett asked.

"He's in. He liked the samples," Finn said. Beside him, Hyde opened her eyes. She looked beautiful, her hair falling across her pillow, her red lips pouty with the annoyance of being woken.

"Good. Make sure he stays happy," Barnett said.

Hyde shifted in the bed, moving closer to him and pulling the covers over her bare shoulders.

"He'll be happy when he gets his shipment. He knows the value of what we have," Finn said.

"Do you?" Barnett asked.

Barnett was an irritating devil at this hour. "It's why I'm in Miami," Finn said.

"Just make it work," Barnett said.

He disconnected the call. Finn hated working with Barnett. His business was despicable, and he was a difficult person. He treated the people around him like servants.

Finn set his phone on the nightstand. Hyde patted his pillow. "Go back to sleep."

What more could he ask for from her? She was a great partner, an amazing lover and the woman of his dreams. They could have many more happy years together. As spies. Not in the happy family dynamic that Hyde seemed to want.

But she had set loose a train of thought he couldn't stop. Was he resisting settling down to spite his father or because he didn't want a domesticated life?

Finn was too old to be playing rebellion games. For years, he had done everything possible to stay off the path his father had walked. Considering that the path wasn't entirely bad was a foreign concept. The path of being a father and a husband wouldn't necessarily mean being the same father and husband his father had been. Finn could do better than cold, withdrawn and demanding.

Contemplating it made him decidedly uncomfortable. The words "slippery slope" came to mind.

After this mission Hyde might change her mind about being a spy. He could help her see that she was good at what she did. Not only that, she was needed. And they had great chemistry together.

Finn hated to get out of bed. Hyde looked peaceful and needed to catch up on sleep. But if Barnett wanted him to meet a contact, he had to get moving. Finn touched Hyde's shoulder. "I need to meet with one of Barnett's contacts at a shipping yard."

Hyde opened her eyes. "What time is it?"

"Six."

Hyde groaned. "You have to meet the contact now?"

"I assume this is Barnett's way of keeping me on my toes."

"Then let's go," Hyde said and threw back the covers.

"You can stay here. I can handle this," Finn said.

Hyde quirked an eyebrow. "Not going to happen. I need to go with you. That's part of the arrangement."

Finn read something in her expression akin to love. Her coldness had melted away and she was again the warm and affectionate woman he'd remembered. How long would that last?

She climbed out of bed. "Quick shower. You need me to tail you? What's the plan?"

She was reading his mind. He followed her into the bathroom, discussing the meeting while looking at an aerial map on his phone. Hyde turned on the hot water and after steam billowed from the shower, she stepped in.

Speaking to her was natural and easy. Bouncing ideas off each other and discussing the merits of pursuing a given course of action. They'd had a rocky start, but now they were meshing well.

Finn left Hyde in the shower to brew coffee and think over their plans for the morning's meeting. Hyde joined him in under five minutes. He loved that about her. She didn't fuss about her appearance and managed to look flawless and beautiful. Her hair was twisted into a bun at the back of her head. Finn wished she would wear it loose.

Finn handed her an earbud and touched his left ear. "Already synced to our phones. Keep the line open so you can hear the conversation."

"What if they check you for bugs?" Hyde asked.

"They will. They won't find this one and my phone displays no active calls when connected to yours." The geniuses at the West Company created imaginative toys to use in the field. It was one of the reasons Finn liked working with them.

He handed Hyde the cup of coffee and she took a sip and smiled. "Thank you. Delicious."

After reviewing their plans verbally twice more and making small changes to account for possible problems, they headed out the door. For the first time

Finn felt they were in sync. No barriers between them and they were working as a team. They were taking separate cars, Finn driving the expensive car and Hyde driving a late-model, nondescript sedan. Hyde would wait and listen and be prepared to enter the situation if Finn required backup.

Finn hoped the meeting this morning meant Barnett was pleased with his discussions with Damien Winslow the night before. Or it could be a trap and he'd be gunned down walking to the rendezvous point.

Hyde wanted to be closer to the action. A gun could go off in a second and she would be too far to help Finn. Barnett was expecting Finn to take the meeting alone, and creeping around the vicinity could raise questions.

Hyde waited half a block from the shipping yard's gated perimeter. She checked her phone. She could hear Finn and his conversation from her earbud. Ten minutes and so far nothing in their exchange alarmed her.

From a driver's-side mirror, she saw someone approaching. The security guard from the shipping yard. She ignored him, hoping he would leave her alone. She wasn't on the shipping yard's property.

He tapped on her window. Hyde smiled and lowered the glass. She had to get rid of him fast so she could concentrate on what Finn was saying and doing.

"Excuse me, ma'am. This is an unloading and loading area. No parking."

Not a single other car was around and nothing was being loaded or unloaded anywhere she could see.

Why was this man making trouble? "My apologies. I think I am lost and I was trying to use my phone to redirect myself." She held up her phone and waved it in the air.

"What are you trying to find?" the security guard asked, his eyes narrowed in suspicion.

"The Brunch and Munch? My friends are meeting me. We were separated last night and I slept elsewhere," Hyde said. She had passed the Brunch and Munch on her way to the shipping yard. It was a nondescript place with a vinyl sign hanging over the door. Easy to miss.

The security guard pointed behind him. "You're close. Follow this road until you reach Palm Avenue and then make a left. Right side of the street."

"Thanks so much. I appreciate it." She pulled her car away slowly, glancing at the guard. The guard was watching her. She'd need to circle around and find another place to park. Showing up in the same place twice would blow her cover. No one was stupid enough to get lost driving in a circle and she didn't want the guard to call the police.

"Finn, I've had to relocate. Give me a couple minutes to find a place and then I'll give you my location." Finn couldn't respond. He was speaking with Barnett's contact. From the tone of the conversation, everyone was calm.

Neither Finn nor the man he was speaking with had mentioned the drug by name. They were still assessing each other. Drugs were big business and the authorities were good. They had surveillance and plants and undercover agents savvy enough that new relationships weren't formed lightly. Even with Barnett's recommendation, both men were cautious.

Hyde consulted her GPS, frustrated at the change of plans. She found another location. It was farther from the first and less advantageous. To get to Finn, she'd need to climb a fence. Climbing would cost her precious seconds in the event that he needed her.

Needed her. He had needed her last night. She'd sensed it in the way he'd touched her and kissed her. Her desire for him had been equally consuming. For the first time in months, she had slept long and deeply. Making the connection with Finn had quieted some of her demons.

Hyde heard a shift in the tone of the conversation. Finn's voice dropped deeper and intensified. Adrenaline fired hard and her muscles coiled to move. Hyde abandoned her plan to find another place to park and returned to her first position, driving her car to the unmanned gate.

Her first luck for the day—the security guard had moved on and was out of sight. Hyde parked, slid on her shoulder holster and checked her gun. She raced toward the entryway.

Finn and his contact were talking about Whiteout by name, and the other man was demanding to know more about Finn. Finn had his manufactured past, but his street credit was missing.

Hyde found a location where the gate was broken, likely from other vandals or thefts. She squeezed through the stiff metal chain, catching her pants on a sharp edge and tearing them. Unhooking the fabric, she hurried inside. She navigated around the large storage containers, mentally picturing the map of the area and where Finn would be.

The situation hadn't escalated further. Finn was doing a good job convincing the man he was a worthy partner.

When she caught sight of Finn, relief rushed over her; she was close enough to help. He was talking to three other men and their postures were aggressive. Finn appeared unruffled, but Hyde knew him well enough to know he was poised to strike.

Who were the other men? Had they just joined the group? She hadn't heard their voices over the line, and Barnett hadn't mentioned meeting with more than one person.

Hyde aimed her weapon, prepared to take out anyone who threatened Finn's life. As Hyde listened, she was amazed at Finn's ability to win people over. He laughed at the appropriate moments, said the right things and within several minutes, the three men across from him relaxed, their posture nonthreatening.

Hyde remained primed.

"We want to show you the location where we plan to store the goods," one of the men said.

Finn nodded. "Barnett mentioned I should do a security assessment. I'm sure you guys have it locked down, but security is my specialty. We'll drive together," Finn said.

"We'll take my car," the other man said.

Hyde shivered. She didn't like the idea of Finn alone in a car with these men, especially when he wasn't behind the wheel. She would tail them, but navigating roads she didn't know well while remaining undetected was challenging. Finn had his phone and his earpiece. That would help, as long as they didn't enter a network dead zone.

Finn followed the men. Hyde couldn't pursue without giving away her position. When they were out of sight, she returned to her car and pulled out onto the main street. She may have missed them or they could have used a different road to leave the shipping yard.

A dark car pulled out and Hyde hurried to catch up. A truck exited the shipping yard, cutting off her visual of the dark car. Hyde kept her patience. Honking at the truck would call attention. She waited. The truck moved into traffic and Hyde darted out behind it and swerved to maneuver around it.

She caught sight of the other car ahead.

As she closed the distance and followed Finn and Barnett's associates through the streets of Miami, Hyde focused on not being too close and not being spotted.

Her mind wandered to the night before. She wondered if she was healing. Finally, really and truly learning to cope with her loss. Before spending the night in bed with Finn, she hadn't considered being with another man. That part of her life felt sacred and private and broken. Last night she hadn't thought about her miscarriage. For the first time in a long while, she had felt comfortable and safe with another person. She hadn't felt judged or punished by the universe. Somehow, Finn had made it right.

Traffic grew heavier. The other car shot ahead. Hyde steered around some slow-moving vehicles and then swallowed her dread when she lost sight of Finn. She couldn't hear Finn in her earpiece. Checking that it was on, she glanced at her phone. A no-signal message blinked. They had been disconnected.

The GPS was still transmitting a signal. Pressing harder on the accelerator, she followed the map on her phone's screen. The moving dot abruptly turned down an unmarked road, either an alley or a private driveway. Hyde slowed and wasn't surprised to see the road adjacent to a warehouse.

Barnett's associates had selected a large building, half-rundown, to store Whiteout, or at least the chemicals for it. Hyde sent a message to the West Company. They wouldn't alert the authorities until they knew more about the warehouse. Better to build a solid case against Barnett. For all they knew, the warehouse was empty and calling the police would tip off Barnett that someone was watching him or he had a mole in his crew.

Hyde parked down the street from the warehouse in front of a beat-up white house with two cars on cinderblocks in the front yard. The neighborhood was a combination of houses and businesses, and the area felt neglected and tired.

Hyde hurried toward the warehouse. Barnett's associate's car was parked outside a rusted door on the side of the building facing away from the street. She could go inside or wait for Finn to signal her. She hadn't heard any parts of their conversation for the last twenty minutes, making it harder to decide what to do.

She waited outside the warehouse, crouched against the side of the building. Two hundred yards away, three black SUVs with dark tinted windows pulled up. Hyde removed her phone from her pocket and recorded. The speed of their vehicles approaching the building and their hard stop worried Hyde. Eight men dressed in black jumped from the SUVs and raced up the rickety wooden steps and into the building.

Panic tore through her and Hyde marshalled her control. Panic led to disaster. The sound of gunfire helped Hyde to focus. She needed to see what was happening inside the warehouse.

Her goal was to make sure that Finn was okay. She would not consider the possibility that he had caught a bullet from one of the intruders.

After pressing the alarm to alert the West Company of trouble, she slipped her phone into her pocket. She hauled open the rusty door to the warehouse. Slipping inside, she pressed herself against the metal wall. The space wasn't as open as she'd expected. Stacks of cardboard boxes and crates about eight feet high filled the room, creating narrow aisles. It was dark; the only light came from windows thirty feet high on the walls. The area smelled like chemicals, but Hyde couldn't identify the specifics. Hyde ran swiftly through the rows on silent feet, watching her back and searching for Finn.

Explosions echoed around the warehouse, making pinpointing a location of the blasts impossible. Adrenaline sharpened her senses. She needed to find Finn, and that would involve her search and rescue training.

Hyde glanced at her phone, hoping for a message from Finn. Only one from the West Company, asking for an update when possible and asking if she needed an ambulance. She wasn't sure what was needed yet. Her connection to Finn was still out.

Hyde slipped her phone into her pants pocket.

She needed a bird's-eye view to find Finn. The warehouse was too big and the boxes were making the search harder. She selected a stack of wooden crates that looked stable and scaled to the top. The darkness in the warehouse and her black clothes helped conceal her. She was careful not to make herself a target for the shooters.

The smell of chemicals was stronger where she stood and she choked back a cough. The scent was acidic and mixed with bleach. Were the chemicals being stored combustible? Hazardous? Poisonous?

Hyde couldn't see Finn, but lights beckoned farther ahead. She climbed down the crates and jogged another ten yards to another stack.

Crouching on top for a better view, she spotted Finn. He was standing with another man and speaking to the men who had stormed into the warehouse. Finn had left the port with three men. She didn't see the other two.

Hurrying back to the floor, she raced closer to Finn. Hyde concentrated on listening to the conversation and waiting for the right time to strike. She didn't see anyone bleeding or on the ground. She snapped several pictures, trying to capture the faces of the people involved.

Finn was smooth-talking his way out of the situation. At least it seemed that way until the leader of the eight aimed his gun at Finn and his associate.

Hyde didn't want to start a panic by firing her weapon. She took another approach and decided a distraction could help. If she gave Finn the opportunity, he would run. His body was tense, ready to take off in a split second.

She selected a pile of wooden crates and pushed hard. Nothing happened. She tried another pile nearby, testing the sturdiness. Going to a third pile, she found those boxes were tippable. She rocked them several times and then sent them over and tumbling into others. The impact was huge; the sound of the crashing crates drew everyone's attention.

The men were demanding to know who was hiding. Hyde moved away from the mess and circled to get closer to Finn.

The chaos she'd created presented an opportunity for Finn to move to a defensible position. Hyde slipped around the piles of crates and saw Barnett's associate in a standoff with the intruders. Finn was gone.

"Hey you." Finn's voice behind her. She hadn't heard his approach. She whirled and grabbed his arms, looking him over and needing reassurance he wasn't hurt. No obvious signs of bleeding.

He took her face in his hands. "It's okay. I'm okay."

Relief rushed over her. "We need to go."

"Bail on Barnett's guy?" Finn asked. "Shouldn't we get him out?"

Barnett would question the sequence of events. Would he blame them if his men were harmed?

"Where are the others?" Hyde asked.

"Dead," Finn said.

Killing another person wouldn't faze the eight intruders. "How can we help him?"

"Not sure yet," Finn said. "Who are those men?"

"No intel. I sent pictures to the West Company. They'll look into it."

The sound of gunfire split the air. Hyde was afraid to look. When she did, her eyes landed on Barnett's associate on the ground. The invaders gathered together.

"Find them. Kill them!" The intruders fanned out to search the warehouse.

"They know someone else is here with you," Hyde said. If they hadn't seen her car parked outside, they had heard her distraction.

"Come on," Finn said and gestured for her to follow him. He approached the man he'd met at the shipyard. Kneeling next to the body, Finn checked the pulse at his neck and on his wrist. "He's dead."

They heard voices and pounding footsteps and ran to hide. The crates provided a protection and a maze through the warehouse.

"What's in these crates?" Hyde asked.

"I don't know. From what Jeff told me, this warehouse was a print factory and a front for a smuggling operation. The crates could be legitimate product or they could be smuggled goods."

"The chemical smell," Hyde said.

"Ink? Glue? No idea."

Hyde suspected it was something more devious, but they didn't have time to investigate. Eight armed men wanted them dead.

They reached the door where Hyde had entered the warehouse. She looked through the door window to the lot surrounding the warehouse. Three men in dark clothing encircled her car, but even at this distance, Hyde didn't recognize them. Feds? More of Barnett's associates? She hadn't gotten a good look at the men who'd arrived in the SUV and hadn't checked their car to see if others had waited in the vehicles.

Exiting through this door wasn't an option.

"Plan B," Hyde said. She hadn't thought of one, but she wouldn't stand around and wait to be discovered.

"Another exit?"

"Even if we have to blast our way out," Hyde said. She and Finn were wearing bulletproof vests, but they didn't have helmets.

She hadn't investigated the full layout of the warehouse but by keeping to the perimeter, they would eventually find another door or window.

Frustrated voices grew closer. Hyde didn't like the odds of trying to shoot their way out of the situation. She drew her gun, enjoying the heaviness in her hand. Being armed increased the chances of survival.

Finn tapped her shoulder and pointed behind them. Along the wall was a stack of cartons that formed an alcove. If they moved into the alcove and watched each other's back, they could better protect themselves.

They hurried into the small space and stood back to back. In the shadows of the crates, they blended. Perhaps they wouldn't need to go on the offensive.

Hyde leaned on Finn to feel his strength. His gun in one hand, he reached to her hip with the other. Slipping her hand into his, she squeezed it.

A shower of sparks lit between them. Their connection went beyond their physical attraction into deeper territory. Finn understood her and seemed to anticipate her needs and desires. Hyde trusted Finn. She had from the first time they had met, when he saved her life.

Voices rushed by and Hyde held her breath, trying not to make a sound.

Questions fogged her brain, but she would work it out with Finn. Whatever happened in this warehouse, they would explain to Barnett. They'd consider carefully what to tell him about the situation and the intruders. She'd been in circumstances before that went off the skids and she had made it through.

The slamming of a door echoed through the air and then quiet. Absolute stillness. Several long moments passed and then Finn stepped out from the alcove. Hyde followed him, walking back to back, covering the spaces around them and checking around corners. The intruders had entered the warehouse with a purpose and they had seemed organized and armed. If they wanted the people inside dead, leaving Finn was sloppy work.

It was silent. Uneasiness passed through her. The intruders could be waiting to ambush them as they fled the warehouse.

Finn was a good shot and a strong and capable operative. However, they were outgunned and outnumbered.

Ahead, a frosted window built only five feet from the ground. As they drew closer, Hyde saw it was nailed shut. So much for adherence to OSHA laws.

"I don't like our odds," Hyde said.

Finn was typing into his phone. "I'm letting the West Company know we might need help."

"Like a medevac?" Hyde asked.

He swore under his breath. "No signal. We must be in a Faraday cage. Message won't go out."

"Think positive. The authorities will show up in time to arrest whoever these men are," Hyde said.

Hyde ripped a board off a nearby crate, earning herself a hand full of splinters. She would deal with them later. She wedged the wood into the window, trying to lift the nails and pry it up.

"Let's push together. We can pop it open," Hyde said.

They pulled on the wood. The wood fractured and broke. The window remained stubbornly nailed and rusted shut.

Finn glanced at his gun. "We could shoot it out."

"Might bring the men hunting us running."

"Let's take our chances." Finn shot the window several times. He lifted one of the cartons and heaved it at the window, knocking out the glass. Hyde removed her blouse, leaving her in a tank top, and wrapped it around her hand, bashing out the rest of the glass. The splinters burned and she ignored it.

She and Finn climbed onto the window ledge and dropped to the ground.

They weren't home free. Their ride was unavailable and they needed to get off the premises without anyone seeing them, a difficult task with little to hide behind. They stayed close to the building.

They waited and Hyde took a minute to look at her palm.

"Hyde, what happened?" Finn asked, taking her hand and examining it.

"One of the crates. It will be fine," she said.

Car engines rumbled. Hyde and Finn rushed to the gate around the warehouse. It was a ten-foot-tall

chain-linked metal fence, with looped barbed wire
at the top.

"We'll need to climb it," Finn said, looking up and
grimacing at the sight of spiky wire.

They could wrap the barbed wire in his shirt and
hope it protected them.

The sonic boom of an explosion detonated behind
them. The shock wave threw them into the gate. The
metal wire pressed into her back. Her eyes felt gritty.
Her hands burned and the heat was intense.

Hyde stood, her back aching as another explosion
sounded. Turning to the warehouse, Hyde's breath
caught in her throat. The warehouse was on fire. If
they hadn't escaped when they did, they could have
been trapped inside. What about the chemicals? If
they were poisonous, they would leach into the surrounding area.

Sirens sounded over the ringing in her ears. She
shook Finn, who was lying on the ground next to her.
"Get up! We have to go!" Hyde dictated a message
into her phone. "Chemical explosion at a warehouse
at my GPS location. Send HAZMAT. Ambulances.
Unknown chemicals. Proceed with caution." Though
she didn't have a signal, while she was on the move,
her phone would attempt to find one and deliver the
message to the West Company.

Hyde's working theory was that the men in the
SUVs were destroying the warehouse in an attempt
to murder Finn and possibly hide the bodies of the
people they'd killed. Hyde had been right to take them
seriously. Destroying the warehouse would bring Barnett's anger and interest from the authorities. No crim-

inal wanted that. Something huge must have been at stake to risk this level of destruction.

Finn's head moved lifelessly back and forth.

"Finn!" Hyde shouted. The fire was loud and Hyde felt dizzy. Sweat rolled down her back. She couldn't carry him easily and she wouldn't leave him. She slapped his cheeks. What she wouldn't do for her field kit now! Her smelling salts could help. She had nothing except her phone, and aid may not arrive in time.

She lifted Finn to a sitting position and looked him over for injuries. Though he was likely bruised, she didn't see bleeding or obvious head injuries. Hyde dug deep for strength. If she had to, she'd drag him with her. She hadn't before left an operative in the field and she wouldn't start now, especially not when it was Finn's life on the line.

He had selected her for this mission because he knew she'd have his back, unyieldingly and incessantly.

"Finn, you need to open your eyes and we need to run."

The sound of car engines terrified her. The men in the SUVs hadn't given up their search.

Hyde looped Finn's arm over her shoulder. She started dragging him. The police sirens were getting closer. If they were arrested, Barnett may cut ties, although after this disaster, that was already a risk.

Hyde spotted another, more imminent danger. The intruders were driving toward the gate. It swung open and five cars were barreling toward it. They had likely heard the approach of sirens and wanted off the premises before the police and fire departments arrived.

She and Finn were out in the open. Someone would spot them! They had no cover.

Finn mumbled under his breath. Some of the weight lessened and Finn stood.

"Run!" she shouted to Finn. They couldn't make it to the open gate without being seen by the men in the black SUVs. They could make it to a small, rundown shed fifty feet away. She and Finn hobbled to it and tried to open the door. It was locked.

The SUVs exited through the open gate and then it slid shut. Tires squealing, the vehicles turned down the road toward them.

Finn ripped the padlock from the door, tearing the metal from the wood, and they slipped inside. Hyde prayed they weren't seen.

"What should we do?" Hyde asked.

"We need evidence about who set off the explosion for Barnett. We can't let the police see us," Finn said. "We're supposed to be criminals."

They looked around the small shed. Little to nothing to work with. An empty gas can, a broom, a roll of trash bags, a bucket and a broken bicycle with the wheels torn off. "The bicycle."

"We can't ride that to safety," she said. The impact from the explosion had jarred his brain.

Finn knelt on the ground next to the bicycle. He ripped off the metal chain and a flat plastic cover from the side. "I'll use this and the trash bags to wrap around the barbed wire. My shirt will help, but it's too thin to protect us."

Carrying their supplies to the fence, Finn climbed like a monkey, tossing the chain to pin down the wire and laying his shirt and the trash bags over it. He had created a bridge, a safe method for their escape. He leaped over and onto the other side.

Hyde followed the path he set and then dropped to the ground next to him. "Your arm!" The center of the white bandage over his gunshot wound was bright red. "You're bleeding."

Finn glanced at it. "I think I tore something climbing. It will be fine."

Hyde wouldn't argue. They had no time. Instead, they ran.

Chapter 10

Police and firefighters swarmed the area around the warehouse. The fire was roaring out of control. A HAZMAT team had been called and no one was entering the building. They likely had the same questions Hyde had about what exactly was in the warehouse. It was a miracle she and Finn had escaped when they did.

The authorities wouldn't yet know the source of the explosions and would proceed with caution.

"We need to lay low," Finn said. "Touch base with HQ."

In every direction were onlookers. Were any of them with the intruders? Would they be watching for survivors of the explosion?

Finn was staggering as he walked.

"Are you okay? Do you need to go to the hospital?"

Finn's injury struck her hard and she felt unusually emotional about it.

"I need to sit for a few minutes. My vision is blurry."

Hyde tightened her grip on him.

After crossing two streets, they entered the back-yards of a residential community. One of the houses had a children's playhouse large enough for them to fit inside. It fit the criteria.

She pointed to it. "A little farther and we'll take a break."

They climbed inside the small yellow wooden house and closed the plywood door. The floor was cheap vinyl tile and the walls were painted white. It was hot in the small space. But it was an unexpected place to hide. Her preference would have been for some cold water and a medical exam, but those would have to wait.

Finn sat with his knees bent and his elbows resting on them. He closed his eyes. Sweat was running down his face and he was too pale.

"I'll call the West Company and get some intel." And some medical aid. His phone had been broken, but hers was working and she again had a wireless signal.

Their contact, Abby, answered.

"I need a car. Finn was hurt in the explosion. I need water and medical attention."

Finn set his hand over her arm. "I'm okay."

"I also need to know who the police are looking for in connection with the fire in the warehouse and I need to know who the men were who set the explosion," Hyde said. After providing as many details as they could to Abby, they heard frantic typing, followed by a cool, professional response.

"We're looking into the pictures Hyde sent over.

The police have no information regarding the source of the fire. They received eleven 911 calls reporting an explosion. They're looking for information about the owners of the warehouse to see if the warehouse was perhaps improperly storing combustible materials. The warehouse is owned by a company called Swift Speed, which looks to be a shell corporation. We're trying to connect it to Barnett." Abby continued typing. "I have your GPS location. I don't see any police activity near you heading west. I have a car coming to pick you up. Red sports utility vehicle."

"Thanks, Abby," Hyde said.

"I'm pulling security camera feeds from the area to look for details about the intruders. Your description fits with a group of drug runners in the area that go by the name the Shadow Crew."

Hyde had heard of them. She didn't like that the operation now involved two drug rings. The more people involved, the harder it was to control the mission.

Hyde disconnected. She pulled a few splinters from her hand and felt immediate relief.

Hyde shifted to move. Being in this small playhouse was a good cover, but she wanted to be somewhere safer. If the police tried to track them with dogs, they'd be discovered and cornered.

Finn grabbed her arm and electricity shot from where his hand met her bare skin. "Hyde, wait. Thank you for saving me back there. I could have been killed."

She didn't like to fixate on that. "Not you. You're invincible."

Finn touched her cheek. The small window of the playhouse let in only enough light for her to see the profile of his features. "I'm not, Hyde. No one is. You saved me."

He kissed her lightly. The kiss communicated so much more than he could have said with words. His appreciation, his admiration and his affection for her.

She broke the kiss. "You saved my life once. Now we're even."

"I was thinking back there, in the warehouse, about you," Finn said. He sounded groggy.

"Stay awake, Finn," Hyde said.

"I am awake. For the first time I feel like I know what's going on. What's important. I want to do this for Simon and then I want to do something for us."

Hyde held her breath. He could be talking about their future, making an actual life with her, or his head injury could be causing him to ramble. "What do you want to do for us?"

Her phone buzzed with a message from Abby. The red SUV was circling the block, looking for them. "Our car is waiting."

Finn pushed open the plywood door and they exited the small space. Hyde wasn't finished with the conversation they'd been having. "What about us? What's next for us?" She put her arm around his waist to support and guide him.

Finn slung his arm across her shoulder. "Something more than this. Just something more than this."

Simon had crossed Finn's mind while he had been inside the warehouse. Simon had been killed in one of Barnett's drug manufacturing facilities, and Finn wouldn't become another of Barnett's victims. Now Finn was struggling to keep his temper while he listened to Barnett rant, as if he was the only victim of the accident today.

"I want names! I want the person or people responsible dead!" Reed Barnett was screaming into the video chat.

He had expressed no anger or sadness over his team dying or about Finn being injured. He was concerned about the warehouse and the chemicals contained within. They were essential to creating Whiteout. From what Finn gathered, the burning of the warehouse presented no threat to the area, but it was a huge impact on Barnett's bottom line.

Barnett would calm down and ask questions. As yet, he hadn't asked Finn much except how the warehouse had exploded. After accusing every major crime organization along the East Coast and in the south of being responsible, Barnett was taking stock of the incident. "Tell me what happened from the point that you met my contacts at the pier to my warehouse being destroyed."

Finn related the story, leaving Hyde out of it. Barnett had many of the same questions Finn did. They didn't have the identity of the men in the SUV or why they had targeted the warehouse.

Their guns, their vehicles and their techniques spoke of experience and professionalism. "I'll find out who they were," Finn said. "They almost killed me. I'll work my contacts."

"Good, good," Barnett said, rubbing his jaw, appearing lost in thought. "Let me know what you find out. Also, I'll need you to scout a new location for the warehouse. I'll send you some leads. Stay in touch." Barnett disconnected the call and Finn closed his laptop.

Finn's focus was on bringing Barnett's criminal organization down, not helping prop it up with a new warehouse. If Finn dragged his feet, Barnett could lose faith in him, select another errand boy and cut Finn out of the loop.

"You look like you're carrying the weight of the world on your shoulders," Hyde said, standing behind the couch. She rubbed his shoulders and some of his stress dissipated. "Tell me about it. Tell me what you're thinking."

Finn had taken on this venture because Simon deserved justice. Finn had been closer with Simon than he was with his biological brother. "I'm helping a man I despise build his drug organization. If I refuse, he'll work around me and I won't be in a position to impede the business and then take him down."

Hyde made a sound of understanding. She wrapped her arms around him. Barnett's request felt distant. Thinking of Hyde brought a swell of emotions. She had been there for him, through this mission and over the last several years. More than not wanting her to quit being a spy, he didn't want to lose her in his life. He wanted her, he needed her and he would go crazy without her. In the playhouse, he had started to tell her that he wanted a future with her. Those words might be irresponsible given that he didn't have a plan yet for how to keep her in his life while keeping his career. But he was working on it.

"I want justice for Simon, too, but I'm questioning if this is worth it," Hyde said.

Finn set his hands on her arms. "It's worth it. Not just for Simon but to keep another drug off the street. I would have been okay. I'm quick with my gun."

Hyde circled the couch and sat next to him, laying her head on his shoulder. "I know that you are great with your gun. But that didn't stop me from being terrified that you could be shot. You couldn't get off eight shots in the time it would take those men to shoot you."

He hadn't liked his odds, either. When his meeting with Barnett's contact had been interrupted by the intruders, Finn had wondered if it was a test. But they had gunned down Barnett's men at the warehouse. Though Barnett wanted to know who the men were who had destroyed his warehouse, supplies and killed his men, he likely had a better idea than Finn did about the enemies who were the biggest threats.

Finn kissed the top of her head, the scent of her hair and her skin overwhelming him. How did she smell fresh and clean after running through the Miami heat? As soon as he had decided to fly to Bearcreek, Montana, he had admitted to himself there was something different about Hyde. She was irreplaceable. Until now, he hadn't realized how far down the rabbit hole he'd traveled. Pursuing her for the good of the mission wasn't the truth. Pursuing her was what he wanted for himself. He needed to convince her that this could work. It may not be the picture she had painted in her mind, but they were real and their relationship was worth fighting for.

Hyde stroked the side of his face. "It's been an intense day. Let's go for a swim."

"Where?" he asked. Their hotel had a pool, but they were laying low.

"Abby arranged for us to use the Lemon Drop Spa

about ten minutes from here. We have the place to ourselves for the evening," Hyde said.

"Why would she do that?" Finn asked. What was at the spa? Contact with someone in Barnett's organization?

Hyde blinked up at him. "This has nothing to do with the mission. She arranged it because it's my birthday."

Finn jolted. He hadn't known and she hadn't said anything before today. "Happy birthday. You should have told me sooner."

Hyde shifted on her feet. "I've been pretending to be so many people for so long, I didn't remember my real birthday. Abby reminded me. Must be in the file the West Company has on me."

"Barnett thinks I'm scouting locations for a new warehouse and gathering information about the incident. We'll go off the grid for a while. I thought spas weren't your thing?" he asked. He wished he had known. He'd have gotten her a gift or made celebratory plans.

"Having my nails done, when I know they'll look chipped and broken within hours strikes me as a waste of time. Swimming and a massage sound pretty great."

"I feel bad that I don't have a present for you," Finn said.

Hyde shrugged. "I don't expect anything."

"What would you have liked?"

Hyde stared at him. "There's nothing I want. I planned for this year to be better. I wanted for my life to be different. I thought I would spend birthdays and holidays with my family for the first time in a decade."

"Then I pulled you into this mess," Finn said. Guilt assailed him.

"I let myself be pulled."

She may have wanted him to pull her into his life, as well. He wouldn't quit being a spy, but they could still have a future.

Two black swimsuits were waiting for them at the Lemon Drop Spa, a pair of board shorts for Finn and a black bikini for Hyde. Special operatives guarded the nearly empty facility and only a few key employees were in the spa. No other guests were permitted inside.

It was an amazing feat pulled off by the West Company. "I can't imagine how Abby arranged this," Hyde said.

"The West Company is well connected," Finn said. "People all over the world owe them favors."

The pool was located on the top floor and enclosed under glass. The lights were dim and most of the illumination was from the pool lights beneath the water.

Having a few hours alone was a nice gesture and a break they needed. It had been a tough few days.

For the last decade, celebrating Hyde's birthday hadn't been an option. Spending her birthday with Finn was a luxury she hadn't before considered.

Hyde changed into her swimsuit, a string halter-style top. She padded to the swimming pool and dipped in her toe. The water was warm and inviting. Hyde dove in. The water felt great against her skin. Smooth, long strokes and flutter kicks got her halfway across the pool. She surfaced for air. Finding her stride quickly, moving through the water, stroke after stroke, she came close to the wall and turned.

Bubbles exploded next to her. Finn had joined her. She kicked off the wall, powering through the water.

He caught her at the opposite wall. "Care to race?" he asked. He set his hand over hers.

She was breathing harder from her swim and from having him close. "You want to race after I'm already tired. That's the only way you can beat me."

Finn threw back his head and laughed. "Confidence. I like it. I think I can beat you and I'll give you a lead."

If she beat him, she wanted it to be fair and undisputed. "No lead. Let's race." She pushed off him. As they swam, the water pulled beside her.

She reached the wall and stopped, grabbing the ledge and meeting Finn's eyes. "We might have to call it a tie."

Finn slid his hand around the back of her neck and kissed her. "You're one of the most competitive women I know."

"Don't we have to be?" she asked. She had been competitive all her life. Being recruited as a CIA agent then transitioning into private spy work had made her urge to win and to succeed stronger. On some missions, only the winner survived.

"You'll always come first with me," Finn said.

His words made her heart race. The word *always* lingered between them.

He slipped his arm around her waist and she wrapped her legs around his body. "I can keep you afloat," he said.

Drops of water dotted his face. His hair was slicked back and she held on to his bare shoulders. His muscles were tense beneath her fingers as he treaded water.

His words held meaning. She leaned close to him and kissed him, open mouth, wet lips and tongues dueling. He smiled and she leaned away.

"Is something funny?" she asked.

"I'm happy," he said.

He was talking about being in this space with her. What they had together was good.

"What would you say about making this a permanent thing?" Finn asked.

Hyde's heart hammered so loud, she could barely hear. "Us?"

"Us as partners," Finn said.

Her racing heartbeat slowed. The work. He was still focused on that. "This is my last mission. That hasn't changed."

Finn stabbed his fingers through his hair. "If you're living in Bearcreek, you'll have different expectations from your boyfriend. You'll want a man who can be around all the time. I'm in the States maybe fifty days a year."

Hyde rolled that thought through her mind. The hours and commitment were familiar to her. "Lots of couples have one half who works too much."

Finn touched her cheek. "I can't imagine you being happy with that arrangement."

This wasn't a conversation to pass the time; this was the most serious discussion they'd had about their relationship. She was feeling him out and he was keeping her expectations low. Hyde shouldn't have ventured onto this conversation now. It was her birthday and Finn had been clear about what he wanted. It was her time to be clear and go after the life she dreamed about.

"Race to the stairs?" she asked.

He nodded.

They took off and hurried up the steps of the swimming pool. Finn took a towel and wrapped it around her shoulders and another around her waist. Then he did the same for himself. They lay on a single lounge chair, head to head, legs entwined. Talking wasn't needed now. Broaching a difficult subject had put enough out in the open. They had no answers, only more to think about.

Hyde pulled at the towel around his waist, lightly, letting the towel part. Finn did the same to her.

"This night has been great. When's the last time you swam for fun?" Finn asked.

"Swimming for fun isn't something we do at the farm," Hyde said. "This is the first time in years."

"I owe Abby a thank-you. I should have arranged this for you," Finn said.

Hyde rolled on top of Finn. "The West Company has a reputation for taking care of the people who work for them. This is an amazing perk. If I didn't know Connor as well, I would think he wanted to lure me back into the spy life."

"Maybe he does," Finn said.

"He'll be a dad soon. He gets it," Hyde said.

"He'd take you on in a heartbeat."

Hyde let that settle around her. Proud of what she had accomplished, it was hard to let go and forge a new path in life.

"I need more breaks like this," Finn said.

"When's *your* birthday?" Hyde asked.

Finn laughed. "So relaxing like this is a twice yearly thing? Only on birthdays?"

"This is the first time I've had the royal treatment on my birthday."

"Queen for the day?" Finn asked.

"At least queen for tonight." Hyde tugged at the strings at the waistband of his swimsuit. Finn lifted his hips and Hyde pulled the wet fabric down his legs. He was gloriously naked and not shy about it.

He had no reason to be. He was a perfect specimen of a man. Strong and ripped, pumped biceps and corded muscles, six-pack abdominals and toned thighs.

She stood to the side of the lounge chair and shimmied her bikini bottoms down her legs.

Desire was a fluid, overheated emotion in her veins. Her encounter with Finn earlier had given her a taste. Unable to think of anything else, she wanted to do it again.

Finn extended his hand and she sat next to him. Her skin prickled in awareness as he tugged the ties holding her top around her neck. It fell away. She unfastened the back and let the suit hit the ground.

She covered Finn's body with her own. His hard strength and lean muscle pressed against her softness and curves. Parting her legs, his arousal brushed between her thighs, making her mad with lust. His eyes were half-lidded and he lay back on the lounge chair. Deep burning desire scorched her.

She straddled his body and ran her hands down his chest, touching the waterproof bandage at his shoulder. "Does this hurt?" she asked.

"No."

"Are you lying?"

"Yes," Finn said. "But the hurt is minor compared to other things I'm feeling."

Hyde kissed his ear and his neck. She stroked his muscles, liking the sensations of the strength beneath her hands. She scooted lower and kissed his chest, brushing her lips across his taut skin.

Finn groaned. "Condom in my bag."

His bag was under a table a few feet away. Wishing it were closer, Hyde stood and grabbed it. She checked it and found the item. "Confident? Or do you always carry protection?"

"Both. I'm prepared. That's supposed to be a good thing," he said.

Hyde tore open the package, rolled the condom on and then positioned herself over him. They'd had mindless sex dozens of times before, but this felt weighted with meaning. This was the meeting of two minds, two hearts. She rocked her hips against his, letting him slide between her legs, his hardness nudging at her. She rose over him and positioned him. Then she pushed down, relaxing her muscles, letting her body accept him.

He moaned and she rose and then lowered herself again, taking him deep. She thought she would burst from his thickness and the emotions filling her chest. She forced herself to move slowly and not get overly excited. Consuming need tore through her. The tease was a favorite of hers. Finn liked to be in control and in bed was one place where he could let go. She liked the uninhibited side of him, more animal than man. She could get that if she played her cards right.

Bracing her hands on his chest, she rode him. Pleasure streamed through her and she rocked, unable to get enough from him. Each time they came together was better than the last. Sensations sizzled her skin. The air was humid and warm and the more she moved, the hotter she felt.

Making this connection with Finn was trouble. It was easy for her to sink into old habits, to become a spy again, to live a life of lies, to sleep with Finn and give herself over to him.

Her body shaped into his and they moved together, the thrust of his hips sending him deeper, his hands working her body. His eyes were bright with passion and excitement, riveted on her.

He moved her, lifting her off him and setting her on her feet. Grasping her hips, he turned her around. She clutched the edge of the lounge chair, one knee propped on it. His hands slid under her rear and then he was moving again. She pushed back against him and his hand went around her waist for leverage.

She inhaled a quivering breath, feeling her muscles tightening. It was too soon for this to be over.

"Arch your back," he said, running his hand along her spine.

When she did, his piston movements touched the spot that made her wild, and a shuddering climax ripped over her. Pleasure rippled through every nerve ending and she reached to touch him, needing the connection. He shoved harder inside her and found his release, too, his fingers digging into her hips. Her legs felt weak and she collapsed onto the lounge chair.

Finn joined her, lying on his back and tossing his arm around her.

"Happy birthday, Alex," he said, kissing her cheek.

"Was that my birthday present?"

He made a sound of disgust. "I have more class than that. Even with no warning, I've managed to acquire something you might like."

She looked over her shoulder at him. "I have long admired your resourcefulness."

"Is that all you like about me?" he asked. He kissed her shoulder.

Hyde shook her head. "You're sexy. And smart. Handsome. The first time I saw you, your eyes were blue. I didn't even know they were brown until a few months later."

"Interesting."

"What's interesting?" Hyde asked.

"My eyes are blue. A strange shade, so I wear contacts to cover them," Finn said.

Hyde rolled to face him. "Are you serious?"

"Yes."

Hyde sat, the impact of what they had done relaxing her, but the emotional impact of losing herself in him rattling her. "I never knew." How could she feel this close to him and not know something as basic as his eye color?

"No one is supposed to know," Finn said.

Blending and remaining utterly typical was one of the reasons Hyde had never bothered with tattoos, even though she had wanted one for some time. Tattoos were ways to identify operatives. Word could spread in the field about especially unique tattoos and blow her cover. Her cover involved wearing what the locals wore, trying to walk like them, mimic their accents and eat their food.

"We've hidden who we are on every operation. I plan to go shopping after this operation and pick out clothes I like to wear," Hyde said.

"You don't wear clothes you like?" Finn asked.

"I wear what's needed to play a part. I am not sure I know what clothes I like. Or what jewelry. Or music. Or television shows. I heard my sisters talking about a television series they've watched and I had no idea what they were referring to. I told them I usually read or watch old movies when I travel. I couldn't tell them the truth, that in the past ten years, I haven't had time to watch movies or read books." Unless the book was a document about a mission, and even those she had skimmed. She had no time to read a thousand-page intelligence report when she was on a two-hour flight into a situation that required an immediate response.

"We could go back to the hotel and watch television."

The idea was enormously appealing. "That seems so normal. And fun."

"It is," Finn said.

She kissed his chin. "Massages first. Then television."

Finn loved watching Hyde relax. She had been tense since the start of the mission.

Tonight she had been the fun-loving woman he remembered meeting between operations. A night off while on assignment was rare. Finn had to work magic to get his present for Hyde delivered to their hotel room. He was looking forward to watching her open it and doubly excited to have thought of a gift for her.

He opened the red door to their hotel room and instinctively stepped in front of Hyde. Alarm shot adrenaline through him. A stranger was in their room. He reached for his gun and snapped on the light.

Chapter 11

A man in his forties or fifties sat on the couch in Finn and Hyde's hotel room. He was short and slender, wearing a suit and drinking a clear liquid from a hotel glass. An open bottle of mineral water from the minibar sat on the coffee table. He didn't have a gun in his hand and he seemed unfazed. Was he in the wrong room? An operative from the West Company? His goatee was tidy and his short hair nothing remarkable.

Finn would take no chances with Hyde's life. "Your name. Two seconds to answer and then I shoot."

Hyde stepped around him. Her hands were near her gun, but she hadn't drawn it.

"Pierce Holt."

"What made you decide, Pierce Holt, that it would be a good idea to break in to my hotel room and surprise me?" Finn asked.

Holt set his glass on the coffee table and stood from the couch. "You escaped several of my men today. Impressive. I hired them to take out the competition and they are well trained. It isn't often that they make a mistake and let a target flee."

Finn didn't remove his hand from his gun. Holt wouldn't shoot him. If Holt wanted him dead, he would have been shot on sight. "What cartel do you represent?" Finn asked.

Holt stared hard at him. "You should answer the same question first."

"I am self-employed," Finn said. He wouldn't tell Holt he was working with Reed Barnett. Not until he knew more about the direction this was headed.

"You chose Miami to look for additional work? This area has enough businesses. Might I suggest you head up the coast? Find another town to work in," Holt said.

A not so subtle warning to beat feet out of Miami. "Our product doesn't compare to others. We're targeting a different market segment. We are not a threat to you."

Holt smiled knowingly. "You're an agent for Reed Barnett."

Finn said nothing. He wanted Holt to know he was a player, but not how close to Barnett he was.

Holt took a step toward them and he and Hyde tensed. "I've heard of Reed Barnett. Never had the pleasure of meeting him."

"Most people have heard of the Barnett cartel," Finn said.

"Pass on a message for me. The Shadow Crew runs these streets. Nothing gets bought or sold unless we approve. In this matter, I want in. If I'm not given an in, bodies will pile up, starting with yours."

"You're issuing Reed Barnett an ultimatum?" Finn asked.

"It's the quickest way to get what I want," Holt said. He was confident.

"I've got the message," Finn said. He would pass it along to Barnett, though it would only anger him.

Holt looked at him, lifting his chin slightly. The man seemed to want more, but Finn stood his ground. No changes to the operation until he had spoken to the West Company and Hyde.

"You can show yourself out," Finn said. He wouldn't lock into a power struggle with Holt, and he wouldn't fold at a threat.

"Good evening," Holt said before leaving. He had been bold to come alone.

Hyde stared at Finn. "I kept waiting for you to kill him."

"If the Shadow Crew wants a piece of the action, once they have it, they'll cut out the Barnett cartel. Or kill them. He killed Barnett's men at the warehouse. Between that and his verbal message, he's made his point."

Hyde rested her head on his chest. "Barnett sent us into a lion's den."

Barnett was a coward. "He's aware of the players in Miami. He stays on his island because he's afraid."

Finn was open to possibilities in bringing Barnett down. Let the drug lords take each other out. Starting a street war wasn't in anyone's best interest—too many innocents would be caught in the cross fire—

but with the right nudging, Finn would be happy to see the cartels carted off to prison.

"Barnett can't be trusted. Holt can't be trusted. I don't like facing off against enemies on all sides," Hyde said.

"We can handle it. The payoff will be worth it," Finn said. "We need to change hotels. But before we leave, I have your present."

Hyde looked around, the worry falling away from her face and a smile replacing it.

Finn kissed the top of her head and released her. He strode to the bedroom. It appeared undisturbed, but had likely been searched by Holt. Finn went to the safe where he'd ordered the item to be delivered. Opening it with a three digit passcode, he withdrew the slim black velvet box.

He carried it behind his back and into the main room. He handed it to Hyde. She glanced at the box and then at him. "Jewelry?"

"Maybe."

She lifted the lid and gasped. Inside was a custom-made pendant necklace, the jewels of her and his birthstones. "I understand my birthstone. What is the other?"

"Mine. My real birthday. This way you won't forget it."

She ran her index finger over the line of jewels. "It's beautiful. Thank you, Finn. How did you have this delivered so quickly?"

"I have contacts everywhere," Finn said.

Hyde lifted the necklace from the box. She strode to the mirror and put it on. He came behind her and wound his arms around her waist and kissed her cheek.

"Happy birthday, Alex."

Her eyes misted and she laid a hand over the pendant. "This is beautiful. Thank you, Finn. I will treasure it always."

Looking in the mirror, his heart stirred. He had the oddest sensation of rightness, of his world clicking into place.

Before the moment took an emotional turn, Finn withdrew his phone. Hyde had been clear about her intentions and he hadn't found a solution to their obvious differences yet. Giving up his work or giving up Hyde were catastrophically bad outcomes. How could he choose?

Hyde preferred the new hotel room. It was a second-floor corner room with a great view of the parking lot. The security breach at the previous hotel was disturbing. They had been showing up in Miami hotspots wanting to be seen, but to already be on a rival cartel's radar was surprising.

Hyde touched the necklace Finn had given her. Why her birthstone and his? He knew where they stood. Their on-again, off-again relationship had suited their traveling lifestyle. Immediately before this mission, they were off again and Hyde had made her peace with that. For him to gift her a sentimental and expensive gift struck her. They'd had fun together in the past. Finn had bought her meals and trinkets, but nothing like the necklace. That made two pieces of jewelry that Finn had given her, each with sentimental value.

Hyde sat on the couch under the window and looked out at the night. Finn was on his cell phone, speaking in hushed tones. He approached and switched his phone to speaker. "Abby has news to share."

He turned the screen to face Hyde. A secure connection provided privacy for their conversation with Abby.

"Happy birthday, Hyde. I trust you enjoyed our gift."

"I did. Thank you," Hyde said.

Abby's face turned serious. "We have confirmed that the Shadow Crew is responsible for the incident at the warehouse. Pierce Holt, the man who visited you, has spent a considerable amount of time in juvenile detention centers and in prison. He's avoided jail for the last nine years. We were lucky that the explosion at the warehouse didn't create a hazardous situation in surrounding neighborhoods. We've sent operatives to the scene and they've collected samples. We believe the chemicals inside the warehouse were nontoxic and nonpoisonous. Working theory is that whatever controlled substance is in Whiteout is either being stored elsewhere or isn't in Miami yet."

Holt was a career criminal with street credit working against Barnett, a pampered prince of his own island. The dynamic was interesting, but no winners would come out of a battle. Casualties would be high on both sides.

"We also have confirmed Swift Speed is a company owned by Reed Barnett. We think he is using that company for his imports and exports," Abby said.

"You've been busy," Hyde said, impressed at the amount of information Abby was providing.

Having intel in the field was critical. Hyde had been thrown into prison overseas because she had been missing important information.

"How do we handle the Shadow Crew? What are their weaknesses? Do we go on the offensive?" Finn asked.

Hyde had the same questions.

Abby typed on her keyboard. "Barnett likely knows about them. Inform him of the incident with Holt and let him know the Shadow Crew torched the warehouse. We don't have a bead on the Shadow Crew's headquarters, but I will email a list of known hangouts. You'll need to be careful. Avoid them if you can. Focus on Barnett. Scope of the mission remains the same."

"Then we wait?" Hyde asked. She would get antsy sitting around. The war was building and she wanted to defuse the parts she could.

"We're looking into locations to replace the warehouse. Keep me in the loop about Barnett's requests as you receive them," Abby said. "And the last item Connor wanted me to pass along is that we're using the information obtained from Ramirez to round up drug caches and dealers. Great job on that."

After discussing a few more issues, they disconnected their call with Abby.

Finn laid his phone next to him. "I didn't expect to be in the middle of a turf war between competing drug cartels."

"Not the highlight of my week." The highlight of her week had been receiving the necklace and the implication of a deeper relationship with Finn. Their birthstones together meant something.

Finn's gaze swerved to her face. He leaned close, his mouth hovering inches from hers. "What was the highlight of your week?"

"The massage," Hyde said. Speaking aloud how much he meant to her rattled her. She might be reading into the meaning behind the necklace. Finn could have intended it as a goodbye gift.

Finn frowned and she pressed a kiss to his lips. "Don't pout. You know I tease. The best part of my week has been you. What about you? What's the best part of the week?"

"I'm on an operation to avenge my best friend with my best girl." A half smile lifted the corners of his mouth. He kissed her, a soft press of his lips against hers, the right amount of pressure and coercion. That quick, he lit her up. She shifted to a more comfortable position and slipped her hand around the back of Finn's neck, drawing him down on top of her.

He balanced his weight between her and the edge of the couch. She loved the feelings he evoked in her. Excitement and heat, and she wanted him so much when he touched her. She might go up in flames.

His thigh nudged her legs apart and she sighed. Contented, happy, relaxed sigh.

Finn's phone rang. He ignored it and kissed her harder. Then hers rang. They'd had a few hours together at the spa, without interruptions. They were back on the clock now and that meant answering the phone no matter how inopportune the time. She groaned and pushed lightly on his shoulders. "Could be an emergency."

Finn sat back on his haunches and answered his phone. "What." He practically growled the word.

After a few seconds of listening, he swore under his breath. "We're on it. Thanks for the call."

"What's happened?" Hyde asked.

"Damien Winslow is reporting a death from White-out at Luminous."

"From Whiteout, or is Holt making good on his promise? Delivering a message?" Hyde asked.

"I don't know," Finn said. "If it was Holt, he's coming at us hard and wants us to know he has reach."

"What's our next move?" Hyde asked.

"Winslow wants to sweep it under the rug. The body was taken to Miami General after an anonymous 911 call reported a woman acting strangely in an alley on Paradise Avenue. By the time the paramedics arrived, she was dead," Finn said.

"Let's get to the hospital," Hyde said. "Find out everything we can."

"This isn't how I planned the rest of the night with you," Finn said.

Hyde touched the side of his face with her fingertips. He needed a shave and his beard tickled her fingers. "I'll take a rain check, okay?" Even interrupted, it had been one of the best nights she'd had in a long time.

Hospitals made Finn nervous. He had learned far too much about the status of enemy operatives from a bored staff member excited to talk about what they knew. Perhaps more unsettling was how easy it was to walk around some hospitals without being questioned.

Finn and Hyde entered the crowded emergency room. A hospital map in the waiting area showed where they needed to go. They went past the admitting desk and down a hallway leading to the morgue.

"This might not be the best time to mention this, but I really hate morgues," Hyde said.

"Phobia?" Finn asked.

Hyde rubbed her arms. "Not exactly a phobia. When I was in La Sabaneta, I worked in the morgue. Not voluntarily. And it wasn't exactly a morgue. It was a place where the guards dumped the prisoners who died. I had to see some awful things," Hyde said. She shivered.

Finn squeezed her hand. He didn't want to call attention to them by being too affectionate, but he wanted to reassure her. She hadn't mentioned the morgue at La Sabaneta before today. "If you don't want to do this, you can wait in the car. I can take care of this. I don't want to put you through anything. This will be sterile and clean." He tried to imagine Hyde dealing with dead bodies under terrible conditions and his heart went out to her.

Hyde hesitated and then shook her head. "I've got your back. I can do this. Totally different situation and circumstances."

Finn didn't press the issue, but he made a mental note to keep an eye on her and give her any excuse possible to stay outside the morgue.

They passed the doctor's lounge and Finn pointed to the ajar door. They exchanged smiles. After confirming the lounge was empty, they stepped inside. They located two white coats and slipped them on. After checking the lockers and finding a few that were unlocked, they borrowed two identification badges.

The West Company would discreetly access the

hospital's records to find out the details of the death, but Hyde and Finn needed to pull a sample of the victim's blood. A toxicity screening would tell them more about Whiteout. Running their own tests prevented Barnett from paying someone in the hospital to cover up the death or rule it unrelated to the new designer drug.

The morgue was located in the basement of the hospital across from the medical records department. The hallway leading to the morgue had several overhead lights out, casting shadows as they walked. Security cameras were positioned in the corners near the ceiling, and Finn and Hyde kept their heads low to prevent the cameras from recording their faces.

"This place is creepy," Hyde said.

Her experience had been traumatic. "Don't be a hero. If you need to stay outside, please do."

Finn waved his badge over the reader at the entryway to the morgue. The lock clicked and he pulled open the door. Expecting Hyde to remain in the hallway, he was surprised when she caught the door and entered with him.

The bespectacled medical examiner looked up from the table where she was working. Confusion and wariness was etched on her face. "Doctors? Can I help you?"

Finn stepped forward and Hyde followed. The name on the ME's lab coat read Styles in blue cursive letters.

"Dr. Styles, the CDC has asked us to look into an issue. They received a report of a death possibly related to an ongoing investigation. They requested we collect a blood and tissue sample from a body that was brought in tonight."

Dr. Styles set down her instruments and peeled off her latex gloves. "I've never had the CDC send a doctor on my shift. I've only worked here a few weeks. Do you have paperwork?"

They could take advantage of her being new and pretend their request was the norm. "It was faxed over to the hospital administrators. The emergency nature of the situation doesn't allow us to delay," Finn said.

Dr. Styles huffed. "The people making the big bucks need their beauty sleep. You'll have to be more specific. I've had four bodies come in tonight."

Hyde's hands were shaking. She put them in the pockets of her medical coat. She got points for holding it together.

Finn was direct. "We're here about the body found in an alley on Paradise Avenue."

Dr. Styles tensed. Her shoulders lifted slightly and her hands moved nervously, like she was looking for something out of reach. "Do I need to be concerned about that body? Was it not an OD? A rare disease that killed her?"

"The CDC didn't indicate we needed to be worried about infectious disease or take any special precautions," Finn said.

Hyde's chest was rising and falling fast. Finn wished she would excuse herself. He would bail on this if she didn't. Worry for her spread across his thoughts.

"Could we take a look at the body?" Finn asked.

"I have not fully processed it yet, and I can't have you interfering with evidence," Dr. Styles said, setting her hands on her hips. "Listen, I have work to do. Come back at eight when the next shift arrives."

"Two minutes with the body and we'll be out of your way," Finn said. "We'd be in your debt." Dr. Styles had a chip on her shoulder. He debated groveling or flirting to get what he needed.

Dr. Styles walked to one of the drawers and pulled out the table. "This is her." Her voice was wavering.

Finn looked at the body. She was pale white, her skin almost tinged blue. Her body was covered with a sheet. He wanted to look at her arms and between her toes for signs of track marks. With Dr. Styles standing over them, it was impossible.

They needed to know if this death was connected to Whiteout.

"I'll need a sample of her blood," Finn said.

"As long as I have a warrant," Dr. Styles said.

Finn could knock her out. Tie her up and take the blood sample from the victim. But he wouldn't resort to that. The West Company could obtain a warrant through official channels, but they preferred for their work to be untraceable, and a paper trail complicated matters. "Your administration has the fax the CDC sent over. They will see it first thing in the morning. Let's save everyone time and effort."

Dr. Styles narrowed her eyes. "I need a warrant or authorization from my boss. I am not getting fired because the CDC decides they can't utilize the proper channels."

Finn tried again. "You can have your boss call me and I'll explain everything. Again, the emergency nature of this requires I take the blood work now."

Dr. Styles pushed closed the drawer and made a

show of locking it. "Warrant or forget it. You can see yourselves out."

With a quick exchange of glances, they exited the morgue. Hyde was breathing deep and slow, likely trying to stay calm.

"Why did you stay in there so long?" Finn asked.

Hyde brushed some hair away from her face. "What was I supposed to do?"

Finn put his arm around her. "Make an excuse and leave."

"I thought she was planning to let us take the sample, then she turned on a dime and got argumentative," Hyde said. "If we have to wait for the official records or a warrant, we're losing time."

"Excuse me!" A loud voice from behind them.

Finn and Hyde turned to see a redhead in her twenties wearing pink scrubs jogging toward them. Her tight curls bounced around her shoulders as she ran.

"Please, just a minute," the woman said. She didn't seem to be carrying a weapon, but Finn reached for his.

The redhead was out of breath when she caught up to them. "I'm Nadine. I work in the medical examiner's office. Paperwork and ordering supplies. I overheard you talking to Dr. Styles about the drug overdoses."

Finn's ears tingled. He and Hyde were on to something and Nadine might fill in some blanks.

"Why does the CDC care about the overdoses? I mentioned something to my boss, but nothing came of it. There's been so many recently and they're different than what we've seen in the past," Nadine said.

Finn flashed a charming smile, trying to set her at ease and establish they could be trusted. "The CDC is concerned. It's why they sent us. Working here, we could get the samples faster."

Nadine seemed relieved. "You know there's been an influx of cases in the last few months. Drug overdoses that are filed as cocaine usage, but the test results are subject to interpretation. It's not clear-cut. I have a friend who works at Miami West Hospital, and she heard the doctors talking about another drug. Not cocaine, but similar."

"What are they calling this drug?" Hyde asked.

"Whiteout," Nadine said.

Whiteout was on the street, attracting users and killing people. Barnett was aware of it and was either covering up the deaths or ignoring them.

Nadine shifted on her feet and glanced over her shoulder. "Don't tell Dr. Styles I said anything. It worries me how many drug overdoses we've had. In the past, when this has happened, the police have spread the word to warn people. But with this stuff, no one wants to admit we have a huge drug problem. Something more dangerous or lethal, I don't know."

Payoffs were involved if the incidents weren't being investigated. Barnett's payroll must be huge, ensuring unchecked distribution of his new drug.

"If people know it's dangerous, why is anyone buying it?" Hyde asked.

Nadine shrugged. "I know about the overdoses and the drug is potent, but not everyone does. When I bring it up, everyone wants me to stop talking about it."

"Thanks for having the courage to tell us about this, Nadine," Hyde said.

"I'm glad you guys are looking into it." Nadine looked over her shoulder. She reached into the pocket of her scrubs and handed them a vial. "The blood from the victim. This should help you. I need to go. I'll be in trouble if anyone sees me talking to you." She whirled away and jogged down the hallway toward the morgue.

Chapter 12

Another hotel room, another frustrating conversation with Barnett. He wasn't a patient man and at times, he was completely unreasonable. This was one of those times.

Finn paced across the plush maroon rug, stifling his frustration. This hotel room was smaller than the last and the geometric print wallpaper—and this conversation—was giving him a headache.

"Have you found a new warehouse?" Barnett's voice was terse.

Even with the West Company's considerable resources, scouring the city and surrounding towns for the perfect location was a sizeable task. The dimensions of the warehouse and the distance from the port were critical. Finding an empty warehouse available immediately added to the challenge.

Finn was learning more about Barnett's network. The closer he got to Barnett, the sooner they could take him down. For now, Finn kept his temper. "I have a few possibilities. I am scouting them and running surveillance. I need to know who's in the area and if our sudden presence will bring interest." Finn had told Barnett about his run-in with Holt and the Shadow Crew, and despite Barnett's promise to handle it, Finn hadn't heard more from him. By handle it, he could mean taking out a hit on members of the gang, like he had on Ramirez, or he could mean ignoring the problem and leaving Finn to fend for himself.

"Hurry up. My contact at the port and in the DEA is costly. It's not like I can make this move in a day," Barnett said.

His DEA contact? Barnett was paying off someone in the Drug Enforcement Agency? Finn was curious about that, but asking too many questions would raise Barnett's suspicions. "Give me a few names of men who can run surveillance for me," Finn said. "I need to know if the location is secure."

Barnett grunted. "I'll email you. Any further provocation from Holt or the Shadow Crew?"

It had only been a day since Holt had shown up in their hotel room. "Nothing." As of yet, they hadn't tracked Holt's location, but he hadn't approached him or Hyde again.

"Stay on top of it," Barnett said. "I've got to go. Don't let me down, Finn."

Hyde looked up from her computer. She was catching up on personal emails over a secure connection. Victoria had posted pictures on a social media site of her and Thomas poolside at their resort. Hyde felt a twinge of jealously at the scenic photos.

When this mission was over, Hyde would take a vacation and treat herself to great food and wine. Her ideal trip would include Finn. He may take a week or two away from work. Then he would move on to the next assignment. A pang of loss struck her.

Finn stood by the window, holding his phone in his hand. "Barnett has someone on the take at the DEA."

Not surprising. "Did he mention who?"

"No."

Hyde shut down her computer and focused on this conversation. "We'll mention it to Abby and keep our eyes and ears open."

"If Barnett has a DEA agent or agents working for him, who else does he have in his pocket?" Finn asked. He leaned on the table next to her computer, folding his arms across his chest.

Barnett knew how to pave the way to what he wanted. Hyde set her hands on Finn's thigh and rested her head against them. "We can't know. We can only trust each other," Hyde said.

Finn ran his hand through her hair. "Just each other."

She had more to say on that thought. Admitting that Finn was the person who knew her best, the man whom she trusted with her life, felt overpowering.

Hyde's phone rang. Lydia was calling. Hyde answered the phone, trying to keep her voice casual.

"They suckered you back in, didn't they?" Lydia asked.

Hyde forced a laugh to cover how close Lydia was to the truth. At the beginning of this mission, her express intent was getting in and getting out without forging any ties. Believing that was possible had been a lie she had told herself. She was involved in this mission and she was getting in deeper with Finn, too. "It's taking longer with the client than we initially thought. But it's just this one client. Then I'll be back in Bearcreek."

"If I asked you to babysit Thea this Friday, you'd be okay with that and not stand me up?" Lydia asked.

Hyde couldn't commit to Friday. She was hopeful about bringing Barnett down, but not that quickly. Lydia was hundreds of miles away. "Not that soon."

A labored deep breath in and out. "Hyde, I need the truth," Lydia said.

Had Lydia stumbled on something about her life? "About what?"

"About what you're doing. I was counting on you to be back here with me. You said you'd help me with Thea. Between the worry when I was pregnant and the last year, I haven't slept through the night in a year and a half. Now Victoria is married and she'll be starting her own family. She'll have this great life with a man who provides for her and I have sleepless nights and money problems and—" Lydia choked back a sob.

Hyde's heart ached for her sister. "Please don't cry."

Finn shot her a questioning look. Hyde closed her eyes and searched for the right words to comfort her sister. Hyde couldn't fully understand what Lydia was going through. Raising her daughter alone, working full-time and not having much help was wearing on her. "I can wire you money if that would help. Use it for whatever you need. A babysitter, a day care or bills."

Lydia scoffed bitterly. "If you could pay my bills eternally, that would help. Oh, and be the person who I can call at two in the morning when Thea has a fever and I can't decide if I should take her to the ER or wait until morning and call the pediatrician. Or you can come over every day so I have ten minutes to myself. Can you do that?" The harshness of the words and Lydia's anger bit into her.

"You can always call me," Hyde said, feeling inadequate and knowing she had let her sister down.

"You're nowhere around," Lydia said.

The guilt nearly crushed her. "I'm sorry, Lydia. I want to make things right for you." It was part of her motivation in avenging Simon.

"I know that. You, Victoria and Mom and Dad have tried to help me. I probably sound hostile, but this has been hard. Thea is the greatest thing that's ever happened to me. I wish it was easier. I wish that Simon hadn't been a lying coward," Lydia said.

To hear those words spoken about a man Hyde knew had been honorable and decent cut to her soul. "Simon wouldn't have wanted this to happen."

At the mention of Simon's name, Finn's eyes met hers.

Hyde wanted to defend Simon without upsetting her sister. "Simon would have done things differently if he could."

Lydia sniffed. "You've said that before. Yet, this man who you brought to visit our family, who you brought into our lives, is gone. You can't contact him. No email address. No phone number."

She had told her sister those things. "Are you blaming me?" Hyde asked. Blame or not, she was carrying the guilt.

"At first, I did. But I believe you would tell me if you knew where he was. I hired a private investigator about six months ago to track down Simon. Victoria gave me the money. She thought that Simon would pay child support."

Hyde hadn't known about this. Simon's cover had been deep. No way could a PI track Simon's identity or find out what he had done for a living. "What did you find out?" Hyde asked. She was almost afraid to hear the answer. Finn knelt on the floor next to her, listening.

His hand was on her shoulder for support.

"It's as if he was a figment of our imagination. If I didn't have Thea, I would question my sanity and if I made up the whole thing. The PI said he was probably a criminal. He fooled you, he tricked me and when the whim struck, he disappeared."

Finn looked at her and his eyes were filled with deep wells of sadness. He didn't want his friend remembered this way.

Hyde's chest ached. Her sister had no idea what she was saying. But if Barnett was no longer a threat, Hyde could tell her the truth and it would free Lydia. She could move on with her life. Hyde heard Thea in the background.

Lydia sighed. "I have to go. I understand you can't come Friday. But when you come home, do us a favor and come home alone."

The line went dead. Hyde looked at the phone and then at Finn.

She fell into his arms and Finn held her. He kissed

her cheek, and his strong arms kept her afloat. The overwhelming urge to burst into tears pressed into her. Simon's memory should be honored. Lydia deserved happiness. Compounded with her feelings for Finn, she felt lost. Her relationship with Finn was confusing and difficult to process. The distance hadn't kept her from wanting him and when this was over, those feelings would persist.

She leaned away and Finn wiped at her cheeks with his thumbs. "We'll make this right, Hyde. I promise you."

Hyde pressed her lips to his, ending the conversation before she told him the truth. Helping Lydia with closure was important and so was bringing Barnett down. But there was something more important. She had fallen for Finn a long time ago, and being with him in the future was what she most wanted. But did she want it enough to give up a family of her own?

Hyde strode into the newly scouted warehouse. It was empty, but a delivery was expected soon. She and Finn were waiting to meet one of Barnett's Miami contacts to show him the warehouse.

The West Company had outfitted it with discreet surveillance devices. They could monitor what went on inside. It would go a long way to building their case against the men involved with Barnett's enterprise.

Hyde hid her shock when James Sydney stepped out of his luxury sports car and strolled to the door. He was tall and slim, outfitted in a Hawaiian button-down shirt and a pair of khakis. A pair of sunglasses was tucked in his shirt pocket and he wore a crisp pair of brown loafers. His hair had begun to recede and he was gray around the temples. Hyde stepped away from the door and occupied herself looking in her handbag and watching from her peripheral.

Sydney pulled the door open and stepped into the building. He extended his hand to Finn. "I'm Sydney."

"Finn. Glad you could make it. This is my girl-friend, Alex."

Sydney glanced at her, but said nothing.

Finn gestured around the space. "Let me show you the place." At the first opportunity, Hyde would message the West Company about this development. The West Company believed that Sydney was involved in the Barnett cartel and had been for a decade. They suspected he was responsible for seven deaths and an uncountable number of crimes. Having him at the warehouse confirmed his connection to Barnett.

"You're new. Let's see if you make it. You're off to a rough start," Sydney said.

Word had spread about what had happened to Barnett's previous associates. Their bodies had been found inside the burned-out warehouse. The cost of doing business with Barnett had gone up.

Finn pointed out the features of the building. He had already sent Barnett the necessary documentation including the access roads, the surrounding area and the building specs. Hyde trailed behind them, pretending to be involved with her phone.

"This place isn't as big as the other one," Sydney said. "I was hoping for something larger."

"We'll move the goods here and ship them as soon as possible. This isn't a long-term storage facility. We want the product on the street," Finn said.

Sydney stroked his goatee. "That's a good point. You know, you look familiar. Have we met before?"

Hyde mentally checked her weapon. Finn and Sydney's families had a connection. The men may have briefly crossed paths. If Finn resembled his father or brother, Sydney may realize who Finn was.

"I've done business up and down the East Coast," Finn said.

Sydney had his hands in his pockets, and on his hip was a prominently displayed gun. Hyde wished she could flash her gun to show him that she would take him out if he hurt Finn.

Sydney shrugged. "You're pressing your luck. You're Barnett's go-to guy for this project. How long can that last?"

"Until the job is finished," Finn said.

Sydney laughed. "This job is never finished. You must know that."

The list of Whiteout customers was long and increasing by the day. "Do you want to sign off on the warehouse?"

Sydney took out his cell phone and snapped some pictures. "Give me a few hours. I'll speak to Barnett."

Finn shrugged as if he didn't care, but Hyde knew what was on the line. They'd tried to sell Sydney on this place. If they had to find another location, it would take additional days.

Sydney left a few minutes later. The sound of his car engine roaring down the street faded.

Finn grabbed her hand and kissed the back of it. "How do you think it went? He doesn't trust me. I don't trust him, either, but it presents a problem if he tells Barnett this warehouse won't work or if his distrust sways Barnett."

Hyde wrapped her arms around Finn's waist. "He was interested. I guess now we wait."

"Any word from Abby about the blood work?" Finn asked.

Hyde looked at her phone. "Nothing yet."

The West Company had confirmed the victim had an unidentified chemical in her blood, but they hadn't matched it to other overdose victims in the area. Those samples weren't available.

"What's the plan for tonight?" Hyde asked. She wondered if they would do something nonmission related, like see a movie or dine out or crash on the couch and watch television.

"Have something in mind?" Finn asked.

"We could grab dinner and go dancing," Hyde said. They had once danced in Barcelona at a club on the water. It had been exhilarating, like four hours of foreplay. A night out might rekindle some of what they had lost and forgotten about each other—the fun, the flirting and the easy affection. They had been spies first and lovers second. She wanted it the other way around.

They took Finn's expensive car, valet-parked and strode into Dazzle, a club in South Beach.

"There have been a number of overdoses in this area," Finn said.

Hyde's heart fell and she looked up from her handbag. She had been searching for her lipstick until his words caught her off guard. This was a date, not another part of the mission. Finn had picked the club.

She hadn't realized he had done so because of possibly related overdoses.

"We're not here for bodies," Hyde said.

Finn cleared his throat. "Right. I got that. You seem tense. Everything okay?"

"I'm fine." If tonight went well, she planned to tell Finn how she felt about him and what she wanted for their future, namely, him in it.

They entered the nightclub. Perfumes, cologne and sweat mixed, the music pulsed and colored lights made it hard to think, which worked for Hyde. No capacity for more deep thoughts.

Hyde held on to Finn's arm. Wearing the short, tight green dress and black heels, she fit in with the women in the room. The pendant Finn had given her for her birthday hung around her neck and she wore his grandmother's bracelet around her wrist.

Their first stop was the bar and they ordered outrageously expensive drinks.

Finn glanced at his phone, and a smile lit his face. "Sydney recommended the warehouse. They're moving forward to purchase it."

Hyde set her finger over Finn's lips. "No work talk tonight." She took a sip of her bright blue concoction. "It's good." Getting Finn's train of thought off work and onto her would take some doing.

Finn sipped his top-shelf Scotch. "Same here."

They switched glasses and took a swig from each other's drinks. Hyde took another nip of hers and then set it on the bar. "Dance with me?"

"Absolutely," Finn said. He took her hand and he led her onto the dance floor.

She brought her mouth close to his neck and kissed

his cheek and inhaled the masculine scent. Heat singed her. They moved easily together. Finn's leg brushed her inner thigh and she leaned closer, drawn to him, a magnetic pull that would not release her. His touch unhinged her, the friction between them electric. Spears of pleasure ignited, leaving no part of her unaffected. Finn brushed his thumbs down her back.

After several songs wrapped in his embrace, her skin was oversensitive and somehow also starving for his touch. Her thoughts were fixated on him, only Finn.

"Do you want something to drink?" Finn asked.

"Water. Water would be good."

Their hips grazing, they moved to the bar.

The bartender glanced at Finn's expensive, borrowed watch and then at Hyde, his gaze lingering on her cleavage. Finn stared at him—hard—and the bartender averted his eyes. Lowering her head, Hyde hid her smile. Territorial when they were together, she had missed spending time with Finn.

"Planning to rent a cabana tonight?" the bartender asked.

Hyde had no idea what he was talking about. A secret upstairs room for trysts? She played along like she understood. "I heard they were hard to come by."

The bartender poured a few shots for a group of customers and slid them down the bar. "They are. But one has become available. Ten thousand for the night."

Finn snapped his credit card onto the bar top. "Put it on the plastic."

Not a part of the mission. He was dropping that money on her. She touched his hand lightly, a small thank-you.

The bartender swiped the credit card and then handed Finn a gold coin. "Double doors. Purple tent, blue entry. Have fun."

Anticipation grabbed at her. As Finn and Hyde strolled away from the bar, Finn took Hyde's hand. "Do you have a guess about this cabana? What is it?"

"I thought you knew," Hyde said. She was curled against him, her body rubbing against his as they walked. She stopped him, standing in front of him, setting her leg between his, entwining their bodies. Kissing the underside of his jaw, she hugged him. Emotions swelled inside her.

"I'm guessing the cabana is offered to their elite patrons," Finn said. His hand brushed her necklace. His eyes glittered; he was happy she had worn it.

"Or we're suckers who got taken for ten grand."

At the glass door, Finn slipped the gold coin into a slot. The frosted glass doors parted and they walked through. The doors closed behind them and drowned out the sounds from the club. Instead, the music being piped into the gated outdoor area was soft and melodic.

Around the perimeter was a ten-foot-high fence lined with palm trees and tropical flowers. The cabanas were situated to provide privacy to each.

"We may have paid a huge amount of money for time alone in a tent," Hyde whispered. "Which we could have had for free at almost any national park."

"You looked interested when the bartender mentioned it. This might be fun," Finn said.

"That's the idea," Hyde said.

They walked toward the purple cabana and moving aside the blue fabric door, they entered. On the floor were large, plush, jewel-toned pillows with gold tassels. The room contained a leopard-print chair and large blue settee. Though the patterns and fabric would have clashed in another space, here, they set the mood. "Is this supposed to be like a harem?" Hyde asked. She was digging it.

"Let's go with it," Finn said.

"I'm assuming based on the privacy this space is made for sex," Hyde said. The words had popped from her mouth before she could censor them. She was thinking about sex with Finn, thinking about how much she cared for him and loved being in his arms, nothing between them.

Hyde looked directly at him. Finn was into the idea. Her body heated, knowing how she affected him. Arranging the pillows on the cloth-covered ground, she patted the cushion next to her. "Join me?"

Finn sat. "Smells like incense. Like cumin and bay leaves."

Before they could discuss the smell or why the room was perfumed heavily, the fabric door fluttered and a man and woman filled the entryway.

Finn and Hyde rose to their feet.

The woman was wearing a nearly sheer robe and holding a large bowl in front of her, and the man was wearing a short robe that fell midthigh and carrying a wicker basket. Were they selling sex? Or was this supposed to set the stage?

The woman smiled and tossed some flower petals from her bowl onto the floor. "I'm Giselle. This is Lucas. We're here to offer you our personalized services."

"What services are those?" Hyde asked.

"Massage. Relaxation. Drinks. Food. *Anything* you need to make the night more memorable," Giselle said. "Name it and I'll make it happen."

Hyde looked at Finn from under her eyelashes, trying to hide her amusement. All she needed was Finn. The pillows and decor were fun, but superfluous. Being with Finn was an aphrodisiac.

"A glass of wine for each of us," Hyde said. "And that's all. Thank you."

Lucas and Giselle bowed slightly and backed out of the tent.

"Hyde, I need to ask you something," Finn said.

Hyde's heart was going to beat out of her chest. He may be feeling the same as her. He might want to escalate their relationship beyond lovers into a word that might cement more meaning. "You can ask me anything." Let him know she was open to it.

"I think Giselle and Lucas could know something about Whiteout."

Her heart fell. His mind was on the mission. She wanted it on her. "What's the question?" Irritation grated at her.

"We can get our hands on a sample if we ask."

Disappointment and frustration mixed inside her. Throwing a tantrum would get them nowhere. But she didn't want to talk about Whiteout. "It's a long shot and tonight is about us."

Finn took her hands in his. "We're close, Hyde. I can feel it."

"Tonight is not about work," Hyde said. Pressing the issue wouldn't get her anywhere. Surrender was settling over her. If Finn was bent on hunting down Whiteout tonight, his mind would be on that and not on her. Maybe if they were lucky, he would track this lead and they could recover the rest of the night.

Giselle returned with their glasses of wine. Hyde and Finn accepted them gratefully, and Hyde tried to hide her hurt and annoyance.

Finn leaned closer to Giselle. "While you were gone, I had a thought. We haven't been in town long, but we've heard about a unique experience. A new substance that will blow our minds."

Giselle blinked at him.

"Something we can take to relax," Finn said.

Giselle set her hand on her hip. "The experience tonight will blow your mind, and our accommodations will be all you need to relax."

"Nothing more unique?" Finn asked.

Giselle moved her tray to her other side. "A night in our cabanas is unique." She smiled and whirled away, leaving them alone.

Hyde hoped it was the end of the discussion. She didn't want to talk about Whiteout. "The lead didn't work out. But we still have this place. I don't think a glass of wine counts for ten thousand dollars. Let's just enjoy."

Finn pulled her hips close to him, setting his left hand at her lower back, holding her against his body. His right hand brushed her soft hair over her ear. Instead of capitulation, she read worry in his eyes.

"I can't forgive myself for what happened to you in Munich. You've been there for me. You've helped me keep my sanity. I'm sorry that I wasn't there for you when you needed me," Finn said.

Hyde threaded her arms around his neck. She had already forgiven him. If they could accept this, they could move forward together. "I don't have the right words to explain how I felt. How I feel now. So many emotions hit me and I'm confused."

"It's okay to be confused," Finn said. "I'm confused about us and what happened, too. I know it must have been terrible and I wish I could make it easier for you. When you're ready, you'll try again and it will work out. You'll be a mother."

He had said *you* not *we*. She might be putting herself through an ordeal, building her hopes, when Finn wouldn't give or change. "It was hard to keep it a secret. If I told my sisters, they would have had too many questions about you."

"Why didn't you tell me?"

"Is that where we were? Was our relationship about confiding in each other?" Hyde asked, leaning away and looking up at him.

"I thought it was. Was I wrong? I thought what we had was good," Finn said.

They were circling a conversation she wanted to have. "We hadn't put words to it," Hyde said.

"Did we need to?" Finn asked.

Hyde stepped away and Finn released her. The dimness of the tent, speaking in whispers, she was finally ready to let him in. She felt the words in her mouth. "Is it wrong, after giving so much of myself, to want some of my life for me? You're the only adult relationship I've had with a man because there's no way I could make it work with anyone else. He would ask too many questions or I'd be gone too much. And my family life. My parents don't say anything to me directly, but I know they miss me at holidays and gatherings. Why can't I have my life now? Let someone else take up the cause."

"It's not wrong. You can change what you want. Is what you want a house with mortgage payments and a car note? Paying bills and weekly trips to the grocery store?"

"You're pointing out the mundane parts of living in suburban America. What about the best parts? Apple festivals and baking cookies, family and friends, parties and celebrations, movie nights and happy hour at the bar."

"You have some of that now," Finn said.

"I don't. But I know that I want it. And I want you. I want you in my life. I know that's putting a lot on you and I understand if you need time to decide on an answer."

"In your life how?" Finn asked.

Hyde swallowed the growing lump in her throat. "Together. As a couple."

Finn stared at her. "You're asking me to stop being a spy?"

Was she asking that of him? Was there something in between? All or nothing felt like an ultimatum, and she hadn't intended for it to come out that way. "No. I just want to see you."

They sat in the quiet for a long time.

"I need some air," Finn said. He left the tent and Hyde followed him, feeling like her heart was breaking. She had told him how she felt and he had retreated and shut her down.

They left the tent and Finn slung his arm over Hyde's shoulders for the sake of appearances. Tension was rolling off Hyde in waves. He had upset her.

But he didn't have an answer for her. She wanted a life he couldn't give her.

His coin was handed back to him as he exited the cabana area. He tossed the coin to a couple dancing close. If he and Hyde couldn't use it, someone else should. The woman with orange hair caught it and smiled, calling out her thanks.

Strolling casually, they exited the club. As they stepped onto the busy street, Hyde drew away from Finn. Physically and emotionally, she wanted space. He owed her a response, a real answer, and he didn't have it.

The sidewalk outside the nightclub was crowded and well-lit by the bars and restaurants open in the near vicinity. Expensive cars were parked along the curb, and men and women mingled in the street, talking, laughing, and some more inebriated were singing. The general merriment and excitement swirled around him and Hyde, none of it reaching them. The heaviness seemed to hang exclusively over them.

"Hey!" A voice from behind them.

Finn exchanged glances with Hyde. They turned. Neither spoke, waiting for the approaching man to speak. Preparing for an ambush, he nudged Hyde behind him.

The man was wearing a pair of jeans ripped at the knees, a black ribbed tank top and a purple and black flannel shirt tied around his waist. He had his hands jammed deep in his pants pockets.

"Can I help you?" Hyde asked.

The stranger pulled his hands from his pockets. Finn tensed, watching the man's movements.

"I have something you might want."

Finn lifted a brow. What did this man think they wanted? "You have a name?"

"Shake."

"Okay, Shake. What do you have?" Finn asked.

Shake jerked his head behind him. "You need to come with me."

He could be targeting them for a theft, thinking they were easy marks leaving a club.

"We're not going anywhere without more information," Hyde said.

"My girl Giselle says you're looking for Whiteout," Shake said. He spoke the name of the drug in a hushed voice.

"No one has it," Finn said. He wasn't sneaking off with a drug dealer until he was more sure.

"Not true. Not true," Shake said. "I have my hands on a stash. Fifty per. If you're not interested, I have other buyers."

Finn internally questioned how Shake had the drug. He could be part of Barnett's network or work for the Shadow Crew. Once a drug hit the street, it could change hands. "How do we know you have what you say? I hear Whiteout is hard to find."

Shake shrugged. "You have to take my word. You won't have other offers. New product is delayed and everyone I know is tapped."

Good information. Barnett hadn't moved his shipment into Miami yet. A quick nod and the trio stepped into a nearby alleyway.

Reaching into his pocket, Finn withdrew two fifties folded into fourths. He pressed them into Shake's hand as Shake slipped him two plastic bags.

Finn glanced at the bags. "You might not know who

I am, but if you screw me on this, I'll find you and I'll make you wish you had never met me."

Shake jammed the money into his pockets. "I'm not lying to you, man. Giselle told me you were a power player. I want to make good on my investment. Cash is king."

Hyde and Finn backed away. Shake didn't follow them.

"You think this is the real deal?" Hyde asked when they had moved away from Shake and were blending with the crowd.

"We'll take it to the lab and find out."

"Do you think Shake is part of Barnett's network?" Hyde asked.

"Can't say. Barnett needs to get the drugs on the streets somehow," Finn said.

Finn called the West Company, requesting a location to drop the pills. If they could connect them to the blood work of the latest known victim, they would know more about the overdose and what made Whiteout so alluring and dangerous.

"Looks like you got your way. We've focused again on the mission."

Finn stopped in his tracks. "You threw something at me that I wasn't prepared for."

Hyde met his eyes. Her sadness was palpable. "Not prepared. For a relationship. For us. I know that work can take over a life, but I'm tired of living that way. I need something more."

For the second time that night, Finn was at a loss for words.

Chapter 13

Finn groaned when Barnett's name lit on his phone display. He answered curtly.

"I need you at the pier on Fourth Street," Barnett said.

It was two in the morning. Finn was exhausted. He and Hyde had delivered the sample of Whiteout to the West Company lab. They were heading back to their hotel, exhausted and hungry. Hyde was annoyed with him, and their need for sleep was adding to her agitation.

Finn kept his voice energized. "We're out now. What's up?"

"My contact at the DEA is on shift at the pier and he's going to green light supplies I need," Barnett said.

Finn looked forward to meeting the DEA contact and making sure he went down when Barnett's enterprise imploded. "Why do you need me there?"

"I'm keeping the location of the warehouse to a few trusted people. I want you to make the delivery. Get the supplies there. I'll send you information on how we'll distribute it to the cook houses."

"Is the warehouse ready?" Finn asked. It had only been a day. Barnett had moved fast.

"Sydney's taken care of it. Stop asking questions. Do as I tell you," Barnett said.

Making the delivery and then setting fire to the warehouse would keep the supplies from reaching their destinations. If Finn was involved in two destructions in the same week, questions would be raised. Blaming the Shadow Crew would take some of the heat off him, but it would also make Finn look incompetent, and he would lose Barnett's trust. "Sure thing, boss."

He disconnected the call. "We're playing delivery people tonight."

Hyde sighed. "Delivery of what exactly?"

"The supplies Barnett needs to make Whiteout, I'm assuming," Finn said. "He wasn't open to questions."

Hyde wrung her hands. "We can't do that. We can't allow more of this stuff to be sold."

"Maybe someone is adding their own ingredients. Maybe one of the cook houses is contaminated." He didn't like the idea of helping Whiteout reach the street, either, but staying involved was the only way to stop it. "Barnett wants us at the pier now. He has a DEA agent ready to approve the shipment. It's too late to call in law enforcement. Barnett will know from the timing we were the rats."

Hyde forked her fingers into her hair. "We'll have to disrupt the supply chain before this makes it to the street."

Twenty minutes later Finn was waiting on the pier. Not much activity at this time of night, and not being able to see over the shipping containers made him nervous. He didn't want another shoot-out with the Shadow Crew or anyone in the Barnett cartel. He'd had no time to prepare or to surveil the area prior to this meeting. Hyde was watching his back, but it was two of them against an unknown number.

Two men wearing dark clothing approached. "Moore?" one of the men asked. He had a trim, gray beard, and his gaze darted nervously left and right.

"Yes," Finn said.

"Truck's at the end of the line. Already loaded. Get moving."

That was it? "You have a plan to keep the authorities off me?" Finn didn't want to drive the streets of Miami with illegal products and into a trap. That amount of substances meant jail time and if he went free because he was undercover, the mission was blown.

The men exchanged glances. Hyde was likely taking their pictures and sending them to Abby. Two more who'd go down with Barnett.

"You don't need to worry about the authorities," the first man said.

Because they were the authorities. Were they DEA agents? Was the other man police? Coast guard? How many pockets was Barnett stuffing with bribes to get Whiteout into Miami?

Waiting around would invite more trouble. Another option had not presented itself and he went with it. Keys were tossed at him. Finn caught them and strode in the direction he'd been pointed. Hyde met him close to the truck. Coming close to him, she grabbed his sleeves hard.

"Something about this feels off," Hyde said. "Why couldn't they drive the truck? If Barnett trusts them with the goods, he should trust them with the location of the warehouse."

He agreed something was wrong. "They don't want to be seen lurking around Miami. You think this is a trap?" Finn asked.

"Why would Barnett want us caught?" Hyde asked.

They climbed into the truck and started it up.

"Send a message to Abby. Let her know what's going on and to watch the police scanners for any activity we need to avoid."

Finn pulled slowly away from the pier. The truck rumbled as they drove down the streets of Miami. "You think we're being watched?" Finn asked.

"Quite possibly," Hyde said. She was checking the interior of the truck for bugs. "We're clear. Nothing in here. Could be a tracking device elsewhere in the truck."

Being thrown into the assignment had taken the focus off her anger for him. She was into the mission now.

"I'd love to look in the back and see what we're working with," Finn said.

"We'll find out at the warehouse," Hyde said. She glanced in the passenger-side mirror. "It might be nothing, but there're three men on motorcycles behind us."

Finn saw them. "I'll change lanes and see if they pass us."

Finn pressed the turn signal and moved right. Taking his foot off the gas, the truck decelerated and Finn waited for the motorcycles to speed by. Instead, they changed lanes and slid behind him.

Finn swore under his breath. "Ideas?"

"They haven't done anything aggressive. If we go somewhere more populated or better lit, they'll back off. There's a chance they don't want the items in the truck or they're three guys, out having a good time, messing with us."

Finn snorted. "I love your optimism. The other option is that they are with the Shadow Crew and will ambush us."

"How could they know about the delivery?" Hyde asked.

"Barnett could have leaks in his organization," Finn said.

One of the motorcycles sped up, its engine roaring. Finn caught a glimpse of the rider. He was wearing the gang colors of the Shadow Crew and their logo of a ghost on his helmet. "Shadow Crew. They must have been tipped off about our delivery. They've made it clear they want in. They're getting the point across."

Hyde reached into her bag and withdrew her gun. "If they don't back off, this won't end well."

Ahead of them on the two-way street, five more motorcycles pulled out of a side road.

"They're trying to box us in," Finn said. They had the advantage of mass, but the motorcycles had speed and numbers.

"Don't let off the accelerator. They'd be stupid to play chicken with us. Ram them if you have to," Hyde said.

Finn pressed the truck's limits. The last thing he

wanted was to hurt anyone and he didn't want to start a gang war. The motorcycles were darting ahead, moving into Finn's lane, threatening to slam into the front of his vehicle.

Before impact, the cycles veered.

Hyde was typing on her phone. "I'm looking for alternate routes. We can't get trapped."

The motorcycles were pursuing them.

"We could be carrying flammable cargo," Finn said.

"I'm calling Barnett. We need to know what's back there," Hyde said.

Finn didn't want to involve Barnett, but they hadn't checked the contents. If they had explosive chemicals, they needed to be careful. "Put the phone on speaker so I can talk to him."

Barnett answered and Finn relayed the situation.

"Evade them. We can't lose that cargo. It will set us back weeks," Barnett said.

"I thought you were handling the Shadow Crew," Finn said.

"I have handled them. I'm shutting them out. I don't cave to threats," Barnett said.

If Barnett had been there, Finn would have punched him. Avoiding the Shadow Crew wasn't a solution. "Who else knew about the delivery?" Finn asked.

Barnett sighed. "Sydney and a few of my men. You're in Miami to be my eyes and ears. Make this right or disappear."

"What's in the truck? I need to know if it could explode, like the warehouse did," Finn said.

"You'll be fine. Don't hit anything and you'll survive," Barnett said.

The call disconnected.

Finn had some choice words. They would have to wait.

"If they start shooting, they could blow our tires and we're screwed. I've messaged Abby, but I don't know if she can send anyone to help us in time."

The sound of a bullet striking metal set Finn's nerves on edge. He had anticipated an attack, but nothing like this.

"We need a defensible position," Hyde said.

Finn looked around the street. On his right, about thirty yards away was the water. On the left, tall condominium complexes and shops filled with citizens who could be caught in the cross fire. Finn pulled the truck diagonally across a side street and slammed to a stop. On the corners of the block were a dry cleaners and an accessories boutique, closed for the night.

They slid out his side of the vehicle. The motorcyclists formed a semicircle around them. They seemed unsure how to react.

Finn belly-crawled underneath the truck. Aiming his gun in their direction, he had the luxury of time to be careful to hit a metal garbage can across the road. Killing a member of the Shadow Crew wasn't in his plan. Finn's shot had the desired effect. Some of the gang members retreated and two fled on their motorcycles.

Others retaliated, shooting at the truck. Finn took cover behind one of the truck's wheels. Finn was lucky that they didn't seem to have much skill in aiming.

"Are you okay?" Finn asked.

The sound of police sirens filled the air.

"I have a message from Abby that a call went out

over the police scanner that a truck and motorcycles are involved in an active shooting," Hyde said.

That fast?

"Fleeing in the truck is painting a huge bull's-eye on us," Finn said. The police would pursue them, especially if they had a correct description of their truck. Based on the number of windows facing their position, Finn guessed it was likely. The dark would only conceal them to a point.

"What's the plan?" Hyde asked. She reached across to Finn and they interlaced their fingers. Then they put their hands back on their weapons.

"I wanted to scare them off," Finn said. "I didn't think they would hold their ground."

"We can run on foot and abandon the truck or we can flee with the goods," Hyde said.

Finn ducked under the truck and fired another warning shot. Hyde stood and did the same over the front of the truck.

"If you want the mission to be over, we run," Finn said. He wasn't sure how he wanted her to answer. Until this point, his first priority was taking down Barnett. Now his thoughts were blurred with Hyde's words. She wanted a future with him, and that meant something. More than that, she meant everything to him. He wanted her. Needed her. Would go crazy without her.

His silence had shut her down. She was again focused on the mission, maybe as a defense mechanism. Now wasn't the right time to discuss this, but the words weighed on him.

Hyde looked at her gun. "Let's take the truck." She sounded resigned to it, but not hopeful.

The police arrived on the scene, approaching from opposite ends of the street perpendicular to their position. Black-and-white police cars skidded to a stop, blocking the street. They exited their vehicles and drew their guns. Three cars in total, and Finn guessed more were on the way to provide backup.

Finn swore. The motorcyclists were raising their hands above their heads in surrender. If he and Hyde did the same, this would end tonight. Barnett would be free, but he and Hyde would be done. Following that thought to a logical conclusion, the picture was blurry: Hyde living in Bearcreek and he was working a job, maybe as a PI or getting a job in the local police department. The picture didn't disgust him. But in the immediate, they needed to get out of this.

"I'm not killing a cop," Finn said.

Hyde wiped a hand across her forehead. "Not me, either."

"Let's get in the truck and get out of here," Finn said.

"It's the only option."

They climbed back into the truck. Finn lay low in the driver's seat. There were six police officers on the scene. They were rounding up the gang members, each officer busy.

Finn hit the accelerator. The truck drove up onto the curb. With a jerk of the wheel, Finn put the truck on the road. He was lucky he didn't pop a tire. He imagined the cargo in the back of the truck was shifting and he prayed nothing ignited, exploding them off the road.

In his side mirror, he saw the police waving and shouting to stop. Finn kept moving.

"Find a place for us to hide the truck," Finn said.

Hyde was tapping at her phone. "I can't internet search that. Places to hide a freaking semi. I'll message Abby."

"If we don't hide it, we'll be located," Finn said. He drove down the road and heard sirens approaching. The police were looking for them and would find them.

Finally, Hyde spoke. "Circle back to the pier. There's a company that says it repairs boats. They may have a big place to stash a truck and even some paint to disguise it."

Hyde gave him the directions and Finn drove as quickly as he could.

The drive to the pier took ten minutes, though it felt like hours had passed. They had heard sirens getting closer and then farther away, which meant the police had not given up their search.

Finally, Hyde and Finn arrived at the boat repair shop, but the entrance was barred by a chain wrapped around a metal gate and secured with a padlock.

"You're better at this than I am." Finn handed her a lock pick kit.

Hyde jumped out of the truck. Her adrenaline was pumping and her hands were shaking. Calling on her training, she took deep breaths and slowed her racing heart. To get out of this without being caught, she and Finn needed to stay calm and alert.

She looked around for a camera and was relieved not to see any. Hyde knelt in front of the fence. Shaking out the last of her jitters, she used the picks to pop the metal lock open. She removed the chain holding the gate closed, thinking it sounded incredibly loud. Someone would hear them and call the police. A residential area was located across the two-lane street, a tall six- or seven-story condominium community with windows lining the side facing the water. With the noise the police sirens had made, people had to have been awoken. Were she and Finn being watched?

Hyde pushed open the gate and motioned to Finn to pull the truck through. The truck's engine was loud and, at this hour, out of place.

The ground around the repair shop was made of crushed seashells. The garages were vinyl construction, pale green and large enough to house the truck. Hyde closed the entryway gate and slipped the chain around it, leaving the lock dangling.

Peering in through a small window on the garage's sliding door, the first two sheds were filled. They were lucky on the third. It was empty. Hyde picked the lock and slid the barn-style doors open.

Finn parked the truck inside the shed, and Hyde secured the doors. She typed an update to Abby. Abby had been tracking the situation with the police and the motorcyclists from the Shadow Crew.

Hyde groaned. "I have no signal. How is that possible?"

"Is there a landline around?" Finn asked.

An inspection of the shed revealed no other way to make calls. They did, however, find a sign indicating the boat repair shop opened for business at five in the morning. Two hours before they needed to move. The room was outfitted with large, overhead lights, but Hyde and Finn used only the light from the truck's interior.

"Let's check the cargo and see what's so important to Barnett," Finn said. He left the driver's-side door open and circled the vehicle. He lifted the gate.

The truck was filled with brown cardboard boxes labeled with the word pineapple and a yellow and green picture of one. Hyde hadn't expected the boxes to be labeled with their true contents, but she credited Barnett with printing something boring on the boxes.

Finn slit open one of the boxes. "Definitely not pineapples." He tilted the box toward Hyde. The box was filled with small plastic zipper-sealed clear bags of white, blue and red chemicals.

"Let's take a sample so we can figure out what it is," Hyde said. She didn't recognize the substances and had little experience identifying ingredients from smell or taste.

They secured their sample in one of Finn's pants pockets.

"We need to paint the truck. The yellow is too noticeable," Hyde said.

"I was thinking the same thing," Finn said.

They searched the shelves and inside a freestanding metal closet along the wall and found a couple of cans of black paint.

"Black would work," Finn said. He removed his shirt.

Hyde drank in the sight of him. His broad shoulders and muscled arms, toned abdominals. She liked a man who was physically fit, and Finn took it to the next level. But checking him out wouldn't lead anywhere. He had made that clear at the club, freezing when she had talked about the future. "What are you doing?" Besides creating a tempting distraction for her.

"I don't want to get paint all over my clothes. If we're questioned, spatters of paint on me and the freshly painted truck I'm driving? Trouble."

He was right and Hyde removed her dress. She had on about as much as she wore to the beach and felt a flash of self-consciousness about it. They didn't have extra time to be sidetracked.

Paintbrushes and a paint sprayer were located in the closets. Finn worked with the sprayer on one side of the truck while she painted the edges, covering the yellow of the truck. The monotonous activity gave her too much time to think, and her thoughts focused on Finn. "We could leave the truck. Let the West Company deal with it. Take a boat and sail away."

"Is that like saying you want to sail off into the sunset? Or sunrise?" Finn asked.

"It's an option," Hyde said.

"We're close to the end. I feel it," Finn said.

That was what she was afraid of. She had come full circle with her feelings for him, but Finn hadn't changed. Hyde directed her emotions into painting faster.

When they'd finished covering the truck, an hour and a half had passed. It was hot and humid inside the shed. Their skin was covered in paint flecks. Finn tossed her a roll of paper towels and she wiped the bits she could from her skin.

Finn tore a sheet from the roll. He folded it in his hand and held it to her cheek. "May I?"

She nodded.

He wiped at her cheeks. He was standing close enough that she felt the heat radiating from his body.

Avoiding making eye contact, she scratched the paint from her fingernails.

"Even with black paint in your hair, you make it work," Finn said.

Hyde lifted her eyes to meet his gaze. "Same goes."

Finn cleared his throat and looked away. Her heart fell. When they got close, he backed away.

She checked the truck for yellow that had bled through; Finn left to find vehicle license plates. Hyde checked her phone. She still had no signal. Were the police ramping up their efforts to find their truck? Would they be surrounded at the shed? Abby couldn't tell the police Hyde and Finn were undercover, not when Barnett could have an inside man on the police force.

With her heart aching, paint fumes nauseating her, Hyde questioned why she was doing this. She wasn't a stranger to difficult operations, but this one was growing more complex and taking longer than she had hoped. Perhaps she hadn't thought it through, but she had imagined doing some surveillance and handing the intel to someone else. Let someone else do the legwork to bring Barnett down. Finn was intent on doing it himself.

When Finn returned, it was ten minutes to five.

"We need to get out of here," Finn said. If the owners showed up for the day, they'd involve the police. As it was, Hyde and Finn owed the shop a check for the paint they had stolen and the paintbrushes and the paper towels and mess they had made. The West Company would send money to reimburse them.

Paint was still dripping off the truck.

"We did what we could," Hyde said. They pulled their clothes on and tidied in the shed.

The smell of the paint would linger. They had no way to air out the shed. The morning air was still and humid.

Finn got into the driver's side and pulled the truck out of the shed. Hyde locked up and they followed the same procedures at the gate, trying to leave the area undisturbed. The longer it took the owners to realize they'd had a break-in, the farther away Finn and Hyde could be.

Driving in the direction of the warehouse, Hyde rubbed at the flecks of paint on her hands. "When you've spoken to Barnett, has he said anything about Ruby? I've been worried about her." Speaking of her and Finn's relationship would sink them deeper into troubled waters, but she felt okay asking about another couple.

"He hasn't mentioned her. You want me to ask directly?" Finn asked.

"I can't imagine she likes living on that island with him," Hyde said.

"He wasn't holding her against her will," Finn said. "If she wanted to leave, we could get her out. Ruby is strong. She seems subservient to Barnett, but she has to have some inner strength or Barnett would have crushed her by now."

Hyde sensed Ruby was stronger than she may give herself credit for.

"I'll take the long way around the city to get to the warehouse," Finn said. "See if I can avoid being spotted by the police."

Hyde looked at her phone. "Still no signal."

They drove in silence. Exhaustion was creeping into her, but she didn't fall asleep on missions. Finn might need her. Hard to stop thinking about a hot shower and bed, taking off this dress and slipping into a soft T-shirt and comfortable cotton shorts.

Not the first time she wished she hadn't come on this mission. She had solid reasons for agreeing to the mission, her sister first among them. But was this worth it?

Outside Miami, Hyde made contact with Abby.

"Where have you guys been?" Abby asked. She sounded out of breath.

"We're laying low."

The familiar clicking of Abby's fingers moving over the computer keyboard filled the line. "I've been watching the warehouse. I sent a few agents to find you and offer support. The police are looking for two people matching your description and driving a yellow delivery truck."

"That's not great news. Hard to hide in a truck," Hyde said.

"Can you ditch the truck in a safe location?" Abby asked.

Safe being the operative word. "Not to our knowledge and not without pissing off Barnett," Hyde said.

"Also, I need to pass along that we have the results from the blood work you sent from the victim from Illumination," Abby said.

Hyde held her breath, waiting for the answer.

"Substance unknown, likely Whiteout. We've added it to our database. If there are more victims, we'll receive an alert. We have a task force looking into past overdoses to make a connection. And since we've been working around the clock, we also used the information we pulled from Ramirez's computer to track deliveries in Selvan. We have operatives on the ground making arrests."

"Great news," Finn said.

Hyde felt less enthused. She was being pulled back into this life. She felt the rush of excitement over each development on the mission pulling her close to their end goal. That high was dangerous and addictive.

"Barnett hasn't withdrawn the money we stole from Ramirez. We can't use that against him," Abby said.

"Do we have enough to bring him down?" Hyde asked, unable to hide the sigh in her voice.

Finn shot her a strange look. If he thought she was cranky, she was.

"We can't tie Whiteout to Barnett yet," Abby said.

"We have samples from our truck," Finn said. "We'll make the delivery and then get them to the lab."

"That's great," Abby said. "Be careful, though. There's a heavy police presence in Miami and some-one got a look at you two. Your likenesses are in the media. We're trying to keep it local."

What if her parents saw them? Or her sisters? Would she be recognized? The mission highlighted what was at stake and everything she had to lose.

When Hyde and Finn arrived at the warehouse, they pulled to the loading dock.

Sydney was standing outside, smoking a cigarette. A soft pack was tucked in his dress shirt pocket, the gold foil sticking up. "Took you long enough."

Hyde tried not to let the comment irritate her.

Finn handed over the keys to the truck. "I'm sure you heard we ran into trouble."

Sydney narrowed his eyes. "You keep running into trouble. We need someone who won't bring the authorities down on us. Someone who knows how to avoid trouble."

Finn's shoulders tensed. "I've done my job."

Sydney sneered. "Maybe. Maybe not. I'm keeping a close eye on you. There's a car out front. Take that and get gone."

Chapter 14

After a meal, a shower, and a three-hour nap, Hyde was feeling better. She needed something to take the edge off the tiredness that fogged her brain. A jog in the Miami humidity would clear her head. Whiteout and Sydney, Barnett and Ruby, Simon and Lydia and Thea, her feelings for Finn and her future. Thoughts ricocheted around her brain and she questioned her decisions. Every mission put a lot on the line. On this mission, she personally had so much at stake and that made everything more difficult and complex.

"I'm going for a run," Hyde said. The exercise would take the edge off her tumultuous emotions and get rid of her nervous jitters. Too little sleep and too much caffeine had that effect on her.

Finn grabbed his running shoes. "I'll join you."

Hyde and Finn had worked out together before.

They stayed in shape for their jobs and Hyde enjoyed the company and the competition, but today, she wanted to be alone.

"I'm okay on my own," she said.

Finn took her hand. "Come on, Hyde. I know I upset you earlier. It's not safe for you to be alone on the streets of Miami. I won't chatter. I'll stay close to be sure you're okay."

She nodded once, knowing he was right. They needed to stay sharp. A mistake this late in the game would make their efforts for naught.

In the promised silence, they took the hotel stairs to the main level.

Hyde stretched the backs of her calves. Her feelings for Finn were clouded by the past, but with him, in the here and now, she felt like she was working with a partner and a friend. With someone who she trusted and loved. She loved Finn. She had from that first moment they'd met. Broaching the subject had gone miserably and he had been clear he didn't reciprocate her feelings. Or if he did, he wasn't willing to change anything between them to make it work.

With that hurt crushing her chest, Hyde took off with Finn on her heels. His stride was longer, and he passed her. Competitiveness urged her to move faster and draw on her energy reserves as she chased after him.

At the end of the block, he disappeared around the corner, and Hyde sped up to avoid losing sight of him. As she slowed at the end of the block, she drew to a hard stop.

Standing in front of her was Finn and Simon. She did a double take. Simon? Was it him? Hyde blinked and shook her head. The heat and her exhaustion might be making her dizzy. But the man before her had the same blond hair, aristocratic nose and tall, slender build. "Simon?"

It felt strange to say his name.

Simon held a gun pointed at Finn. "Alex, how good of you to join us. Turn around and walk into that parking garage. If you run, I will shoot you in the back. I will shoot if I think you're signaling anyone. Hands on the back of your heads," Simon said.

Hyde glanced at Finn. He subtly shook his head. They couldn't try anything. She had her gun under her shirt, strapped tightly to her waist to keep it from bouncing as she ran. It would take an extra few seconds to get it out, seconds they didn't have. Simon was a trained operative, one of the best.

Hyde and Finn did as he asked. They walked into the garage, moving around a concrete wall, out of sight of the sidewalk and street. Simon could be reasoned with. Something had gone terribly askew for him to be in Miami holding them at gunpoint.

"We thought you were dead," Hyde said. She tried to gauge his temperament. If the truth didn't work, she would try something else.

"Turn around and let me see your hands," Simon said.

She and Finn faced him, holding their hands in front of them.

"Simon, what's going on?" Hyde asked.

"I'll ask the questions," Simon said. "Tell me what you're doing with Barnett."

She and Finn remained silent. Simon may still be

an operative or working for someone. He could work for another cartel or against Barnett.

"Answer me or I'll kill you for betraying me," Simon said.

"Betraying you? We're not the ones waving a gun in your face," Finn said.

Simon's brown eyes darkened. "You thought that partnering with Barnett wasn't betraying me?"

"Simon, calm down. Let us explain," Hyde said.

"Calm down? That's what you have to say to me," Simon said.

"We are not partnered with anyone except each other," Finn said.

"You're running around Miami helping Barnett set up his drug enterprise," Simon said.

Confusion spiraled through her. "How do you know that?" If Simon had been working for the West Company, Abby would have warned them. The West Company had control of this operation.

"I've been watching Barnett. Imagine how surprised I was to learn two of my closest friends were working with the man who tried to kill me," Simon said.

How much of what they knew of Simon's demise was a lie? He was alive, but she didn't know how.

Typically rock steady in the field, Simon's hand was shaking. He wasn't himself. Whatever had transpired in the last two years, he was a different man.

"Simon, we were told that Barnett trapped you in one of his drug factories and set fire to it." She waited several beats.

Simon rolled his sleeve shirt up. His forearm was

marred with burn scars. "True. Which still doesn't explain why you are working for Barnett."

"Before you do anything you'll regret, I need to tell you something about Lydia," Hyde said.

"Careful," Finn said under his breath.

Hyde glanced at Finn. If she told Simon about Lydia and Thea, he could lash out. He could go after Lydia or Thea. But they needed the truth out in the open. "I need to tell him."

"Tell me what?" Simon asked. He was shouting. "What's wrong with her? Did Barnett get to her?"

Hyde recognized worry in his words. He didn't want to hurt Lydia. Hyde shook her head. "I am careful about protecting my family. Barnett won't come near them. But Lydia fell for you hard. After the night you spent with her, she found out she was pregnant." Hyde held her breath, afraid what Simon might say.

"Pregnant?" Simon asked. He ran his free hand through his hair. "Where is she? What did she do with the baby?"

"The baby is named Thea. She's healthy and fantastic," Hyde said.

Simon stared at them, his mouth agape. Hyde couldn't read his emotions.

"Lydia was heartbroken when you didn't return. We thought you were dead. We were told you were dead. What happened?"

Simon took a step away. "I can't believe this. A child? I have a child?"

"Yes. And Lydia would like to see you. There will need to be a lot of explaining, but she's had a tough time. She would want you to meet Thea and be in her life."

Simon forked his fingers into his hair. "Thea. What a beautiful name."

"Tell us where you've been, Simon," Finn said.

Simon seemed to collect himself. "You know I was working to take down the Barnett cartel. Barnett found out I was a spy and he knew I was closing in on him. He wanted to destroy evidence. He didn't care who he killed and all the better if I'd died. Some of us made it out of the fire. Others died in the explosion. I was taken to a hospital. I didn't have identification and because I was undercover, no one came looking for me. I was in a medically induced coma for six months while I healed. After that I was taken to a rehabilitation center. I worked harder than I've ever worked recuperating. And now I want Barnett dead."

Hyde had much to say and many questions she wanted answered. "You have to know we're not working with Barnett."

"It doesn't look that way. Word around town is that you're Barnett's go-to guy," Simon said.

"You can't believe that," Finn said. "Look deeper."

Simon lowered his gun thirty degrees.

"We're undercover," Hyde said.

Simon shook his head. "You and Finn don't work in the United States. You did the same work I did. Overseas."

"No," Hyde said. "We've started working for another firm. We're trying to stop Barnett and bring down his entire enterprise. For you. Payback for what we believed Barnett did to you and to give closure to

Lydia. I thought if Barnett was dead, I could tell her the truth about you."

Simon's eyes misted and then his face grew hard. "You're lying."

"I am telling you the truth," Hyde said.

"An hour ago I wanted to kill you. Now I don't know," Simon said.

"Call Lydia," Hyde said.

Simon took his phone from his pocket. He looked at it. "What would I say to her? I've thought of calling her many times. I didn't want to bring her into this."

"She hasn't moved on. She has Thea and she does her best, but it's been difficult," Hyde said.

"You have to trust us, Simon. We aren't working for Barnett. We're working for the West Company."

"I've heard of them," Simon said. He seemed to be thinking over what they had said. He put his phone in his pocket. "Tell me how this is going down."

Finn clapped Simon on the back and put his arm around Hyde. "We end this with Barnett. Together."

Finn considered his options. Simon was alive. The driving force behind this mission was gone. If he and Hyde quit, Barnett's drug Whiteout would hit the street. Was that Finn's problem? He and Hyde could turn the information they had over to the DEA.

Except Barnett had the DEA, or at least some agents, in his pocket. The West Company could mobilize a team to bring Barnett down.

Finn's phone rang and he answered.

"Where are you?" Barnett asked.

He was in his hotel room with Simon and Hyde, talking, sorting out their next move. "In my hotel room, sleeping. If you recall, I was up all night making a delivery with the Miami PD on my back."

"We have big problems. Sydney is dead," Barnett said.

Finn glanced at Simon. He was talking to Hyde about Lydia and Thea. Was Simon responsible for Sydney's death? He had come at him and Hyde. Who else had he taken out in the Barnett cartel?

"How? The Shadow Crew?" Finn asked. Throw suspicion elsewhere.

"I don't know who. That's why I'm calling you," Barnett said.

"The last time I saw Sydney, he was at the warehouse handling the delivery," Finn said.

Simon and Hyde's gazes were now pinned on him.

"What is happening over there?" Barnett asked. He was yelling and swearing, having another tantrum.

"Let me look into it," Finn said. "I'll head over to the warehouse."

"If Sydney is dead, it's been compromised. I've already secured a team to move the goods elsewhere. I'll be there in a few hours," Barnett said.

"In Miami?" Finn asked. That didn't fit the mental timeline he was composing. He wanted to hand this mission over to the West Company. They couldn't mobilize in hours.

"Yes, Miami. Clearly, you and Sydney do not have this handled. Do you know how much money is on the line? This screwup will cost me." Barnett said.

No concern for his dead business partner. Classic narcissist. "I get it," Finn said. "Tell me where to meet you."

"I'll call when I'm closer." Barnett disconnected the phone.

Finn relayed the information to Simon and Hyde.

"Did you kill Sydney?" Finn asked. He wouldn't blame Simon. Finn needed to know what they were dealing with.

Simon shook his head. "No. That weasel runs around doing Barnett's bidding. The guy is scum, but I wouldn't have wasted my time with him. He doesn't make decisions. He's Barnett's lapdog."

Finn believed him. Simon wouldn't have a reason to lie about it. He had killed before on a mission. In this case, Simon was working under his own rules. The kill wouldn't have been sanctioned.

"When Barnett steps onto US soil, we can arrest him," Hyde said.

"Abby isn't sure they have enough evidence to tie him to Whiteout. He has a team moving the chemicals from the warehouse," Finn said. "If he's arrested, he won't tell us where he took them. They'll hit the street."

"Simon and I will go to the warehouse and see if we can track the goods. He couldn't have emptied the warehouse that fast," Hyde said.

Finn didn't like Hyde being without him. Simon had been a good operative, but he was out of practice. He wouldn't be as careful with Hyde. He didn't love her the way Finn did.

Love? Finn loved her. Looking at her intense face, his love for her swelled to the point he felt dizzy. Inevitable, perhaps, but absolutely for sure, Finn loved her.

"What's wrong?" Hyde asked.

His mouth felt dry. Finn swallowed. Now was not

the time to declare his love. His love for her didn't change the mission. But it would change him. He could stop doing a job he loved so he could be a husband and a father. The idea didn't repulse him, but he couldn't make a major life decision on the heels of a soul-shaking realization. Hyde seemed convinced she could find a happy, satisfying life in Bearcreek. He could, too. If he was with her, they would make their own adventures. "Thinking about our next steps. I could go with you to the warehouse."

Hyde looked at her phone. "If Barnett calls, you need to be here. Simon and I will run this down. Abby is calling." She answered. After a few seconds her face paled. "I understand. Yes, I'll tell Finn."

She looked at Finn and took a deep breath. "The Whiteout we bought on the street contained a lethal poison. The same poison was found in the victim who OD'ed on Whiteout. One of the chemicals on the truck is poison. If that shipment makes it to users, people will die."

Hyde and Simon waited in the car a block away from the warehouse. In a desolate part of town, Hyde hadn't expected traffic, but the street was dead.

"Is this a trap?" Simon asked.

Hyde understood his concern. After what he had been through with Barnett, he was right not to trust and to be suspicious. "Could be. Do you want to wait here and I'll check it out?"

Simon was staring straight ahead. "I'll go with you. But Alex, wait." Simon set his hand on her arm. "Are you telling me everything about Lydia and Thea?"

Hyde read the pain in his eyes. "I'm sure there's

lots Lydia wants to tell you about what she's been through and is going through, but yes, I'm on the level with you."

Simon rested his head on the seat. "She changed me. That one day and that one night with Lydia changed me. I didn't want to do this work anymore. It didn't seem worth it, not when I thought about having a life with her."

Hyde's stomach clenched. It was how she felt about her life. It was how she felt about Finn. Ignoring her feelings for Finn had only made them roar louder and grow impossibly stronger. Attraction had crossed over into love. It had been for some time, Finn on her mind, Finn in her heart.

"What's wrong?" Simon asked.

Hyde marshalled her expression. "Thinking."

"About Finn?" Simon asked.

No point in lying when he had followed her train of thought. "Yes."

"What's going on with you two?" Simon asked.

"When this mission is over, I'm returning to Bearcreek to be with my family. Finn will go on doing this work. It will be over between us," Hyde said. Her stomach bottomed out and pain tightened her chest.

"That's hard to believe," Simon said.

"It's what we discussed would happen," Hyde said. Not in those terms, but it was inevitable.

"Has it changed since you talked about it?" Simon asked.

The circumstances hadn't. How she felt hadn't. The main difference was that she was ready to admit to herself that her dream of having a home and family of her own included Finn. "Not for Finn." She'd need to rework those dreams.

"He looks at you like you're more than partners on a mission," Simon said. "I think you might be selling him short. Have you told him how you feel?"

She had and he had fled. The life she wanted scared him. Which was strange, considering the life he led scared her.

A gun appeared in her peripheral vision, the metal glinting in the sun. Her blood pressure soared. Before she could react, the driver's-side door was pulled open. Hyde reached for her gun, but it got tangled in her seat belt. Releasing the belt, Hyde angled her head to get a better look at the person aiming a gun at her.

Reed Barnett grabbed her arm and dragged her from the car. His expression was menacing.

Struggling to her feet, she swung her gun in his direction. He stopped the motion with a swift kick. Her gun went flying and Hyde cursed herself for letting it happen. Simon stood on the passenger side, his gun drawn and aimed in their direction.

"Alexandra. Why don't you tell me what you're doing here? Are you the reason Sydney is dead?"

She decided to play stupid. "Please don't tell Finn. He's been busy and when I met Roger," she inclined her head to Simon, who was now standing with two of Barnett's guards, a gun to his head, his own gun missing from his hands. "I wanted to talk to someone." Would Barnett recognize Simon?

"The stupid act doesn't suit you," Barnett said. "I'll get to the truth. You'll help me. And Simon. How wonderful to see you. I should have made sure you were dead. I won't make the same mistake twice."

* * *

Finn couldn't wait in the hotel room for Barnett to call. He had to talk to Barnett and find out why White-out contained poison. Before he could call, his phone rang with a restricted call. Finn answered. "Yeah."

"I have your lover with me at the pier." Barnett's voice was threatening. "I don't know what you two, or should I say three, were planning, but if it was to cross me, you have made a grave error. Come to the pier. I want the truth."

Finn felt anger welling inside him. "Alex is with you?"

"Yes. And Simon. You have ten minutes."

Finn alerted the West Company on his way to the pier. They couldn't help him in time. Finn pictured Hyde injured, and terror shot through him. When he had met Hyde, she had been escaping prison. She had looked wild and petrified and the image was burned into his brain. Was that how she felt now?

Finn had wanted to step away from the mission and he hadn't. Now Barnett had the woman he loved and Simon. The situation was spiraling out of control.

Finn could handle this. He had been in tight spots before. But never when Hyde's life was on the line. Finn had three weapons strapped to his body and he would use them as needed.

The rocking motion of the boat nauseated Hyde. Combined with sitting in the Florida sun, she felt ill. She closed her eyes, but it didn't help. Barnett was forcing Finn to come to the pier. He would be thrown onto the boat with her and Simon and the drugs laced with poison.

When Finn arrived, Barnett would kill them. Or, more likely, have his guards kill them. Why keep them alive? He knew he had been betrayed. Barnett would clean house.

Hyde wouldn't go down without a fight.

When Finn appeared alone with his hands tied in front of him, Hyde's heart dropped. She had hoped that Finn would ignore Barnett or wait for backup. He hadn't abandoned the mission. He hadn't abandoned her.

Their gazes connected, and emotions spiraled between them. With a look, she felt and knew so much. Finn cared for her. Loved her? They were more than partners on the mission, and they were more than blowing off steam between assignments. This was real and this meant something to them. Their futures would converge somehow.

The boat jerked. Panic settled over her. The boat was moving away from the pier. Hyde couldn't guess the destination. Her phone and weapon were gone. She was sure Finn's had been taken. With their hands bound, swimming would be impossible. They needed a way out of this.

Barnett looked at them, a sneer on his face. "Who will tell me who killed Sydney? Whoever tells me first gets killed the quickest."

Simon, Hyde and Finn exchanged looks. They hadn't killed Sydney.

"The Shadow Crew," Hyde said. "Like I've been telling you."

Barnett looked at his gun. "Wrong answer," Barnett said. He shot in her direction. She waited for the searing burn of pain and feeling nothing, relief passed over her. He had missed.

A second shot. She was hit in the leg. Finn roared in anger and launched himself at Barnett. Barnett's guards intercepted before he could make contact. He was shoved onto the ground next to her.

"You're outgunned," Barnett said.

Finn pressed his hands over her leg. The bleeding didn't stop. Dizziness surged through her and she struggled to stay alert.

"I need to stop the bleeding. She needs medical attention," Finn said.

If Barnett was a better shot, she'd be dead.

"That's too bad. We're not turning around," Barnett said. "I want answers. The longer I'm kept waiting, the more bullets I fire and the more she bleeds."

"Stop this." Ruby appeared in the doorway. "They said they don't know." She took Barnett's arm, turning the barrel of the gun away from them.

Barnett shook Ruby off. "This doesn't involve you, Ruby. Go," Barnett said, jerking his thumb behind him.

Ruby's face changed. Her mouth drew into a hard line and her eyes narrowed. She lifted her chin and squared her shoulders in an uncharacteristic display of aggression. "I won't. Let them go. We can do what's needed without more bloodshed."

Barnett turned and backhanded Ruby across the face. She stumbled back, falling against the doorjamb. Crouching low on the floor, her shoulders hunched forward. Her strength had turned to a posture of defeat.

"Answers!" he said, firing again in their direction. His shot missed. They wouldn't get lucky again.

"Why did you poison the drugs?" Finn asked. "What's the point?"

"Are you worried about a bunch of junkies dying? Thousands dead, thanks to me."

Thanks to Barnett? A terror plot to rid Miami of junkies?

"It will take the authorities months to make the connection. By then, Whiteout will be everywhere. Junkies will be dying to get some. Literally. Call it what you want, but I'm doing the US a favor. Cleaning up the streets."

Ruby stood. She seemed unsteady on her feet. Her cheek was red where Barnett had struck her. No outrage on her face, only cold indifference.

Hyde willed Ruby to run and run fast. Even jumping overboard would give her a better chance of survival. Sometimes, those were the best odds to play. Instead Ruby approached Barnett from behind in two long strides. His eyes grew wide and then blood exploded from his chest. Barnett fell to the ground, and Ruby held a small gun in her hand, pointing it up toward the sky.

Finn reached for Hyde, tucking her against him. Hyde waited for Ruby to turn the gun on them. A complete break with reality or maybe she'd snapped and lost her mind. Finn and Simon were on their feet, moving toward Ruby.

Ruby faced each of the other guards and killed them with the small derringer in her hand. "Sorry, Reed. I beat you to the punch. I'm cleaning up the streets." She checked Barnett's pulse. "He's dead." Ruby untied Simon, Finn and Hyde.

Finn removed his shirt and belt. He wrapped his

belt around Hyde's thigh to slow the bleeding and pressed hard against the wound with his shirt.

Hyde stared at her, the pain in her thigh second only to her shock. "Ruby? What did you do?"

Ruby tucked the gun in her waistband. "I've been waiting months to do that. I got the go-ahead from Connor West to kill Barnett once we'd secured the drugs. I've secured the drugs."

Simon, Hyde and Finn didn't move. Surprise had rendered them mute.

"Come on. We need to destroy this boat." Ruby tossed a bag at Hyde.

Hyde opened it. Inside was C4, a detonator and wire.

"Do your thing," Ruby said. "Make it fast before you bleed out."

Standing on the Miami pier, Hyde pressed the detonator. The boat carrying Barnett's drugs exploded. She watched, wanting to be sure the drugs were demolished. Barnett's body had gone down with his ship and his guards were handcuffed on the pier.

She turned to thank Ruby, but the woman was gone.

An ambulance was waiting at the end of the pier. Finn lifted Hyde into his arms. "Allow me to carry you to your chariot."

"Finn, wait. I have something I need to say before this is over." They'd have debriefings and medical evaluations and reports to write to wrap up the mission. She wanted to tell Finn how she felt before all of that. She had nothing to lose except him.

"You're bleeding. You need medical help," Finn said.

"It's a superficial wound. What I need to tell you is important," Hyde said.

Finn stopped walking, the boards of the pier creaking under his weight, but didn't put her down. "Say anything you want to me."

Hyde threaded her arms around his neck. "I came back to this life for this mission. I'm glad I did. I realized something."

Their gazes connected. "That you're a great spy?"

She shook her head. "That I love you."

Finn's arms tightened around her. "I love you, too."

Not the response she had expected. Her heart filled with joy. She smelled the salt air and heard the sound of the water lapping against the pylons. Simon, the ambulances and the police waiting seemed far away and completely unimportant. It was her and Finn. Finally, the pins had clicked into place and they were on the same page. "I thought I would need to convince you that being together was right. I had a speech planned."

Finn kissed her. "As fun as that would be to hear, we could go back to the way things were. Spy or not, I can still meet you anywhere, anytime."

It wasn't what Hyde wanted. "I'm not looking for an affair or a series of affairs around the world, even if they are with you."

"Neither am I. I'll do my job. You'll do yours. And we'll call Bearcreek home. Our home. Together."

Surprise rolled over her. "You want to live with me?" Hyde asked.

"Live with. Be with. Come home to. All of it," Finn said.

Hyde kissed him. "Then I would say yes to that."

* * *

Lydia made a beautiful bride. As Simon stood at the altar, committing himself to Lydia and Thea, Hyde's chest filled with happiness. It had taken eight months of talking and explanations, but her sister understood why Simon had disappeared. She and Simon were starting their life together as a family with their daughter.

Hyde was working for the West Company in the same capacity that Abby had served on their mission. It was exhilarating from the safety of her living room.

Finn was somewhere in the world. He had promised to try to be back for Lydia and Simon's wedding. It hadn't happened. Hyde brushed away the disappointment.

She missed him and today was a special day for her family. She wanted Finn with her. Hyde scratched her palm where her bouquet was itching her. Yellow daisies, Lydia's favorite. Hyde's dress was pale yellow, too, and the pendant Finn had given her for her birthday hung around her neck, a symbol of their togetherness. Soon she would add another birthstone to the necklace. She hadn't told Finn yet. It was a conversation she'd wanted to have in person.

The church was decorated beautifully today, although few flowers were needed to accent the natural exquisiteness of the small community church.

Hyde sensed him before she saw him.

She turned her gaze from her sister, and her eyes met Finn's. Across the church, he was standing in the vestibule wearing a sexy black tuxedo and looking unbearably handsome. She fought the urge to run to him and throw herself into his arms. It had been three weeks since she had last seen him.

The preacher was proclaiming Simon, Lydia and Thea a family. As everyone stood to clap and the new family walked down the aisle, Hyde raced down the side of the church to Finn.

She threw her arms around his neck and kissed him. "Welcome home," she said.

"Happy to be home," he said against her lips. His arms were banded around her, holding her to him.

"You're looking dashing in that suit."

"Glad you think so," Finn said. "Want to stop home and catch up?"

"We don't have time." Catching up in their home would land them in bed. "We have wedding pictures to take."

Finn ran his hand down her side, stopping at her hip. "I can wait until tonight. I have something important I want to ask you. I was a day late because I stopped in Washington, DC."

Hyde inclined her head. "What's in DC?"

"My family."

Hyde gasped. She had called Finn's mom a few times, trying to break the ice without much success. Had Finn finally spoken to them?

"They want to fly to Bearcreek and meet you," Finn said.

Excitement and happiness spiraled through her. "That would be wonderful. I have so many preparations to make, but yes, please tell them to come anytime." She had been decorating their home and she had a room in mind for a guest bedroom.

The wedding party and guests had proceeded outside. She and Finn were alone in the chapel. Even with the lights off, the sunlight streaming through the stained-glass windows bathed the room in a warm glow.

"I figure they should meet the woman I'm planning to marry."

The word echoed around the raised ceilings. Hyde's heart thumped. "Marry?"

Finn set Hyde on the hickory floorboards and dropped to his knee in front of her. "Marry me, Alex. Have a family with me. A life together."

No questions in her heart. "Yes, I'll marry you!" Hyde said.

Finn slipped a ring on her finger and Hyde looked from it to Finn. "This saves you from being forced into a shotgun wedding."

Finn's eyes flashed with excitement. He touched her stomach lightly, his fingertips barely brushing her. "Are you sure? You're pregnant?"

Hyde nodded, happy tears springing to her eyes. "Four months along. I was waiting to tell you in person. I've already been to the doctor to confirm it."

Finn kissed her and pulled her against him. "I better take you on that vacation I promised while you can still travel. I know of a certain private island that's now an asset of the West Company. We can take a trip there." He winked at her. "I have an in."

Hyde laid her head on Finn's shoulder, enjoying his strength and the security and love she felt in his arms. "Anywhere I can be with you is paradise."

* * * * *

REQUEST YOUR FREE BOOKS!
2 FREE NOVELS PLUS 2 FREE GIFTS!

ROMANTIC suspense

Sparked by danger, fueled by passion

YES! Please send me 2 FREE Harlequin® Romantic Suspense novels and my 2 FREE gifts (gifts are worth about $10). After receiving them, if I don't wish to receive any more books, I can return the shipping statement marked "cancel." If I don't cancel, I will receive 4 brand-new novels every month and be billed just $4.74 per book in the U.S. or $5.49 per book in Canada. That's a savings of at least 12% off the cover price! It's quite a bargain! Shipping and handling is just 50¢ per book in the U.S. and 75¢ per book in Canada.* I understand that accepting the 2 free books and gifts places me under no obligation to buy anything. I can always return a shipment and cancel at any time. Even if I never buy another book, the two free books and gifts are mine to keep forever.

240/340 HDN GH3P

Name _____ (PLEASE PRINT) _____

Address _____ Apt. # _____

City _____ State/Prov. _____ Zip/Postal Code _____

Signature (if under 18, a parent or guardian must sign) _____

Mail to the **Reader Service:**
IN U.S.A.: P.O. Box 1867, Buffalo, NY 14240-1867
IN CANADA: P.O. Box 609, Fort Erie, Ontario L2A 5X3

Want to try two free books from another line?
Call 1-800-873-8635 or visit www.ReaderService.com.

* Terms and prices subject to change without notice. Prices do not include applicable taxes. Sales tax applicable in N.Y. Canadian residents will be charged applicable taxes. Offer not valid in Quebec. This offer is limited to one order per household. Not valid for current subscribers to Harlequin Romantic Suspense books. All orders subject to credit approval. Credit or debit balances in a customer's account(s) may be offset by any other outstanding balance owed by or to the customer. Please allow 4 to 6 weeks for delivery. Offer available while quantities last.

Your Privacy—The Reader Service is committed to protecting your privacy. Our Privacy Policy is available online at www.ReaderService.com or upon request from the Reader Service.

We make a portion of our mailing list available to reputable third parties that offer products we believe may interest you. If you prefer that we not exchange your name with third parties, or if you wish to clarify or modify your communication preferences, please visit us at www.ReaderService.com/consumerschoice or write to us at Reader Service Preference Service, P.O. Box 9062, Buffalo, NY 14240-9062. Include your complete name and address.

HRS15

"Your time would be better spent coming up with answers regarding our dead woman," she said in a no-nonsense tone.

Our.

Her slip of the tongue was not lost on Chris. The grin on his lips told her so before he uttered a word. "Our first joint venture. We should savor this."

"What I'd savor," she informed him, "is some peace and quiet so I can work. Specifically, some time away from you."

The expression that came over Chris's face was one of doubt. "Now, if we spend time apart, how are we going to work on this case together?" he asked, conveying that what she'd just said lacked logic.

Suzie had only one word to give him in response to his question. "Productively."

With that, she went back to doing her work, but that lasted for only a few moments. A minute at best. Though she tried to block out his presence, he still managed to get to her.

He was standing exactly where he had been, watching her so intently that she could feel his eyes on her skin. It caused her powers of concentration to deteriorate until they finally became nonexistent.

Unable to stand it, she looked up and glared at him. "What do you want, O'Bannon?" she muttered. It took everything she had not to shout the question at him. The man was making her crazy.

Chris never hesitated as he answered her. "Dinner."

She clenched her jaw. "You can buy it in any supermarket," she informed him coldly.

He sidestepped the roadblocks she was throwing up as if they weren't there.

"With you."

This time Suzie was the one who didn't hesitate for a second. "Not at any price. Now please go before I take out my manual on workplace harassment and start underlining passages to get you banned from my lab."

"It's the crime scene lab, not yours," he reminded her pleasantly, taking a page out of her book. And then Chris inclined his head. "Until the next time."

"There is no next time," she countered, steaming even though she refused to look up again.

"Don't forget we're working this case together," he told her cheerfully.

He thought he heard Suzie say "Damn" under her breath as he left the lab.

Chris smiled to himself.

Don't miss
CAVANAUGH IN THE ROUGH by Marie Ferrarella,
available February 2017 wherever
Harlequin® Romantic Suspense books
and ebooks are sold.

www.Harlequin.com

A *Romance* FOR EVERY MOOD™

JUST CAN'T GET ENOUGH?

Join our social communities
and talk to us online.

You will have access to the latest
news on upcoming titles and special
promotions, but most importantly,
you can talk to other fans about your
favorite Harlequin reads.

Harlequin.com/Community

 Facebook.com/HarlequinBooks

 Twitter.com/HarlequinBooks

 Pinterest.com/HarlequinBooks

Turn your love of reading into rewards you'll love with
Harlequin My Rewards

**Join for FREE today at
www.HarlequinMyRewards.com**

Earn **FREE BOOKS** of your choice.

Experience **EXCLUSIVE OFFERS** and contests.

Enjoy **BOOK RECOMMENDATIONS**
selected just for you.

PLUS! Sign up now
and get **500** points
right away!

Earn **FREE** REWARDS
HarlequinMyRewards.com
Join Today!

MYR16R

THE WORLD IS BETTER WITH

Romance

Harlequin has everything from contemporary, passionate and heartwarming to suspenseful and inspirational stories.

Whatever your mood, we have a romance just for you!

Connect with us to find your next great read, special offers and more.

f /HarlequinBooks

🐦 @HarlequinBooks

www.HarlequinBlog.com

www.Harlequin.com/Newsletters

⬥HARLEQUIN®

A *Romance* FOR EVERY MOOD™

www.Harlequin.com

READERSERVICE.COM

Manage your account online!

- Review your order history
- Manage your payments
- Update your address

*We've designed the
Reader Service website
just for you.*

Enjoy all the features!

- Discover new series available to you, and read excerpts from any series.
- Respond to mailings and special monthly offers.
- Connect with favorite authors at the blog.
- Browse the Bonus Bucks catalog and online-only exculsives.
- Share your feedback.

Visit us at:
ReaderService.com